KRISTMAS COLLINS

BY DEREK CICCONE

OTHER BOOKS BY DEREK CICCONE

Painless

Officer Jones

The Trials of Max Q

The Truant Officer

SUNDAY DECEMBER 22

CHAPTER 1

Sunday December 22

Christmas in Connecticut—

Was the name of a campy 1940's comedy starring Barbara Stanwyck. But there was nothing funny about the modern version I was living out this afternoon—a horror film that made me want to return to the safety of prison.

My cab passed through the electronic gates and drove up the Belgian-block lined driveway. We passed rolling, snow-covered lawns, before coming to a stop in a circular drop-off area in front of the ivy-draped English manor. I was here for the Wainwright holiday party, held every year on the Sunday prior to Christmas. I was unable to attend the past three years, and I would have pushed the streak to four if not for some business that needed attending to.

I secured the envelopes that contained my gifts, placing them in the pocket of my suit coat, and grabbed the pastry dish that I'd purchased at a bakery along the way. I then stepped out into the late afternoon—the sky was a dreary gray, and a light snow had begun to fall.

I was met by a portly man in an elf costume. I didn't recognize this particular greeter/security-guard from my previous times on the property, going back to when I used to live here with my ex-wife, Libby, during our first years of marriage. This surprised me, since the Wainwrights always made it a point to surround themselves with loyal soldiers, even if loyalty had never been a two-way street for them. Perhaps they had added extra security this year since a convicted felon was on the guest list—their favorite former son-in-law.

I started to walk in the opposite direction. This predictably upset Buddy the Elf. "Sir, the party's this way," he commanded.

"I'm going to take a shortcut," I replied without looking at him.

I braced, expecting to be wrestled to the ground and kicked with the curled-up tips of his elf shoes. But as luck would have it, I noticed a longtime Wainwright security guard named Lonnie—windbreaker, winter hat, no elf costume—who nodded at Buddy, instructing him to back off. Lonnie knew from firsthand experience that Kris Collins was capable of creating a scene on a moment's notice, and the last thing the Wainwrights wanted to do was to call attention to my presence.

I ventured over a slate path, which was lined with sculpted boxwood and ornamental trees that were decorated for the season. In the summer, the formal landscape of the estate was breathtaking, filled with magnolia trees and kiwifruit arbors. But for the party it had been transformed into a world of Christmas fantasy.

Music was being pumped out through speakers—"Winter Wonderland" was currently playing. *The weather outside is frightful,* the lyrics informed me. And while I would agree that it was a tad on the frosty side, I found it downright delightful compared to what was awaiting me inside.

I walked past elaborate ice sculptures, then an empty tennis court and pool house, before I began to smell the real party. I trudged through another frozen acre until I arrived at the Lake House.

It actually sat next to a pond, not a lake, and it would be more accurately described as a mansion. Like most things on this property, it was more about perception than reality. As a former attorney, who was once known as the "lawyer to the stars," I understood the concept of "perception over truth." And now it was likely the only thing keeping me alive.

Outside of the Lake House, sitting in lawn chairs on a brick patio, and enjoying the warmth of a fireplace, were the self-proclaimed Amigos—Tomás, Gustavo, and Berto—spending their final Christmas on the Wainwright property.

Alexander Wainwright had always referred to them as "the Mexicans"—his name for all those of Spanish descent—but they actually emigrated from Peru as children. And what I've learned over the years about these Peruvian house parties, called *tonos,* is that you don't arrive *manos vacias*—empty handed. So after exchanging warm greetings with the Amigos' wives and large extended family, I handed over a panettone cake to Tomás' wife, Mia.

I then moved to the patio area, and attempted to spread more holiday cheer. I handed each of the Amigos an envelope that contained a Christmas card. Inside the card, besides a sappy holiday greeting, was the final information regarding a project of mine—one that the Amigos had agreed to lend their considerable talents to. I'd been plotting it since my time in prison, and now we were just days away from the big moment.

Tomás motioned for me to take a seat and join them.

"I don't have much time," I cautioned. "I need to make an appearance at the big-boy party. Then I have a few more rounds to make tonight."

"Just like Santa Claus," Gustavo said with a chuckle.

"If that's the case, you're going to need a drink," Tomás added. He got up and poured me our traditional Christmas drink—Mountain Dew and tequila, hopefully heavy on the latter.

Berto brought me a plate from the barbecue, what Gustavo referred to as a "Peruvian specialty." I was fairly certain that a cheeseburger and tater tots wouldn't qualify as Peruvian or a specialty, but I wasn't about to argue.

"I'm surprised you didn't get an invite to the party ... sort of a going away present," I said between bites, but wasn't really. The Amigos hadn't been invited in the thirty years they'd lived here.

"We didn't fit the 'white Christmas' theme they got going this year," Gustavo said with a grin.

"Same theme as every year … the Wainwrights are traditionalists," Berto chimed in.

The volume of the surrounding festivities muffled our voices, which made this the ideal place to go over the final preparations. Children were ice-skating on the pond, while the teenagers were shooting off fireworks like it was the Fourth of July. Gustavo's college-age son, Angel—a dead ringer for his father—headed up a salsa band that had attracted a group of dancers on an adjoining patio. Many of them were attractive girls in outfits that didn't appear to be weather-appropriate.

I pointed at the envelopes. "The disc inside the card contains a complete route of all the houses and their floor-plans." As much as technology had advanced communication, it also left proof, which is why this old-school drop and chat was the still the best way to transfer information.

I viewed the large house in the backdrop, along with all their friends and family who were reveling in the holiday spirit. Things had changed a lot since they'd first arrived here. "I'll understand if you don't want to go through with it. You have a lot more to lose these days."

"What's the point of having our gifts, if we can't share with others. Tis the season of giving," Gustavo responded with another sly grin. The others nodded.

The gift he spoke of was the ability to break into houses like few who'd come before them. And not just any houses—the biggest and wealthiest estates in the area. That was, until Alexander Wainwright's security team apprehended them. But luckily for the Amigos, eleven-year-old Libby Wainwright was convinced that there was good in all people, and just as importantly, she had her father wrapped around her finger. She convinced him not to turn them over to the police. Instead, a compromise was reached in which they would live on the Wainwright property and pay for their crimes by living as indentured servants—performing tasks ranging from keeping up the fourteen acres, to serving as the Wainwrights' personal chauffeur.

I'm an admitted skeptic of most things Wainwright, so I've always had my doubts that this agreement was completely about granting a daughter's wish, or saving a few bucks on lawn care. It would be very convenient for an institution like Wainwright & Lennox to have access to the Amigos' talents, if they were in need of gaining private information from their competitors.

But their working agreement with the Wainwrights took an unexpected turn this year. They were being kicked to the curb so that the Lake House could be sold off. This was supposedly related to W&L's 600 million dollar loss in a business deal gone wrong with Kerstman Publishing a few years back.

This was not news to me, since I was the one who represented Diedrich Kerstman at his trial. This didn't sit well with the general public, as Kerstman had become the poster-child for corporate greed, and it went over even worse with my former father-in-law. When the smoke cleared my client was dead, I was in jail, and Alexander Wainwright was still out over half a billion dollars. So it went without saying that I was surprised to receive an invitation to this year's Christmas party. Although, I was starting to get the feeling that the case was still pending … and I was the one on trial.

CHAPTER 2

With each bite of the cheeseburger and sip of my drink concoction, I came closer to blowing off the Wainwright bash and remaining here for the evening. Libby and I attended a couple of these *tonos* back in the day, usually held on *Noche Buena*—the night before Christmas. They often went until four or five the next morning, and really picked up after the children were put to bed.

But just as I grew comfortable in my rickety lawn chair, I noticed a female in a fancy party dress awkwardly gliding over the snow in a pair of uncomfortable heels. It was still hard for me to believe that she was this grown up. It seemed like just thirty seconds ago she was crawling around the floors of the manor house in her diapers.

Since Taylor would always be six years old in my mind, this womanly stuff was a big adjustment. I noticed Gustavo's son, Angel, whom I've heard is no angel, staring at her. This made me want to make another big adjustment … to his nose. But beyond getting me sent back to jail, it would have also garnered the wrath of my teenage daughter, claiming that I was "embarrassing" her, followed by Dad receiving the silent treatment until I displayed proper remorse—a much tougher punishment. So I chose restraint, which had never been my first instinct.

When Taylor reached the Lake House, the women circled around her. She let out a big smile—as amazing as her mother's—and pirouetted to show off the dress. They analyzed and admired everything from her purse to her heels. Taylor had always been like family to them—her first couple of years of life were spent on Wainwright Manor, and frankly, I thought she'd pick up less bad habits hanging out in this section of town than being around her grandparents, so I made it a point to bring her down here at every opportunity.

After the fashion show came to a close, Taylor made her way to the patio area. She traded greetings with the Amigos, and then informed me, "Dad—I've been ordered to bring you to the party … ASAP."

"And this order came from?"

"Grandmother wanted to call the FBI and demand that they revoke your parole for storming past the party police, but I talked her off the ledge. She gave me ten minutes to bring you back, before she sends in the troops."

It would be no surprise if the FBI had already found their way onto the property. Not only would it allow them to monitor my moves, as they'd been doing since my release, but they could kill a whole flock of birds with one stone, considering the white-collar-crime festival inside … and that was just the Wainwright clients. But I decided to keep this information to myself.

Taylor plopped in the lawn chair next to me. Like her father, she didn't appear eager to return—she was going to use the entire ten-minute allotment. She yanked at her dress. I could tell that she couldn't wait to shed it in favor of a sweatshirt and jeans when she got home. In that way she was very different from her mother, who found a formal gown as comfortable as a second set of skin.

After a few minutes of reminiscing about the "good old days" spent at the Lake House, most of which Taylor was too young to remember, we said our goodbyes, and my bounty hunter daughter dragged me back for my public flogging. The good news was that the walk provided another opportunity for some father/daughter bonding.

As strange as it might sound, we grew much closer during my stint in prison. In the prior years, I'd been too busy with my career, hobnobbing with celebrities, and cheating on her mother. Taylor visited me almost every week, and to prove that she'd inherited her sense of humor from the Collins side of the family, she would occasionally bring me a gag gift like a Hostess cupcake with a nail file stuck in it like a birthday candle. The guards didn't always find it as funny as I did.

"Thanks for my Christmas present, Dad … it's the best gift ever! At least until you buy me that private jet I've had my eye on," she said with a smile.

I looked at her with surprise, which she read. "Mom didn't mean to give it away, but the camp called to confirm this week and I answered. I'm so excited to go!"

"Well, now that your grandparents are claiming to be destitute, you're going to need to get that field hockey scholarship if you want to go to college."

"Yeah, they'll probably have to sell their kidneys just to scrape by."

Or sell mine.

"And Dad," she flashed me her patented look of disappointment. "It's lacrosse camp, not field hockey. You only went to like ten of my games last fall."

"Lacrosse—that's what I meant." The T-shirt she often wore popped into my head. "Chicks with sticks, right?"

"Ewe … when you say it, it sounds like tranny porn."

There is no prouder moment for a parent than hearing your little bundle of joy utter the term 'tranny porn' for the first time. When I stopped beaming, I said, "Your mom said this camp is the one you really wanted to attend, and it fits perfectly into your winter break from school."

"The coach from Clemson is going to be instructing there. I really want to impress her … and get that scholarship. That's where I really want to go."

"Clemson? I thought Syracuse was your top choice?"

"It was … like last year! Do you ever pay attention?"

Obviously not.

"I'm thinking I wanna go to a warm-weather school. And it's only like a few hours from Grandpa's place in Hilton Head—he said I can use the place when I'm on break."

That didn't sound like such a good idea, but I couldn't quibble with the warm weather part. I took notice that Taylor was shivering, so I removed my suit jacket and placed it over her bare shoulders. If I were a better parent I would have thought to do so about an acre ago, but I was making progress, and I think she respected that I was giving an honest effort. At least that's what her smile told me.

We entered the party area, which led me to think that warning signs should be posted, like at the beach when the surf is too rough. The speakers were now blaring "Silent Night." I could only hope.

"Seeing you in a suit reminds me of way back when we were kids. You were so Don Draper back then, always all dudded up," Taylor commented.

Way back … as in a whole four years ago. "I can't believe how much older you look in that dress. You're turning into a woman, no matter how much I want to hold you back."

She smiled. "Speaking of old, I love how you're rocking the gray goatee."

My face still gave off that boyish innocence that was always very effective with juries, and occasionally got me carded at the liquor store. But the recent addition of the gray in the facial hair did make me appear closer to my age of forty-one, closing in on forty-two—maybe it's a sign that I was finally growing up. The hair on the head was still its natural dishwater blond. I grew it out after my release, after having it cut to the nub while doing my time.

Physically, I came out of prison in the best shape of my life. But after suffering through three years of prison food, I fell off the wagon after my release, and gained twenty pounds in nine months, most of it in my gut. Luckily, my custom-tailored suit hid it well … along with the bulletproof vest I was wearing.

CHAPTER 3

Taylor escorted me through the marble foyer into the grand reception hall. When we entered the ballroom, my eyes immediately went to its signature double-staircase that cascaded down from the balcony. I'd always assumed the reason for two was so that neither Alexander the Great and his wife, the lovely Beatrice, would be forced to sacrifice any of their spotlight during their entrances.

A large orchestra was playing on the other side of the room, accompanying a Celine Dion wannabe singer. Or maybe it was Celine Dion. You never know who will show up at these parties. "Do you see what I see," she sang as I entered. As if to warn the others that "the felon" had returned after a three year absence—like a neighborhood watch program for stuffy parties.

Maybe I was being paranoid, but Taylor noticed it too, mentioning, "I guess 'Jailhouse Rock' woulda been too obvious."

I would have taken pleasure in my entrance creating one of those moments where the crowd froze in horror, and a hush came over the room. But most of the guests were too distracted by their revelry ... and alcohol ... to notice.

I did spot a couple of my former brothers-in-law with their bra-bursting second wives, who were trying to put the ho, ho, ho back into Christmas. The rest of the guests appeared to be the usual hodgepodge of old, money, and old money. Despite reports of it being a "down" year for Wainwright & Lennox, which was connected to the lingering martyrdom from the Kerstman debacle, there was no evidence of it in this room.

W&L is an investment bank that dates back to the Civil War. It holds a pristine reputation in the world of high finance. Mainly because its reviews had always been written by the clients they'd made gobs of money for. The investors, the ones who were often bilked by the fraudulent IPOs that W&L underwrote, had another tale to tell. But luckily, W&L employed an in-house law firm that worked endless hours to fend off lawsuits and bad publicity to keep the firm's pristine image unsullied. I had firsthand knowledge of this, since it was my first job out of NYU Law School. They preferred family members to work there—a club that they reluctantly admitted I was a member of during my marriage to Libby—because they were less likely to risk their inheritance by having a heart to heart with the feds about some of the firm's tactics. But working for Wainwright wasn't all bad—it actually made my job representing celebrities seem authentic.

In the center of the room an enormous Christmas tree towered over the partygoers. But in keeping with the party theme, this tree was a fake. Next to the plastic pine, fittingly, was a throne. It was occupied by a Santa Claus, who held two six-year-old girls on his lap.

After Taylor ran off to meet up with a few of her cousins, I made a surprise attack on the throne, sneaking up behind the two girls. They felt my presence, which blew my cover. But that didn't stop me from pulling them into an embrace, causing them to giggle. I received a dirty look from Santa, not that it affected my standing with him—I'd been on his "naughty list" since my first date with his daughter. I shot one right back at him, but quickly looked away—the sight of Alexander Wainwright dressed as Santa Claus was always too much for me to take. It was the equivalent of Bernie Madoff playing the role of Baby Jesus in the upcoming Nativity play.

The twins were the result of the never discussed "save the marriage" crusade led by my former wife. It didn't work, and we learned the lesson that all parents should be taught in Marriage-101—never drag your kids into your problems, especially ones that aren't even born yet. But so far the girls haven't held it against us, which we're thankful for.

We named them Franny and Zooey, because our devotion to Salinger was one of the few things Libby and I could agree on at that stage of our union. Alexander and Beatrice still held *Catcher in the Rye* responsible for Libby's rebellious streak, which was blamed for her marrying a middle-class schmuck from Tarrytown, and gasp, becoming a lowly prosecutor. Although, a rebellious streak for a Wainwright was much differently defined than one for normal people. She would never be compared to James Dean, and as far as I know, doesn't even have a parking ticket to her name.

I took a long look at the identical twins. I often mixed them up, which made me feel like a horrible father. But Libby recently mentioned that she'd often done the same. This made me feel better, since her mothering skills and devotion to our children was beyond reproach.

"So what did you ask Santa for?" I inquired.

Zooey answered for both of them, "A castle!"

I could tell she wasn't referring to a plastic, toy version of one. They were definitely more Wainwright than Collins. But I was trying to make up for lost time in Collins-izing them. Over the last nine months, I'd gone from being a total stranger to "Daddy," which I'm sure hadn't gone unnoticed by their grandfather.

"Nice suit," Alexander said to me. "I was concerned that you might wear prison stripes out of habit."

I noticed a smile peering through the opening in his Santa beard. It seemed that they'd added some extra snark to the eggnog this year. But I refused to let him bait me in front of the girls. "I was honored to receive an invitation."

He leaned in close to my ear. "I like to keep my enemies close, and those who steal my money even closer."

To be fair, I didn't steal his money. But Alexander suspected that I knew where it was, which was no different to him than if I robbed him at gunpoint. The FBI also suspected me in such matters, as did Alexander's former business partner, now rival, Stone Scroggie, who was the mastermind behind the initial heist. It was irrelevant if I knew the location—the important thing was that they thought I did, and were convinced I was the only one who could deliver it. It was more effective than any life insurance I could have purchased.

I reached the maximum two minutes I could spend in Alexander's presence without blood shooting out of my eyes. And since I thought that might scare the girls, I decided to move on. But just as I was about to slither away, my former mother-in-law cornered me. Alexander looked as annoyed by this turn of events as I was.

Beatrice was a Lennox, the other wealthy Connecticut family that had its name on the stationery. The Wainwright and Lennox families were constantly marrying each other—I could count six marriages off the top of my head—which was either creepy, or a well-organized plan to maintain the species, and eventually take over the world.

The not-yet-corrupted Franny and Zooey greeted their grandmother by running to her. They hugged each of her legs, which were covered by her designer gown. I hoped that this might dislodge her robot limbs, and the Stepford Wife scheme would be publicly exposed ... but no such luck. And Franny and Zooey couldn't catch a break either, as Beatrice made them aware that their affectionate act was not acceptable etiquette for young ladies, especially since they almost spilled Grandma's drink. She threatened to lock them in the coal cellar if they didn't drastically alter their behavior.

This was not an idle threat. The manor house did contain an actual working coal cellar, which Alexander liked to brag about. It was dormant when I'd lived here, but it was revived after W&L made a large financial investment into clean coal technology this past year.

Once Beatrice was done scaring the dickens out of my kids, she turned her contempt on me. She admonished the "rude behavior" I exhibited upon my entrance, and informed me that I was lucky she didn't revoke my parole, which apparently she had the authority to do. Having seen the Wainwrights in action, I would never bet against their power and how far it reached.

Out of habit I put my finger on my nose, which had always been the distress signal between Libby and me when one of us was trapped at these parties. But when I caught a glimpse of her across the room, engrossed in a conversation with her current boyfriend, Ned Blaine, I remembered that I was living in a whole new world these days. One that I would have to survive all on my own.

CHAPTER 4

As I made my way to the door, Libby busted me from across the room, effectively ending my attempt to slip out unnoticed.

I've adored Libby from the moment I laid eyes on her, and after having a couple years in a small cell to reflect on it, I had even more respect for her. So technically, I wasn't avoiding her. But my work was done here and I had a train to catch, and honestly, nobody really wants to see their boss on the weekend.

While I was enjoying the normal undergrad life at Iona College, my best friend since childhood, Zee Thomas, had rocketed to stardom with the New York Yankees. The teenage, phenom pitcher had captured the hearts and imagination of the city, but still struggled in social situations, as had been the case since we were kids. So he dragged me along one night to a party that his marketing agency had thrown for him in the city, to play the role of security blanket. Libby Wainwright, a sophomore at NYU, and an intern at the agency that represented Zee, also attended the party. The rest was history. And the historical record read: Twenty-two years, fifteen years of marriage, four children, a messy affair, one divorce, and a prison sentence.

It wasn't hard to figure out what attracted me to Libby. She was beautiful, smart, and funny. Okay, she was never very funny—laughing had always been frowned upon in the Wainwright house … literally. I've always taken great pride in that I was her first, at least when it came to making her laugh. But what really drew me to her, besides the beauty and brains combo, was that just being around her made it seem that anything and everything was possible. Maybe that was why I didn't realize how over my head I was dating the daughter of Alexander Wainwright.

As I got closer, I could hear Ned Blaine talking up Wainwright Manor to a couple of party guests—the "exquisite" French wallpaper of the ballroom, the "spectacular" thousand bottle wine cellar, and how it resonated a homeness, even though it was over eighteen-thousand square feet and had eight bedrooms and eleven-and-a-half baths. I wasn't so sure about the homeness part—that half a bath was ten times bigger than any room we had in my house growing up in Tarrytown.

When Ned spotted me he raised the charm to an even higher level—a skill that had helped make him one of the top realtors of upscale properties in Manhattan. If I was the lawyer to the stars, then he was the one who sold them the best places to live. In fact, he sold Libby and me our first apartment on the Upper East Side, which we bought after fleeing for our lives from her parents' place. At least I felt that way; I think Libby was actually sad to leave.

Ned almost tripped over himself to greet me with a friendly handshake. I should probably despise the man who moved in on my ex-wife like she was a luxury condo overlooking Central Park, before the ink was even dry on our divorce agreement. But Ned had always been generally harmless—he reminded me of one of those polished politicians with the perfectly coiffed hair and sparkly white teeth, who would intently look you in the eye when they speak to you and overuse your first name like they'd learned it in a seminar. And it wasn't like he was standing in a way of a reunion between us. That ship had sailed, and all the Christmas magic in the world couldn't turn it around.

Ned and I had also been collaborating on a secret project that he calls "Operation Farmer on the Roof." He covertly let me know that things were going as planned with it, and we had a meeting with our contact set for Christmas Eve in the city. I nodded, hoping I'd be alive to attend.

Ned then strategically stepped away, so that Libby and I could talk about whatever Libby needed to talk to me about. Ned understood the dynamics of closing a deal, and he knew he wasn't going to close one with Libby unless she was comfortable with his relationship with her children. And unfortunately for Ned, her children came furnished with a father that she was determined to keep relevant in their lives.

After exchanging the cold cheek-kiss of divorced parents, she said, "So you were really going to skip out of here without saying hello?"

"I wasn't skipping out on anything," I replied a little too defensively. "The only reason I came was to see the Amigos one last time before they were thrown out on the street. I was going to leave straight from the Lake House, but Taylor dragged me inside to surprise the twins."

She looked at me with skepticism. "They were hardly thrown out on the street … and you also came because you knew it would irritate my parents."

"I must say, one of the hardest things during my time away was not getting to piss them off every year," I replied with a smile.

"Now that sounds like the old Kris Collins. And in that suit, you are starting to look like him again."

"By old, are you referring to the gray beard?"

"I meant, as in the past. You would wear a suit to the beach if we had let you," Libby replied, and once again reminded me that she was the most literal person I'd ever met.

"My daughter said I used to be 'all Don Draper.'"

Libby never watched TV, so the remark would've had the same effect if I'd referenced Homer Simpson. But she wasn't listening to me, anyway. Her mind was where it always was these days when it came to me—focused on my relationship with our children.

She gazed across the room at Taylor. "I can't believe how grown up our daughter has become."

"Time flies when you're having fun … or even when you're not."

"Tell me about it. It's hard to believe that she's not much younger than we were when we met."

I nodded, enjoying the impromptu trip down memory lane, and let her continue.

"On the subject of college, will you be joining us for her visits this spring?"

"If my boss will give me some time off—she's a real slave driver."

A smile escaped her lips—it was nice to know I still had the touch. "I think that can be arranged."

"Taylor told me that she's leaning toward Clemson."

She sighed. "Last week it was Virginia, next week it will be UCLA."

A brief quiet came over us—the thought of our little girl living in California was overwhelming. But from a safety factor, I'd still prefer her near the San Andreas Fault than Alexander's winter residence in Hilton Head.

"Have you completed your Christmas shopping?" Libby asked.

"Well, I know I'm sending Taylor to lacrosse camp in Florida. Rumor has it that *she also* knows this."

"I'm sorry, it couldn't be helped. The camp called to confirm and she answered. It was an honest mistake—I guess I'm not very good at keeping secrets."

For what it's worth, she'd always been much better than me at it, but that would be stating the obvious. She moved on, "What about the others?"

"I still have a couple of days … I do my best work under deadline pressure."

"You only work under deadline pressure. So you have no basis to say for sure if it's your most effective way to work."

"I was thinking about wrapping up Zee with a bow for Alex."

"That's not really funny," Libby said, looking queasy. "I love Zee like family, but I'm hoping that Alex discovers a new male role model over the next couple of years."

By the uncomfortable stare she sent in my direction, I got the feeling that she was referring to me.

Alex is my only son. I didn't have a choice in the name, since all first born male Wainwrights are named Alexander, which explained why there were so many Cousin Zanders and Uncle Als running around at this party. Unlike his older sister, Alex never came to see me once during my time away, and we've rarely spoken since my release. But being sort of an Alex expert, in that she's one of the few in the human species that he actually communicates with, Taylor assured me that his silence has nothing to do with my time in prison, or "the thing with Mom," as she calls it. She informed me that we are on good terms, and promised to let me know if the status of our relationship changes.

The other person he frequently corresponded with was Zee, who was a combination father-figure and best-friend to him. I never took offense to this, but I sometimes worried about Alex following a similar path. Especially since Alex reminded me so much of Zee, including, but not limited to, their shared social awkwardness and communication issues. I've had a recurring dream for years about being ambushed on one of those daytime talk shows where the true paternity of the child is revealed. Although, it would better explain things.

The mention of Zee reminded me of our meeting tonight, and I attempted to hurry things along, "So what am I getting Alex for Christmas?"

"I'm glad you asked. You and your son will be doing a tour of spring training baseball in Florida this February. You know what a baseball fanatic he is. And I'm hoping that you can use some of your connections with professional athletes so that Alex could meet some of the New York Yankees players, which is his favorite team."

She pulled the itinerary from her purse and handed it to me. The trip had been meticulously mapped out to the hour. "I'm guessing that it's not a coincidence that Taylor will be in Florida at the same time for her camp."

"The three of you will drive home together. I think it will be a good chance for you to bond with them."

I remained impressed by her effort to make me important in our kids' lives. That was her gift to me, even if she would never think of it as a gift.

Two down, two to go. "So what will Franny and Zooey be receiving from Daddy?"

"They will be getting ponies. I think it will be a good chance for them to learn about responsibility, and I think there's no better way to do that than taking care of another living creature."

Goldfish would have sufficed, but when it came to Wainwright gifts this was downright frugal. Libby and her brothers were all bought a thoroughbred racehorse as children, costing well into the six figures each. So as long as it wouldn't require Daddy to be scooping up pony poop on the weekend, I was on board with it … not that I had much of a choice. And Libby and the kids had plenty of space at the house in Pound Ridge to keep them, including a barn. We bought the place right before the twins were born. But I spent most of my time those last few years in Manhattan, schmoozing my celeb clients and writing a cautionary tale.

As if they had an internal alarm clock that beeped every time we discussed their Christmas gifts—for all I know, there might be an Apple app to do that these days—all four of our kids suddenly joined us.

Gathering everyone in the same place had never been an easy task with the Collins clan, so it was a nice moment … until Franny exclaimed, "Look, Daddy—I got a candy cane." She proudly held up her striped sugar stick up for me to see, as did Zooey.

Just as she said it, as if orchestrated, Celine-Lite began singing with gusto, "O Come, all ye Faithful."

A few of the guests had the nerve to send a dirty look in my direction. In this room, I was squarely in the top percentile of faithfulness, having had just one affair, albeit, a very public one.

"I'm sorry about that," I whispered to Libby.

"It was bound to come up. Especially this time of year."

I meant I was sorry about everything, but now was hardly the time for such mea culpas, especially ones that were already understood, and frankly, were too late.

When my public mocking concluded, the kids dispersed to prepare for the Nativity play—a requirement for all Wainwright children each year. I jokingly slipped Taylor the "Get out of Jail Free" Monopoly card that she'd given me during one of her prison visits, and that I'd carried in my wallet since being released. She'd always hated performing in these plays.

But she surprised me with her enthusiasm. "I'm playing the lead this year—the Virgin Mary—it can't go on without me!" she exclaimed, before heading off to Wardrobe.

I'd given up on trying to figure out teenagers, so I didn't give the change of heart much thought, and my mind wandered again to my return trip to the city. Libby caught me glancing at my watch. "Not going to stick around for the play?"

"I'd like to—I hear it's up for a Tony. But I have a train to catch."

"Say hello to Zee for me," she said, showing off her prognostication skills.

"I will."

Before I left, she reached into her purse one more time and took out a folder. "Can you give this to Alyson when you go home tonight? It's for the Morzetti case. We have a meeting coming up, and she's off tomorrow, so she wanted to do some prep work."

I looked at the folder, but didn't say anything.

"You are going home tonight, aren't you?" she asked with a suspicious look.

She always knew when I was up to something. And I was. But that wasn't the reason for my silence. It was the realization that while I might be living with Alyson, home was a place that I'd never have again. So, no, I wouldn't be going *home* tonight.

CHAPTER 5

I took Metro North from Greenwich to Grand Central, and then hopped a subway to Penn Station. The journey took an hour, and ended with me standing outside a door marked "Authorized Personnel Only," and watching weary holiday travelers pass by me without a second look.

After another half hour dragged by, Zee stepped through the door. He was wearing his Amtrak engineer uniform that consisted of of matching blue jacket and pants, along with a winter hat over his shaved head. He had a red bandana tied around his neck like he was a cowboy, but its purpose was to cover his tattooed artwork, a company policy, not a fashion statement.

There was no emotional greeting. Or even an audible one. He just read my look and followed me through the train terminal. We had the ability to communicate solely through gestures and eye contact, as only people who've been connected at the hip since kindergarten could do. Using the touristy Christmas crowds as cover, we were able to avoid the New York media, which had been hounding Zee since it was discovered that the onetime prince of the city was now working as a train engineer—the technical word for the guy who drives the train. I could relate, as they followed me relentlessly when I first got out of prison, but like most people, they quickly grew tired of Kris Collins. But this city had been fascinated with the ups and downs of Zee Thomas for over twenty years, and showed no signs of losing interest in him.

But even I would admit that there was a troubling side to Zee's sudden career move. His father—the one who spent endless hours with Zee in their backyard, grooming his son to become a baseball star—committed suicide during our senior year of high school. Instead of taking the train to the city, as he had done each workday for his job as a commodities broker, his father had leaped in front of one that day. It was why the "train thing" had all those who care about Zee very concerned.

Just a year removed from high school, Zee took the mound in Yankee Stadium. Armed with a 99mph fastball and a burning pain in his heart, the teenager led the Yankees to an improbable playoff appearance. But his rise was like a shooting star. A severe arm injury and a legendary fall from grace sent him on a journey to Milwaukee, San Diego, and even a stint in Japan, as he carved out a fifteen-year baseball career. He was never a star again after the injury, and I think he liked it that way. But New Yorkers never forgot the thrills he supplied them that one summer. They would always have his back, no matter how many indiscretions and court appearances there had been since.

The adversarial media was a different story, and they soon had us surrounded as we stepped out of Penn Station. A photographer snapped shots right in his face, blinding us with the flash. The scene reminded me of when Zee and I would walk up the court steps each day during his murder trial, which became the catalyst for my career.

But Zee remained calm, continuing his methodical stride as if they weren't there. Chaos was Zee's natural habitat—he'd literally been surrounded by it since the day he was born. His father was forced to deliver him while they were stuck in traffic on the Tappan Zee Bridge, desperately trying to get to the hospital. Mother and child survived the ordeal, and thankfully they didn't name him Tappan, but it would be a harbinger of things to come.

A police officer stepped in to play interference, allowing us to break from the hungry pack. We chose walking over a ten-dollar cab ride. Times

Square was only eight blocks away and Zee preferred to stretch his legs after his trip to and from Vermont, driving the scenic train-line aptly named "the Vermonter."

As we walked up Eighth Avenue, and the snow started falling harder, we had one of our usual conversations. In other words, I did all the talking. I told him about the party, getting the information to the Amigos, and bemoaned how fast my daughter was growing up.

Zee listened intently, adding something only when necessary. He had never been a great conversationalist, to say the least, which made it all the more surprising that he would give passionate speeches to schools about the dangers of drugs and alcohol. It was like watching a different person.

He was equally passionate about his involvement in my plot, even though I had reservations about his participation. I didn't doubt he was perfect for the job—the main requirements were loyalty and the ability to keep one's mouth shut. Who better embodied those qualities than Zee? But if things were to go wrong, there would be a lot of collateral damage, and it had always been my instinct to protect Zee. I think this time he believed he was returning the favor.

We soon arrived at the glitzy lights of Times Square, and just like a lot of folks this holiday season we headed to Temple.

CHAPTER 6

We walked into Temple of Duma's. The combination of the loud music, laser-show lighting, and gorgeous naked women left me dizzy, and searching for my bearings.

If you like your strip clubs dark and dingy, with a permeating haze of cigarette smoke, then this place probably wouldn't be your cup of tea. It more resembled the theme-park motif of most of the current occupants of the modern Times Square. The place even had a gift shop. Sometimes I missed the sleaze of yesteryear in New York City—it had a certain authenticity to it.

Just as I was about to fall over, I felt a large paw on my back, steadying me. I turned to see the club's owner, and former Jets defensive lineman Justin Duma—all six-four and three hundred pounds of him.

I was no longer Duma's best customer, but I was a big reason why he was still in business. He first hired me to represent him when the NFL tried to force him to shut down Temple of Duma's, based on a very subjective "morality clause" in his contract.

But that was just the warm-up. The next opponent was a former mayor of New York, who'd made it his mission to clean up Times Square. As a business owner in the area, Duma found this commendable. At least until they tried to shut him down as part of the clean-up plan.

We argued that besides being the owner of a *legal* business, Justin Duma had courage to invest in the seedy, pervert-filled area known for its peepshows, and had been bringing upscale clients into Times Square long before the mayor's grandstanding began. The fight went on for years, but in the end, Temple of Duma's was still here, the mayor was long gone, and Times Square, by any definition, had been scrubbed clean.

Duma spoke over the music, explaining that he needed to attend to some business in his office, and we could meet there in about an hour. In the meantime, he suggested we do some window-shopping, and he wasn't talking about the storefronts on Fifth Avenue.

He called over a girl named Jade, one of the few women in the place wearing clothes. She led us by smaller stages that were scattered throughout the club like islands. They were surrounded by tables of gawking men, who appeared desperate to get their lifeboat to land.

Our destination was the VIP area right in front of the large rotating stage in the center of the room. There appeared to be a Christmas theme tonight, as the dancers gyrated to seasonal music, uniformed in Santa hats and not much else. A slow, rhythmic version of "Santa Baby" accompanied the bumping and grinding.

The uniformity was typical, as Duma ran a tight ship that more resembled boot camp than your usual strip club. Every dancer must be enrolled in college or grad school, and be passing their classes. There was no fraternization with customers outside of work, and there was a zero policy for drugs, which included weekly testing.

Some liked to advance the myth that he opened the club as a tribute to his own mother, who had gotten him and his siblings out of their crack infested neighborhood in Oakland, California by stripping. And maybe the son of one of these dancers would turn out like this Berkeley educated, financially independent businessperson, who once inspired seventy thousand fans to chant *Doooooma!* when he'd sack the quarterback. But having worked with Justin Duma over the years, I knew that the only thing he cared about is the bottom line, and this was a very profitable business. And having disciplined, reliable, and upwardly mobile employees was good for his profit margins. It was this emotionless business sense that made him a perfect partner for my plan.

Before I could take my seat, I was met by a stunning woman wearing *only* a pair of Christmas-themed thigh highs and five-inch heels, to go along with her Santa hat.

"Hey stranger," she greeted me with a flirtatious smile and a hug, pulling me close to her soft body.

She rubbed her hand over my goatee. "Look who's Santa now, baby."

"You don't think it makes me look too old?"

"I like the gray ... but not the white on top," she said, and knocked off snow that had settled on my head during the walk over.

She then seductively ran her hands over my chest like I was one of her typical customers—making a strange face when she came upon the bulletproof vest. "God, you're all wet, Kris. I can't believe you're walking around in the snow without a coat."

It made me think of the coat-less Taylor from earlier. It was a sobering thought, as Taylor wasn't much younger than Sophie.

Then once again proving that all strippers are failed actresses, Sophie looked to Zee and casually said, "Long time no see, ZT. Good to see you again."

"Spending time together"—which was Zee's term, and sounded more like a day at the DMV than dating—was against the rules. But Duma had made an exception in this case, and gave his blessing on the condition that nobody found out ... and he was clear that Sophie would be out of a job if anyone did.

I was the one who set them up last summer. It was reminiscent of our younger days when the antisocial Zee needed his talkative wingman to close the deal for him. Which was sort of funny, since females had been throwing themselves at him since we were in the sixth grade.

But as his wingman, I should have been there for his dangerous ascent into the stratosphere and the predictable fall that followed. The new "friends" he collected after his baseball career took off consisted of hanger-ons and enablers who made it their business to make excuses for him as he continued to careen down the fast-lane toward the concrete barrier. Just like they did when he was arrested on the pot charge. He was still college age, and what kid that age doesn't smoke a little weed? *Baked ZT* was the newspaper headline, almost making light of the situation. But those who really knew him, like myself, understood how out of character that was.

By the time of the home invasion, we had become distant strangers, and I barely recognized him. But he found his way back home, needing his wingman more than ever. When he asked me to represent him, I told him that he needed an experienced trial attorney—I was barely out of law school, and working for my father-in-law. He told me that if he was going to go down, he was going to go down with the last person left on the planet that he trusted.

And when I pulled off the legal miracle of all miracles, that trust was rewarded. And in an ironic twist, the not-guilty verdict sent me into that same dangerous atmosphere. And like Zee, I hit the accelerator onto the fast-crowd highway. Zee had been at the end of his rope, but little did I know as I walked triumphantly down those courthouse steps that I was just beginning to tie my own noose.

CHAPTER 7

When the next song ended, the guy seated to my right turned to me with a shell-shocked look, and said, "I think that girl you were talking to … Sophie … is one of my students."

I couldn't help but laugh. "If you can concentrate with her in your class, you should get some sort of 'teacher of the year' award. What school?"

"I teach in the graduate psychology program at Brooklyn College. She doesn't dress like that for class, or I probably wouldn't be able to."

"You mean she wears clothes for class?"

He chuckled nervously. "Um … I meant she looks a lot different, but I'm sure it's her."

He looked like a college professor with his tweed jacket and glasses. His gray hair lent him a distinguished look, although it appeared to be a toupee. And he was correct—Sophie was pursuing a masters degree in psychology at Brooklyn College. But I didn't want to add to the awkwardness of their future teacher/student relationship, so I told him, "It's probably not her. And after working in a place like this, she wouldn't need to take a psychology class—she would know all there is to know about human behavior."

He nodded, looking closely at me. "I know you from somewhere."

"Zee Thomas. I used to pitch for the Yankees," I said and offered my hand to shake. I received a small smile from Zee.

"No, you're that lawyer. The one who helped Diedrich Kerstman escape."

Since Kerstman ended up dead, I'm not sure that escape would be the proper term, but I didn't push the subject. After we formally introduced ourselves, he asked, "So do you really know where the treasure is hidden, like some people claim?"

I smiled. "I must. How else could I afford to spend time in a place like this?"

Our conversation was interrupted by start of the next song—"I saw Mommy kissing Santa Claus," the John Mellencamp version.

Sophie worked her way over to me. "You look stressed, Kris," she said over the pounding music.

Not as much as her teacher probably was at this moment. I subtly nodded in his direction, but she didn't pick up on my signal. I figured such information might come in handy, especially if her grade ever needed a boost, and let's say, the professor's wife was under the impression that he was at the office correcting papers tonight. "I just came from a party at the Wainwrights, I might need a couple weeks in the Caribbean to de-stress."

"I got a better idea—how about a dance?"

"Zee gave me one earlier, and it didn't really work," I replied with a grin.

I could tell that it wasn't a question, and she began to grind up on me—her excuse to remain nearby Zee. "ZT must not know how to do it right," she said and they smiled at each other.

I lightly pushed her away. "I'm going to have to pass, Sophie."

She looked strangely at me—this probably never happened before—then she grabbed me by both sides of my face like my grandmother used to. Her eyes bulged like she'd had an epiphany. "Oh my God, Kris—you're in love. I see it in your eyes. You are head over heels in love!"

A correct psychological analysis—I wondered if her professor was equally impressed. I never thought I could feel this strongly again for someone after Libby. Then one day she swept into my life—actually my courtroom—and I haven't been able to get her out of my mind since. But the reality was I had more of a chance of remarrying Libby with Alexander and Beatrice's blessing, than even getting a date with this woman. So there was no reason to discuss it.

"I've heard of love causing a man to do stupid things, but never anything as foolish as turning down a dance with you," a voice rang out. I was surprised that it came from her professor—I figured he would want to keep a low profile.

Sophie didn't become the highest grossing girl at Duma's by turning down easy business. She moved to her professor and began dancing in front of him like nobody has ever danced to John Mellencamp. She whipped her leg around him and pulled him into a straddle—a classic move they must teach on the first day of stripper school. She didn't seem to recognize him, but after they'd been doing this job for a while most girls focused on shaking what they've got, rather than who they're shaking it for.

On the other side of me, Zee was also attracting some attention. A guy in a replica Zee Thomas Yankees jersey came up to him and introduced himself as Paulie his "biggest fan." He began excitedly recounting some game he was at years ago, where Zee struck out the first nine batters of the game. Strangely, he told the story as if Zee wasn't present for it. This was outside the lines of etiquette at Temple of Duma's—the VIP clientele weren't to be bothered—and security moved in. Paulie understood the error of his ways, and backed off without incident.

This didn't stop another person from approaching, this time a female, but not a dancer. She had spiky black hair and was wearing a black tank top and tight jeans. One arm was a complete sleeve of ink.

She opened with the typical "I'm a big fan" intro, telling him her name was Jacqueline, before turning around and raising her shirt to show him the 'ZT' she had tattooed on her lower back. She then started moving her hips like she was one of the professionals.

She began to grind her hips into Zee's midsection. Moments later, the tank top flew off. Zee appeared too stunned to react.

Sophie had lost interest in the professor. She was going through the motions while keeping both eyes on Zee and the woman.

Jacqueline stared right back at her, and shouted over the music, "Mind your own business, tramp. This one's all mine."

Sophie, who normally couldn't bring herself to kill a mosquito, was now glaring at the woman like she wanted to introduce her to the art of pole dancing. As in, if she didn't get away from Zee, she was going to stick a pole somewhere that would make her dance.

When Jacqueline went in for the kiss, Sophie lost it—to hell with Duma's rules. She left the professor high and dry, and leaped in the direction of Zee and the woman.

But the professor grabbed Sophie's arm, yanking her back in his direction. "We're finished when the song's finished," he said sternly.

She tried to squirm away. But when that didn't work, she sent a mule-kick into his chest, which would probably cost her on the final exam.

Zee was now trying to push the woman away, but her lips were locked on him like a dog to a bone. She wouldn't let go … until Sophie tackled her, and they begin to roll around on the floor. Security was slow on the draw, which was likely on purpose. This place sold male fantasy, and what do men find more fantastic than two topless women rolling around on the floor and pulling hair? And to make my point, some caveman yelled out, "Cat fight!" Except he used a different word for cat.

A security guard reached the scene and pulled Jacqueline away. "You need to leave him alone," he yelled. But on further review, it wasn't security—it was Zee's fan in the Yankees jersey. Paulie.

I did my best to remove Sophie from the situation, but she continued to kick and scream—arms, legs, and other appendages flying everywhere.

When the song ended, the real security finally arrived. They kicked Paulie and Jacqueline out of the club. Sophie was sent to the dressing room to calm down, like a child getting a timeout. But Zee and I got the worst of it. "You two are going to the principal's office," one guard said, as he dragged us up the stairs. I looked back, noticing that the professor had slipped out, undetected.

We were ushered into Justin Duma's office. Our presence interrupted a meeting between him and the woman who runs the day-to-day operations of the club, his mother. Also present was a former feature dancer at the club who went by the name Wintry Mix. She was now in charge of the dancers. She also happened to be Duma's longtime girlfriend and the mother of his two sons.

The minute they left the room, the smile vanished from Duma's face. "I told you two to do some window shopping, not throw a rock through the damn window," he barked.

I tried to explain that it wasn't our fault, but he cut me off with the raise of his large hand. "That's the problem with you two—trouble always seems to find you."

When he finally allowed me to speak, I got down to business, providing him all the information he'd need to complete his role, including detailed information on all the former Kerstman employees. The office was one of the few places I felt secure to talk these days without feeling the need to hire an exterminator to remove the listening bugs.

When I finished, Duma instructed Zee to wait outside. He then voiced his concerns, "Zee's a good dude, but a black cloud follows him. And I don't like Candi being involved … how many times are you going to let her eff up your life before you learn your lesson? If I'm going to put myself on the line for you, I can't have you thinking with your dick."

I attempted to explain that wasn't what was going on here, but the hand went up again. "And when it comes to Zee, you're thinking with your heart, which might be worse."

Duma's motivation was clear from the beginning—this was solely about business, and he saw Zee's unreliability as a threat to his bottom line. I respected it, but didn't agree.

When he finished lecturing, I did what I've always done—I served as the mouthpiece for Zee Thomas, and defended him to a skeptical jury. If I was going down, I was going down with the last person left on the planet that I completely trusted.

CHAPTER 8

Zee and I walked south on Broadway until we reached 42nd Street. We hung a left, and continued on foot until we arrived at Bryant Park, where we waited by the skating pond for Sophie. To avoid any scrutiny, she would always leave through a different entrance, twenty minutes after Zee exited the club. To keep their relationship under wraps, I might also suggest avoiding public wrestling matches.

A few people spotted Zee. Like always, he didn't have much to say, but he was accommodating with the fans and politely signed a few items, using his once-famous left arm.

Sophie arrived on schedule, having gone from no clothing to now being dressed like an Eskimo. Her cheery demeanor had also returned, and she apologized profusely for her out-of-character behavior. "Look who's the one in love now," I whispered to her. Two could play that game.

It seemed as if we'd escaped unnoticed, but as we attempted to hail a cab on Sixth Avenue, a flashbulb grabbed my attention. Zee noticed it too, and turned toward the source.

The grinning photographer called out, "Are you sure you don't want that dance, ZT?"

Zee and I usually had our paparazzi antennas up, so I was immediately kicking myself for not pegging the woman in the club as a plant.

She took a couple more shots, seemingly enjoying the cat and mouse game. "Say cheese, ZT," she yelled out, her attention then shifting to Sophie. "I thought Duma's didn't allow its whores to go home with the clients? Maybe I should send them a few of these shots, Blondie."

When another flash went off, Zee looked ready to pounce. I tried to position myself in front of him, hoping to stave off another altercation. But Sophie had beaten me to it. It seemed that he had a new protector.

Another voice rose from behind us. I looked to see Zee's other fan from the club—Paulie. He now wore a trench coat, with a winter cap pulled over his thick helmet of hair. It looked like we were right back to where we started. *Where's that damn cab?*

"I thought I told you to leave him alone … you got wax in your ears, sweetheart?" Paulie shouted, moving closer.

"That's more than you got between yours," she fired back.

"I said get lost."

"It's a free country."

When they stepped toward each other, Paulie reached under his coat and pulled out a gun. "I'm gonna say it real slow this time, so you can understand. I. Said. Leave. Him. Alone."

They stared at each other for what seemed like a minute, but the gun won out. She took off in a slow jog and mixed into the crowd. The hustling and bustling crowd on Sixth Avenue seemed unconcerned by the incident, as if it was just a typical case of holiday stress in the big bad city.

Paulie put his gun away and turned back toward us. I wasn't sure if we should shake his hand or run for our lives.

I was hoping that he was just an overzealous fan, but I knew his arrival was no coincidence, nor was what he said next, "I think it's a beautiful night for a walk. The lights, the snow … I love the city at Christmas time. I suggest you take your girlfriend for a romantic stroll, ZT."

When he didn't move, Paulie opened his coat just enough for us to get another look at the gun. Zee gave me an unsure look. I nodded that he should go for that walk. This was between me and them, and I wasn't going to allow Zee to be taken down in the crossfire.

He didn't appear convinced, but put his arm around Sophie and began walking away. He glanced over his shoulder with another concerned look. I waved to indicate that everything was going to be okay. But I wasn't sure that it was.

CHAPTER 9

A cab pulled up alongside us. I didn't take it as a sign that my luck was changing.

Paulie pointed for me to get in. In spite of the many hours I'd spent watching mob movies, I still chose to enter the vehicle. The driver was wearing a denim jacket and a skullcap. He looked like Paulie's chubby little brother.

Paulie piled in next to me in the backseat and we were off. My best guess was that they were a couple of Scroggie's thugs, but so many people were after me at this point I couldn't be sure.

"Court Street, Brooklyn Heights," Paulie instructed the driver, which just happened to be where my apartment was located.

He turned to me. "That is where you're going, Collins, isn't it?"

"I appreciate the ride home—the subway can be a zoo this time of year. But I'm not the only person living there. I'm sure you're aware that with each body you have to clean up, the chances of you getting caught go up dramatically." I couldn't let Alyson get trapped in this, anymore than Zee.

The driver laughed. "Who's gonna catch us … the FBI?"

Paulie grinned at the comment. "I know that Alyson Rudingo is working late tonight, and Robbie is staying with his father. So it'll just be us, Collins."

"And who would *us* be?"

Paulie reached under his trench coat and pulled out a badge. It identified him as Paul Falcone, a special agent with the FBI. The driver held up his badge—Larry Boersch, also with the FBI.

Not what I'd expected, but the lesser of the evils. They would just grill me, while the Scroggie thugs would likely have cooked me on a grill and served me for Christmas dinner.

"If this is about the fight at Duma's, I didn't start it. Come to think of it… I believe you did, Agent Falcone."

"No—Jacqueline Helada did. Do you know who she is?"

"I think she's that photographer that you almost shot on Sixth Avenue."

"It would make your life a lot easier if she was … or if I shot her. Jacqueline Helada is a longtime associate of Stone Scroggie, and is no stranger to guns. You are aware of who Stone Scroggie is, correct?"

"I think I overheard someone talking about him at the Wainwright party. A business partner that might have embezzled from them, or something like that."

Falcone began laughing. "Funny guy, ain't he, Larry?"

"A real crack up," Boersch replied. "Like he makes me wanna crack up his skull."

"Don't mind him," Falcone said to me. "He's just a little pissy because he spent his Sunday squeezing into an elf costume and parking cars for a bunch of rich pricks. He even had to chase down a guy who decided he'd rather hang out by the lake, instead of at the nice warm party."

"Trust me, if you were inside that party you'd understand."

"I don't trust anyone, especially felons like yourself, Collins. But I was inside that party, and I agree—it was a pretty scary place."

Boersch added, "Not as scary as where you'll be going if you don't start telling us the truth."

Since that wasn't an option, and lying to federal agents seemed like a good way to end up back in prison, I decided to just stare out the window. The cab was headed south on FDR Drive, a road named for the man who once uttered the words, "The only thing we have to fear is fear itself." I begged to differ.

Falcone filled in the downtime by making a call. "Any word on Gooch?" he asked into his phone.

After a short pause, he responded, "I was distracted breaking up a fight... when I looked back he was gone ... keep looking."

After the call ended, we again sat in silence. Finally curiosity got the best of me. "Gooch?" I asked.

"Short for goochelaar," Falcone answered. "It's the Dutch word for magician. And you got to see one of his disappearing acts tonight. One minute he was chatting it up with you and getting a lap dance from your buddy's girlfriend, and next thing we know, he's gone."

"The professor?"

Boersch chuckled. "Professor ... now that's a good one."

Falcone didn't seem to share his partner's humor. "Gooch could teach a class on how to take a body apart, piece by piece until he gets the information he's looking for."

"And this Gooch works for Scroggie?"

Falcone nodded. "He grew up with your old pal Diedrich Kerstman in the Netherlands. That's how he was able to bring the two of them together. And when I say he works for Scroggie, I mean he kills for him."

If he was trying to scare me it was a waste of time—I was already scared. Hence the bulletproof vest. "So what do you want?" I asked.

"What I want," Falcone said, "is to take my wife out to dinner on New Year's Eve."

"Why didn't you say so? I know Sal Morzetti—represented him in some legal matters. If I pull a couple strings, maybe I can get you a reservation at his restaurant."

"That's nice of you to offer, but I've promised to take her out every year since we were married, and I've always ended up having to work on New Year's. And this year I'm stuck on the job until the Kerstman money is recovered. So if you would let us know where it is before then, I'd really appreciate it … as would my wife."

"You guys think I know where the money is?" I asked with a surprised look.

The comment caused a ripple of laughter, but not the friendly kind.

"You know who also thinks you know where it is?" Boersch asked.

"Scroggie, Alexander Wainwright, and this Gooch fella come to mind, but I'm probably leaving someone out."

"The difference between us and them, is after we get the money, we're going to put a roof over your head and feed you three meals a day. But a guy like Stone Scroggie is going to send you through one of those chippers like they do with dead Christmas trees."

"What Agent Falcone is trying to say in his *eloquent* manner, is that if you return the money, and help us put Scroggie away, we can put in a good word with the judge for you," Boersch clarified. "And I'm sure your time served will be factored in."

That sounded more like a death sentence than an olive branch. "Even if I knew where the money was, anything Kerstman told me during the course of the trial is bound by the attorney/client privilege, and I wouldn't be able to tell you."

"The good news for you, Collins, is that you're no longer an attorney, and Kerstman is no longer a client … at least not a living one. And since we're your new BFFs, we'll keep your secret. That's what friends do, right?"

"You know it doesn't work that way, Falcone. I have nothing to say."

"Just like your client had nothing to say at trial. And you were quick to take that plea before you ever got to trial."

"Sounds like something's going down to me," Boersch got the last word in. "And I'm not just talking about that boat Kerstman was on."

I might not have been a lawyer anymore, but I still knew that anything I said at this point could and would be used against me. That's why I was practicing a new type of law these days—the law of the jungle.

CHAPTER 10

We passed over the East River with an assist from the Brooklyn Bridge. Its many suspension cables were lit up for the season, making it look like a Christmas spiderweb that connected the bridge's Gothic towers.

Traffic had slowed to a crawl. The bridge had originally been built for horse-drawn carriages and trolleys, which probably crossed faster than we were doing.

Since I wasn't talking, Falcone decided to speak for me, outlining how he believed we got to this point. I stared emotionless at the brake lights in front of us, not wanting to tip him off whether he was getting hot or cold.

"Since you aren't familiar with Scroggie's work, or so you say, let me give you a refresher course. He made his fortune off the desperation of struggling companies. Ones similar to Kerstman Publishing, which was bleeding red ink—a combination of too much overhead, and the drying up of the Harry Crawford pipeline. And as luck would have it, your new friend Professor Gooch had an in with Diedrich Kerstman from their days in the Netherlands, and was able to introduce the two men.

"Being the nice guy that Scroggie was, he offered Kerstman an interest-free loan. All he wanted in exchange was the personal details of his employees, including Social Security numbers, which he would sell to companies who were looking to use the info to market their products to specific audiences, mailing lists and such. Scroggie would make a nice little profit, nobody would know, and Kerstman would buy time to get back on his feet."

I continued staring straight ahead, forcing my lips shut.

"Of course, Scroggie had other plans for the information—using it to steal the identities and finances of the Kerstman employees. He drained bank accounts, got loans and credit lines in their names, and cashed out 401Ks. But that was just small potatoes for Scroggie. Where he makes his money, is by informing the owner, in this case Kerstman, that he was complicit in a scheme to rob his employees. He then extorted him into selling the company, in which he would take the money from the sale. In return, he would keep Kerstman's dirty little secret from ever seeing the light of day, and allow him to ride off unscathed into retirement. The only other choice was jail, and as we've learned, Kerstman would rather be anywhere, including the bottom of the Caribbean Sea, than in jail.

"But the thing was, who was going to buy a struggling publisher that was headed for bankruptcy? The answer was what it always was for Kerstman Publishing—Harry Crawford. You know, the same Harry Crawford that you've visited on numerous occasions since your release from prison."

Harry Crawford was once one of the biggest selling authors in the world, writing the famed Gin Rumy series. I'd successfully defended him some years back on a charge of growing large quantities of marijuana on his Vermont ranch. And even after he stopped writing, he remained loyal to Kerstman for giving him his first chance, when nobody else would publish him. So when Kerstman was arrested, Harry recommended me to represent him, which is how I ended up on the life-changing case. But I'm not sure if he would have made the same recommendation if he knew Kerstman and Scroggie were using him as part of their scam.

And Falcone was right—I still visited Harry, which he knew because he'd been following me. But visiting an old friend was hardly a crime, and what Falcone really wanted to know is what was said in those conversations inside the confines of the ranch. But Harry already has enough elves working for him, so it wouldn't be as easy to get a man on the inside.

Falcone continued, "So Scroggie went to the investment bank he's worked with all these years. The one that looked past his unscrupulous methods of business—Wainwright & Lennox. And to return the favor for all the money they'd made him over the years, he shared a tip—Diedrich Kerstman was looking to retire to his home in Sint Eustatius, and wanted to cash in on the Harry Crawford gravy train one last time by selling the company. He claimed Crawford was coming back to sign a five book deal, it was on the hush-hush, but Scroggie was able to learn of it because of Kerstman's connection with his associate Gooch.

"Wainwright and Scroggie would partner 50/50, each putting up six hundred million in cash, meant to blow Kerstman away with an offer before word of Crawford's return got out. It raised a lot of eyebrows in the industry when the struggling publisher sold for 1.2 billion, but Wainwright was convinced that with Crawford back on board it would be the bargain of the century. And this wasn't his first rodeo, so he didn't just blindly trust Scroggie. But he was convinced that Scroggie would never put up so much of his own money—over half a billion dollars—if he wasn't sure of Crawford's return.

"If anyone should have been aware of what Scroggie was capable of, it was Alexander Wainwright. So it should have been no surprise to him that once the sale was complete, Scroggie planned on taking it all—recouping his money, and taking Wainwright's 600 mil—and since there was no Crawford comeback, the company wasn't worth squat. And when Kerstman handed the money over to Scroggie, he would get something more valuable than money—his freedom. But he was smart enough to call Scroggie's bluff, knowing he'd be the one to take the fall for the dirty deal.

"Kerstman never handed the cash over. He double-crossed the double-crosser. He liquidated the money, hid it, and turned himself in before

Scroggie knew what hit him. He then hired a lawyer he was sure would get him off. But when the trial began to go south, Kerstman and his lawyer decided to take matters into their own hands. How'm I doing so far?" he asked with a cocky grin.

"He wasn't trying to escape. He wanted to go out on his own terms. So I gave him the opportunity ... and I paid for it with three years of my life."

"Like his employees got to go out on their own terms? The ones who had their lives ripped apart? They're the real victims in this!" He looked like he wanted to toss me out of the cab into oncoming traffic. "I think it was a leverage play by an unscrupulous lawyer who'd proven in the past that he would go to any length to get his clients off."

"What kind of leverage could have possibly been gained from him taking off? His flight made him look even guiltier than everyone already thought he was."

"If Kerstman was able to hide the treasure, then he could cut a deal. He could offer the return of the money and agree to testify against Scroggie, in exchange for a light sentence ... basically the same one that's being offered to you. And since you haven't taken it yet, I'm thinking that Kerstman offered you a better deal."

"A better deal than getting an FBI escort home in the snow? I don't know how he could have topped this," I said with a shrug/smirk combination that further irritated Falcone.

"I think he was going to give you half the money if you could get him to Sint Eustatius, where he could hide it offshore. And I think that's where it is, which is why your girlfriend made a recent trip down there."

He held up a copy of the *Inquisitor* tabloid from a couple weeks back, featuring Candi Kane on the cover. It showed her frolicking around in a bikini on the beaches of Sint Eustatius.

"But I don't think you can wear one of these on the beach—it'll cause some weird tan lines," he said, and patted me on the bulletproof vest to make his point.

The cab stopped near the Brooklyn Heights Promenade. There's no better view of the city than from the Promenade—Libby and I used to come down here all the time when we were dating. But I was in no mood for sightseeing tonight—I was too busy watching my back.

"I thought you were taking me home? I guess the moral of the story is never trust the FBI."

"Like I said, it's a beautiful night for a walk," Falcone said.

"Just watch out for the boogieman ... or Gooch," Boersch added with a cryptic grin.

I stepped out of the cab and turned back to Falcone. "I'd love to stay and chat, but I have to be at work bright and early tomorrow. My boss has been on my ass ever since she stopped sleeping with me."

"How the mighty have fallen—was that part of your divorce agreement?"

"The good thing about my new job is that I don't have the responsibility like when I was the boss. When five o'clock rolls around, I'm out the door. And I won't be working on New Year's Eve this year ... like you will be."

I slammed the door shut and began walking.

CHAPTER 11

I entered the dark, third-floor apartment. The barking dogs startled me, as they always did.

The first thing I did was remove my shoes. It was one of Alyson's non-negotiable rules. And since she spent ten years in the army as a sharpshooter, along with flying Black Hawk helicopters into enemy territory, I tended to go along with her rules.

I turned on a lamp and Olive and Oil, her two pugs, made a run for me. I petted them, which was more of a defense mechanism to stop them from scratching my legs, and other areas. I then re-filled their bowls, which was the real reason for the enthusiastic reception.

After leaving the military, Alyson pursued a career in law. But to support her son while she attended law school, she provided security for celebrities. She was working for one of my clients—a famous actor accused of assaulting a tabloid cameraman—and she spent the trial questioning my strategy, and generally telling me how to do my job. This didn't mesh well with my gargantuan ego, but as the trial went on I found myself incorporating her ideas into my defense. I would never admit that she was the reason I won an acquittal, so I did the next best thing, which was to hire her.

I had to match what she made from the security job, which was steep. But it was worth every penny. Since I'd always taken a seat-of-the-pants approach to law, her militaristic detail balanced me, and helped take Kris Collins Esq. to new heights. Her broad range of duties included everything except actually trying the cases, and she had nothing to do with the crash and burn—that was all me.

She finished law school while I was in prison, and she and Libby took over my practice. It's now Wainwright-Collins & Rudingo. The dash, which Libby still uses in her professional life, makes it sound like I'm still a partner, but I was stripped of my license to practice law as part of my plea bargain. And in a twist that only Shakespeare could love, I now worked as a paralegal for Alyson and Libby.

I removed my wet shirt and the vest underneath. I felt like I could breathe for the first time since I left for the Wainwright party. My growing gut was now also free of restraints. The sight of it should have sparked me to grab a carrot stick, but my mind went right to the oatmeal raisin cookies my mother had made for me. The same ones she used to bring to me in prison because I looked "too skinny."

In the kitchen was a note from Alyson that informed me of what Falcone had already filled me in on—that she'd be working late tonight, and Robbie was with her ex-husband, Herm. He stayed at his family farm on the Pennsylvania and Ohio border when he was on leave—the property split between both states. Alyson referred to it as Pohio.

I found the plate of cookies on the counter, and began to salivate—I hadn't eaten since my Peruvian cheeseburger. I needed something to wash them down with, and began searching the refrigerator for a beer. When I located a bottle of Sam Adams left over from the recent Wainwright-Collins & Rudingo office Christmas party, I noticed his reflection in it. It was too late to respond.

I felt a sharp blow to my kidneys. I crumbled to the floor and the assailant pounced on my neck.

"My boss wants to know where his money is," Gooch calmly stated with a slight Dutch accent—sounding different from when he was the professor. He had also removed his hairpiece, revealing a healthy head of slicked back hair.

"If I had any money, would I be living here?" I said, and barely got the words out of my mouth before receiving a chop to my windpipe.

"Because I'm in the Christmas spirit, I'll give you one last chance."

When I didn't answer—I wasn't even sure I could after the blow to the neck—he began shoving oatmeal cookies into my mouth. Not what I had in mind when I got the craving. When I tried to close my mouth, he pried it open. It felt like he was going to remove my jaw from my face.

I began to choke, and when he held my nose shut the room started to get hazy. I could hear the dogs barking, but they sounded far away. I was certain I was going to die.

Suddenly Gooch's head snapped back. Then a boot knocked the Cookie Monster to the ground. I spit up the cookies and sucked in as much oxygen as I could cram into my lungs.

When the room stopped spinning, I realized that Alyson was my savior. I was thankful to see her, but also concerned for her safety. Falcone's scare tactics didn't do this lunatic justice.

Gooch rolled away like a cat and sprang back to his feet. He stood about six-three, while Alyson was a foot shorter.

She lunged at him, and he moved away like a bullfighter. He grabbed a chunk of her dark curly hair on her way by and drove her to her knees.

She spun around like she was break dancing, and applied a martial arts kick to his knee, just enough to loosen his grip and regain her fighting position. Showing no fear, she came at him again.

His fist snapped so fast that her blood was already pouring onto the hardwood floor by the time she saw it coming. That was the end of the fight.

But instead of coming back after me, he retreated toward an open window, and disappeared down the fire escape.

Alyson staggered to her feet. I remained bent over and grasping for air. But as much as she would never admit it, she was the one who needed the help—the blood gushing out of her nose was impossible to conceal.

I grabbed the first thing I could find—my wet shirt—and held it over her nose.

Once the bleeding was under control, she said, "What would you ever do without me, Collins?" It was about as sentimental as she got.

"Probably die of cookie asphyxiation," I replied. But as much as I appreciated her courageous effort to save me, I was starting to doubt that it would have affected the final outcome—if Gooch wanted me dead, I'd be dead. This was a warning shot—not much different than the one from the FBI … just more painful. And he wanted me to know he could get to me anytime, anywhere.

"Looks like you scared another man out of your life, Rudi," I tried to joke.

"I can't seem to get rid of *you.* "

"How'd you know someone was in here?"

"I use the fire escape at night, because it freaks Olive and Oil out when I come through the front door. I noticed that the window was slightly cracked—I never leave the window open. I'm obsessive about shutting it."

What wasn't she obsessive about? But as much as I've teased her about her anal-retentiveness over the years, tonight was another example of how the small details might mean the difference between life and death over the next few days.

"I should move out. Everyone except Seal Team Six is after me. What if Robbie was here?"

"The people after you are trained killers. They're targeting you, and will attempt to lessen any collateral damage. The more bodies, the more complicated their mission becomes."

So that's where I learned that. "Very comforting."

"And besides, Robbie will be staying with his father through Christmas break."

Herm and Alyson met in the military. Herm was still active, just returning from another tour in Afghanistan. I've always got the feeling that their divorce was about logistics, rather than lack of love. But it wasn't something she ever discussed with me.

She took a long look at me, making me uncomfortable. "What?"

"Can you please either put a shirt on, or lose that gut. You really need to get yourself in better shape if you're going to fight off these guys."

That sounded like a good New Year's resolution, when hopefully all this would be over. And preferably I'd be alive, and not back in jail.

"And what's that sticking out of your pants?" she asked.

"I guess I'm just happy to see you," I replied with a smile.

"You should be—I don't sacrifice my cute nose for just anyone. I meant the folder." The bleeding had stopped, but her face was still a big red and purple mess.

I followed her point to the Morzetti file that I'd stuck in the waistband of my suit pants. "Oh, Libby said you wanted to get a jump on it for an upcoming meeting."

I handed it over to her. "If you need any assistance from your favorite paralegal, just give me a shout."

"You need to concentrate on getting some rest, Collins. You've had a long day, and we have an even longer one tomorrow."

She was right. But before I could take her advice, my phone rang. I knew who it was, and Alyson's disapproving look told me that she did too.

"Just give me a few minutes to change, and I'll meet you there in an hour," I told the caller.

CHAPTER 12

I met Candi outside of the club Vida's in the Meatpacking District. Once upon a time the area was known for being the section of the city where meat was butchered and packaged. Now it was a different type of meat market, filled with Manhattan's trendiest clubs.

I kept my dress minimalist with a checkered gingham shirt and khakis, along with a pair of Chukka boots. On most occasions this getup wouldn't get me past the velvet rope, but I brought a shiny accessory with me—Candi Kane.

She used her celebrity to avoid the wait with the other schleps out in the snow. She wasn't the same level of star she was when her stage-mother-from-hell hired me to get her out of the first of what turned out to be many brushes with the law, but she was still a rock star when it came to things like the club scene and making tabloid headlines.

Once inside, I shouted over Snoop Dogg's "Everyday is Like Christmas to Me," "I guess we have a different idea of what discreet means."

A proud look came over her face. "It's from my new clothing line!" She then provided a detailed description of the stretch-leather Santa mini-dress with zipper front that might be considered too risqué for Temple of Duma's. A thick black belt was hooked around her midsection, as if Santa's gifts—and by Santa, I mean her plastic surgeon—needed to be elevated any more than they already were. Her heeled leather boots, the type my fellow prisoners had another name for, came up to her lower thigh.

She pulled down the satin-lined hood and her blonde hair extensions fell down past her shoulders. She then removed her necklace and held it over my head. The last word I heard before she kissed me was "mistletoe."

I did what I should have done the first time this happened, and pulled away.

She looked mystified. "I was just playing, Kris—what happened to your Christmas spirit?"

A good question. Some of my best childhood memories centered on Christmas, and I remained a Santa believer long after my classmates busted the myth. So I couldn't pinpoint why or when it no longer was the season to be jolly for me. Maybe it was when my father died almost ten years ago, or my sister moving away to Seattle with her family. Or that I married a woman so literal that if Santa came down the chimney she might have him arrested for breaking and entering. But it most likely stemmed back to the shock factor of seeing Alexander Wainwright in a Santa suit for the first time, ruining the myth forever.

She grabbed my hand and led me upstairs, jiggling all the way.

Vida's was a multi-level club. The first floor featured a large dance floor and a DJ that Candi mentioned was famous. I wasn't familiar with him, but admittedly, the last time I thought about DJs was when Libby and I were trying to find one for our wedding. When Snoop Dogg finished ushering in the holiday, the "famous" DJ broke into regularly scheduled club music to announce that Candi Kane was "in the house." He then played "Candy Cane Children" by the White Stripes to mark the moment.

Candi looked smitten by the attention and waved to her fans. She was most comfortable in the spotlight, which shouldn't be a surprise. When a mother names her daughter Candi Kane she is looking for attention, and using her daughter as a vehicle to get it. And when Candi spent her childhood going to auditions instead of birthday parties, it became a self-fulfilling prophecy.

And while I'd been very critical of Julia Kane over the years, to be fair, her daughter did achieve great success in her chosen field. And if she had pushed her in science and she became a surgeon, she would have been applauded.

Candi's big break came when she joined the cast of *The Candy Stripers*—how could she not get the part with that name?—a Saved by the Bell-ish teen hit about a group of teenage candy stripers in a hospital and all the dramas that went with that. She quickly became the star of the show and Julia negotiated to have the name changed to *Candi Kane & the Candy Stripers*.

Julia had followed my work at Zee's trial, which led to her hiring me to defend her megastar, sixteen-year-old daughter when she was arrested for her first DUI. Over the next decade I practically became her assistant, as she went from teen idol to an out-of-control twenty-something, charged with everything from petty theft to assaulting a former boyfriend, to the more serious drug charges. Yet, of the two of us, I'm the only one who'd ever done prison time.

While the first floor was full of urban hipsters with their bohemian fashions and messy shag cuts, on their eternal quest to find the world's most obscure indie band—I'd become an expert on hipsters since moving to Brooklyn—the second floor was staked out by the "career clubbers," whose entire existence was built around the club scene. They had more of a reserved cool—goatees and oval rim glasses seemed to be the trend this year. Although, it was possible that my eyes were deceiving me, based on the overzealous work of a fog machine.

We arrived at the third floor "tree fort" section that was VIP only. I noticed a few celebrities, but none of them were attracting the attention that Candi Kane and her sexy Santa outfit was receiving. She dragged me to a leather couch near the railing, where we could look down on the steerage that was mingling below. I took a seat beside her, but kept an arm's length between us.

A waitress brought us a couple of drinks called Frosty the Snowmen. It was a mixture of red and green liquid and a pile of ice. As long as it had enough alcohol to make me forget the last few hours, I was good with it. But Candi pushed it away, announcing, "I've been sober for three-and-a-half years!" She then paused, as if waiting for applause.

After the waitress left, Candi exclaimed, "I'm cleared!"

This was not an uncommon phrase between us, usually followed by a dramatic hug, and me reminding her that she was, as long as she completed her community service. "I didn't know you had any charges pending."

"No, sweetie—I've been cleared to go to Afghanistan to perform for the troops for Christmas."

"I'm impressed—that's a really nice gesture."

"I've been thinking a lot lately," she said, which was always dangerous. "My whole life has been about me. My career, my desires, doing whatever would make me feel good for a moment … so I decided to dedicate the rest of my life to helping others."

I waited for the catch, but none came. She had "dedicated" herself to every quackery known to man over the years, so I found it best to take a wait-and-see approach with all things Candi. But she did seem genuine about it.

"And ever since I did, amazing things have been happening. First the new *Candy Stripers* show, and then this great opportunity you offered me!"

In the new version, Candi had graduated to a doctor who was now in charge of the new young cast of candy stripers. They'd been holding tryouts all over the country this month, including this upcoming week in New York, so I had to schedule around this surprising career rebound. Usually once you start making Skinemax movies—most notably the infamous *Candi Kane & the Candy Strippers*—the career doesn't pull out of the nosedive. And it also shows how much of a difference one 'p' can make.

The good fortune in her life had me rethinking her involvement in the plan. Duma's warnings about my motives for including her were also still fresh in my head, as was the knowledge of the FBI monitoring her trip to Statia.

"Are you sure you want to go through with this, Candi?"

"I told you, sweetie—I'm dedicating myself to helping people, and by helping you, maybe I can make up a little bit for all the damage I've caused."

She looked me deep in the eyes, sealing the deal with the look that I never could resist, even though I always knew I'd regret it in the end.

CHAPTER 13

Candi ran her hand up her thigh and subtly pulled up her skirt. She then removed what looked like a business card that was hooked to her garter, and handed it to me.

I reviewed the number of the bank account that she'd opened during her trip to Sint Eustatius. She had traveled to the sleepy island in the Netherlands Antilles, better known as Statia, on an official visit to perform for St. Nicholas Day, which was as important a holiday on the island as Christmas. And Falcone was right—it wasn't a coincidence that Candi happened to book an appearance on the island where Kerstman owned an estate, and where his boat sank.

Candi pulled out her phone and showed me a photo of her with Sinterklaas, the Dutch version of Santa, and Black Pete, his not so politically correct assistant, throwing treats to children. The tabloid seemed to focus more on the bikini shots. "It was so much fun!" she exclaimed.

I was glad she enjoyed her visit, because she'd be making a return trip very soon. I couldn't argue with those like Duma who thought I was insane to have involved such a loose cannon, and one that I have an unholy history with. But in some ways she was a perfect fit. She freely traveled the world for her career, now including Afghanistan. And she'd accumulated … and snorted away … and re-accumulated millions, so it wouldn't be a total red flag if she opened up an offshore account that became filled with a very large Christmas bonus in the next week.

But most of all, when it came to Kris Collins, she was loyal to a fault. Three people visited me every week that I was in prison—two of which were my mother and Taylor, neither of whom I would include in this at gunpoint. The other was Candi.

I pulled out a glossy travel brochure from Statia and handed it to her. "I circled the location where you will meet your contact on New Year's."

Her excitement bubbled over. "It will be just the type of relaxing vacation that I'll need after the tryouts, and then going to Afghanistan. The perfect end to a perfect year!"

We also had a different definition of relaxing. I kept on task, "Over the next week the treasure will be loaded into the account."

"So I won't be digging for it?" she said with a laugh. "I've been going to the gym to work out for it. Feel my muscle."

I obliged, lightly squeezing her bicep as she flexed it. It was impressive. "No—your job will be to transfer the money into different accounts around the world. Like hitting a diamond with a hammer and the pieces spraying in all different directions."

"That's beautiful … you've always had such a way with words, Kris," she gushed, before proving that no matter how much she spoke of helping others, the world still revolved around Candi—it's how she was programmed. "And I get half … that's our deal, right?"

"I just wouldn't go on a spending spree right away. The FBI is monitoring all of us. Once the new *Candy Stripers* show takes off, you should be in the clear."

She smiled at the thought of being back on the top of the mountain. She then proceeded to unzip her top and tuck the brochure safely next to her bosom.

I looked away, causing her to smile. "It's not like you haven't seen my jingle bells before, Kris."

Nobody knew better than me that those bells came at a very high cost. I had hoped that the court would see my indiscretions as a moment of weakness and lessen the charges. And I pleaded mitigating factors; such as I'd held off Candi's advances for years, basically since she'd turned legal age, which was much longer than most mortal men could have. But the court of Libby found my defense laughable, and gave me the maximum sentence. The court of public opinion was equally harsh, understandably. I was the married man with a wife and twin baby girls at home. I became a public punching bag, which was further exacerbated when I chose to represent fellow social outcast, Diedrich Kerstman.

"Besides, I'm seeing someone," she added. "Do you want to know who he is?"

"Not if he's another controlling, father figure type."

"Then I guess you don't want me to tell you," she said with a shrug. There was nothing more predictable than a Candi Kane boyfriend.

"I have a long day planned tomorrow, I think I should go home and try to get some rest," I said.

She grabbed my hand and pulled me up off the couch. "I've got a better idea—come dance with me, Kris."

Since I rarely danced, even at weddings, doing it in a packed club in the Candi Kane spotlight was pretty much the last thing I wanted to do. But I needed her right now more than she needed me. I agreed to meet her downstairs after a bathroom break.

I made my way to the men's room as a techno version of "Santa Claus is Coming to Town" began to play, which I didn't think either Santa or Springsteen would have been happy with. "Let it Snow" would have been a more appropriate tune for the bathroom, as all the sinks were taken with clubbers getting their cocaine fix. Through my many bad decisions, one good one I made was never getting involved with drugs. I've seen what they've done to the likes of Zee and Candi, and no matter how much they both seem to have it together today, the demons were always looking to make a comeback.

I found Candi in the center of the dance floor on the first level. She was surrounded by a bunch of twenty-something males, all vying for her attention. But she only had eyes for the old guy in the khakis, who was rocking the gray goatee and soft belly. She pulled me close to her as Mariah Carey's "All I Want for Christmas is You" played. She whispered in my ear, "All I want for Christmas is you, Kris."

"You can't have me," I said. For some reason it was much easier to turn her down now that I was single.

"Maybe not, but that doesn't mean I can't ask Santa for the one I love this year."

I've never doubted her claims of loving me. I was the father she never had after he ran out on them when she was three. And I was one of the few people who actually took an interest in her best interests … at least up until that fateful night in her hotel suite in Beverly Hills. I could have brushed off the comment, but I chose to make sure my intentions were clear. One of the most merciful things Libby did for me was to make it known that there was no hope of reconciliation. Hope can be a dangerous thing, leading us to believe in things that have no chance of happening, and sending us down the path to a dead end.

My firm rejection didn't seem to lessen Candi's mood. She continued to dance like nobody was watching, even though every eye in the club was on her. I, on the other hand, was watching everybody else. I noticed a woman snapping a photo of us with her cell phone. She looked like a *Jersey Shore* extra, with her hair almost reaching the third level. In this day and age of camera phones there was no way for celebrities like Candi to stop people from taking unwanted photos. But this was different … I'd met this woman before.

I excused myself from our dance and walked straight toward the woman. She didn't move.

"Hello Jacqueline. I like the wig."

She smiled. "Did Zee's girlfriend send you to beat me up?"

"No, I just wanted to send my regards to your boss Stone Scroggie."

"You're playing a dangerous game, Kris. And when you become too connected to someone in this game, you can get them hurt. It's pretty obvious that you still care about her."

I glanced back at Candi. "You leave her alone—this is between me and your boss."

"I'm not talking about Candi," she said and held up her phone so I could view a photo. It was a picture of Libby.

CHAPTER 14

Edmund Woods sensed danger as he walked down the deserted Yonkers street, sometime between late night and early morning. It was like an extra sense he'd picked up since they began living on the streets three weeks ago.

He arrived at the Range Rover that was parallel-parked in front of the dark apartment building. He brushed the snow off his heavy winter coat, took another glance behind to make sure he was just being paranoid, and then entered the vehicle.

Dora's computer illuminated the inside like a street lamp, and she remained focused on it as he entered and took a seat on the driver's side. In the backseat, sixteen-year-old Payne was doing a thousand-yard-stare out the windshield into the dark night—Edmund could tell that he'd been fighting with his mother once again. The one saving grace, as usual, was his six-year-old beacon of light, Susie.

"It's snowing, Daddy!" she said excitably.

"I know, sweet pea. The weatherman said there's a good chance it will be a white Christmas this year."

"I'll bet Santa's sleigh works much better in the snow. I can't wait for him to come! He brought me everything I wanted last year … and I was even gooder this year!"

"I think he's going to make it a really special Christmas for a special little girl."

Dora finally looked up from her laptop, perturbed. How dare he not tell his daughter the truth that Santa might not be stopping by the Woods' this year due to budget constraints. And that jolly old St. Nick probably wouldn't know where to find them anyway, since their new "home" was parked on a different street each night.

Dora reached into the bag of items he'd just purchased from the 24-hour pharmacy down the street, and pulled out a plastic bottle. She shook her head. "We need to get him to a real doctor, not give him antacids."

Payne spoke up, "I have a stomachache—that's all. Every time I get a normal pain doesn't mean the cancer is back. Who's stomach wouldn't hurt after all the shit we've been eating?"

This reminded Edmund. He reached into his bag and pulled out candy bars and bags of chips, and handed them around. He was convinced that hunger was the cause of tonight's angst, and hoped to temporarily calm the tensions. But he knew it was just a Band-Aid—the only real solution would be to get their life back.

"If it doesn't go away by morning, we're going to take him to the free clinic," Dora said.

"I'm not going to the free clinic," Payne rebutted. "That place is loaded with nothing but homeless crackheads!"

A lump formed in Edmund's throat. Payne's words slapped him with reality—they were homeless! And smoking crack might not be far behind … just to tolerate each other.

Dora warned Susie that she wouldn't be able to sleep tonight if she had any more chocolate—as if sleep was actually a possibility—and swapped a pack of breath mints for the candy bar. It was hard to upset Susie, but she didn't look happy about the tradeoff.

Dora opened a bag of Doritos and mocked Edmund by smacking her lips and making *mmm* sounds as she ate the chips. He no longer recognized her. He kept a clipping of their wedding announcement from the *New York Times* just to remind him of what once was, even if he doubted that it would ever be again.

They'd met at Kerstman Publishing—the first job out of college for both of them. He worked his way up to VP of Finance, while Dora went from an intern all the way to editor, and even worked on the last Harry Crawford book. Edmund had seen the signs of the financial struggle at Kerstman after Crawford stopped writing. When it got to the point that Edmund feared they wouldn't be able to make payroll, he went to Diedrich Kerstman. He told Edmund in confidence that Harry Crawford had agreed to make a comeback, which would solve any financial problems, but in the meantime he would use his own money to keep things afloat … and proved it by handing Edmund a large check. He would learn at the trial that this was a lie. There was no Crawford comeback planned, and the check was extortion money connected to a shady business deal in which Kerstman sold out his employees' personal information.

Once Payne got diagnosed, all their focus and energy went to him. So maybe that's why he wasn't on top of things like he normally was. The first alarm went off when they were rejected for a loan to cover the cost of an experimental treatment that their insurance wouldn't pay for. Their credit had been destroyed, and their savings siphoned away.

The house they fought to keep for three years was just a material object, same with their lost retirement fund, and thankfully Payne didn't need the experimental treatment to survive. But the doctors told them that there was a 50/50 chance of a relapse within three years, and in Dora's eyes, Edmund had left their son vulnerable, and he doubted she would ever forgive him for that.

A knock startled everyone. Edmund looked to see a police officer, and rolled his window down. He gulped a deep breath, trying to remain calm. "Can I help you, officer?"

"Don't get many Range Rovers in this neighborhood, so I thought you might be lost, or having some car trouble."

"We were coming back from my sister's in the city, and my son was having some stomach issues—he gets carsick—so we stopped off at a pharmacy to get him some antacid," Edmund said. Payne held up the bottle to back up the story.

The officer's eyes roamed around the vehicle. It was packed like they were headed for a cross-country trip, not a visit to a sister that didn't exist.

"Take a few minutes until he feels better, and then I suggest you move on. This isn't the safest neighborhood," he let Edmund keep what was left of his dignity.

When the officer left, and things began to settle down, Edmund shut off the vehicle.

"What are you doing?" Dora asked him. "It's snowing out—we're going to freeze without the heater."

"I don't want to call any attention to us and get another visit from the cops. Let's use the sleeping bags, and the kids have heavy coats."

"You got to be kidding me. Well, at least now I know our son won't die of cancer ... because his father is going to freeze him to death!"

"C'mon, Dora, you think this is easy for me?"

"I don't even know who you are anymore."

"Maybe because you avoid talking to me at all costs."

She opened her window and a cold breeze blew through the car. "Are you happy now? We can all freeze to death together—right after we finish eating some more shitty food!" She shoved another handful of chips in her mouth, and again did the lip-smacking thing.

She was about to take another handful, when the bag disappeared out the window.

A voice boomed, "A lot of people don't got no food around here, so maybe you should be a little more appreciative."

The voice came from an enormous man wearing a ski mask. "What do you want?" Edmund asked, trying to shield the fear in his voice.

"You're in my neighborhood."

"We were just moving on. I'm sorry to have bothered you."

"You ain't going nowhere until I'm through with you, Mr. Range Rover."

"Please don't hurt us," Dora called out.

"A minute ago you were hoping to freeze to death, and now you're all worried about your well-being? I don't think you know what you want, lady."

"Just don't hurt my children. My son has cancer."

Those were fighting words for Payne. "For the last time, Mom—I don't have cancer anymore."

"Maybe right now you don't, but the doctors said it could come back."

"Right now is the only time that matters."

The man peered into the backseat, his eyes landing on Payne. "You're a brave kid, it takes a lot of courage to whip cancer's ass."

"He's my role model," Susie chimed in. "And my brother."

"Sounds like a good person to look up to. I think your parents could learn a lot from him. Not only is he courageous, but also smart. Especially when he said that right now is the most important time. For example, *right now*, your mom and dad are going to hand me their wallets, and that way nobody will get hurt."

Edmund reached into his pocket and handed his over. Dora resisted at first, but when the man displayed a knife she begrudgingly handed him her purse. He did a quick search through it until he found the wallet. He took nothing else.

She tried to hand him her laptop. "Go ahead … take it. They've stolen everything else from us, you might as well have it."

"You don't get it do you, lady?"

"What's that supposed to mean?"

"As far as I can tell, nobody took any of your important stuff."

"Don't you tell me what's important!" she screeched, and again pushed the laptop toward him.

"Do I look stupid to you? I don't want nothing that can be traced, so keep your computers and phones." He looked in the wallets and pulled out their driver's licenses, which he studied. "I wish you a Merry Christmas, Mr. and Mrs. Woods ... just don't be spending it in my neighborhood."

And just like that, he was off into the night.

Dora looked at Edmund with fire in her eyes. "If you don't go after him, I will."

"He has a knife, Dora."

"If I get stabbed you can buy me some antacids and I'll be fine," she said and began to open the door.

He reached out and grabbed her arm—it was the first time they'd touched in months. "I'll go find that policeman—they probably know who this guy is ... he said it was his neighborhood."

Edmund again entered the cold. But he didn't look for a policeman. He walked a couple blocks away and found a bench. He cleared off the snow and sat by himself. He just stared out into the dark night and cried.

Almost an hour later, when his tears began to turn to icicles, he returned to the vehicle. Everybody was asleep—they'd been conditioned with Payne's sickness to get their sleep between emergencies and disasters, and now it was between fights and muggings. But one person awoke, huddled under a blanket with her sleeping brother.

"Hi Daddy," she whispered.

"Hey there, sweet pea."

"Did you find the policeman?"

"I did ... you know what he said?"

"What?"

"That Susie better get some sleep, because she has a big day tomorrow."

Edmund reached into his pocket and pulled out the flyer he found when they stopped at the post office to pick up their mail yesterday.

"Why is it gonna be a big day?"

He took another look at the flyer. "Because you're going to meet Santa Claus.

MONDAY DECEMBER 23

CHAPTER 15

I hid behind the morning edition of the *New York Globe*, as I peered out at the suburban Ossining street from my Volvo SUV. Mothers stood at the ends of snowplowed driveways, waiting with their children for the arrival of the school bus. But there was one I was specifically interested in.

Her long red hair fell out her winter cap. Her heavy overcoat covered up an athletic physique that was the result of her training for her first marathon last year. But I worried that the sudden affection for distance running was her trying to run from the pain of the past. Her son, Peter, looked just like her with similar red hair and collection of freckles around his nose. His younger sister, Janie, reminded me very much of the twins. I thought they might hit it off if they met, but it was doubtful that would ever happen.

I questioned my sanity coming here. But after a day that included a return to the Wainwright estate, an FBI ambush, and almost being cookie'd to death by Gooch, I sought out the one person who always made me feel like the world was going to be alright. Not that she'd ever see it that way.

I first came in contact with Nicole Closs during the Kerstman trial, when her sharp wail interrupted my cross-examination of a witness. I turned, as did the rest of the courtroom.

"You're a murderer!" Nicole shouted. "You killed him!"

While the courtroom was a new venue for these types of verbal assaults on Kerstman, the attacks were not. He had become the face of corporate greed, right up there with Enron and Madoff. As his lawyer, I pleaded with him not to be seen in public as the trial neared, but he continued to walk the streets of Manhattan and take his medicine from the angry public ... and occasionally a fist.

But I quickly realized that Nicole wasn't just talking to him—her comments were also directed to the man who was defending the evildoer. Her fiery eyes locked on mine as she cried out, "Did you use the blood money he paid you to buy your children Christmas gifts this year, Mr. Collins?" She then held up pics of Peter and Janie for me to see, adding, "There will be nothing under our tree this year."

The next day the *New York Globe* led with the headline "Nothing Under Our Tree." It included an artist's rendition of our showdown in court, accompanied the caption: "Blood Money!" Nicole became the face of the victims' pain.

The story shed more light on the motive for her outburst, which went deeper than the usual animosity—her husband had committed suicide the previous day.

Our brief encounter changed me. I know it would be hard for people to believe that, especially after I went on to help Kerstman attempt an escape, and my failure to return the money. But when I looked in Nicole's eyes that day, I saw my own life crumbling around me—their intense pain and vulnerability providing a glimpse into my grim future. But when I looked closer, there was also a twinkle of hope. A small diamond floating in an ocean of pain and destruction. It was that small flicker that had kept me going in the darkest days in prison. I hadn't been able to get her out of my head since that day.

A clinking of metal on my window woke me from my daydream. I turned to see the barrel of a gun pointing right at me. Since I never took Alyson's advice to get bulletproof glass installed, I rolled down the window.

"What are you doing here, Rudi?"

"I just came to wish you a Happy Festivus, Collins. Are you airing grievances or performing a feat of strength? Because from my vantage point, it just looks like you're trying to get people hurt."

"Speaking of which, put that thing away. There are children here!"

"If you were really concerned about their safety you wouldn't have dragged that bullseye on your back down here."

"You shouldn't sneak up on people … what if I had a gun?"

She began to laugh. "You wouldn't have a chance against me. Or more importantly … Scroggie's people."

She pointed in the direction of a driveway, two houses down from where Nicole was standing with her children. "Does that mother look familiar?"

I squinted at the woman with short bob haircut and heavy overcoat, flanked by a couple of preschoolers. She looked like a typical Ossining soccer mom. "Should she?"

"Remember your friend Jacqueline from last night? And FYI—when she pretends that she's taking pictures of her kids with her phone, it's not a coincidence that she makes sure you're in the background.

"I'm going to put an end to this—it's harassment."

"This isn't a court case, Collins. The best move right now is to lay low."

"She threatened Libby last night. That's crossing the line. If she wants me, I'm here, but leave my family out of this."

"Libby isn't the Kris Collins love interest that I'm worried about."

"What do you mean?"

"They're stalking the stalker," she said, while glancing in the direction of Nicole. "And before long they'll figure out who you're stalking."

"I'm not stalking anybody," I said defensively.

Coming here might not have been the healthiest way to spend my morning, but I associated stalking with the sick and depraved. No matter what people think of many of my former clients, if they'd seen some of the threatening letters from their stalkers, or the photos to prove that they could get near their children, it would have been hard not to have empathy.

"Do I need to remind you, Collins, that you're one slip-up from heading back to jail? And you know very well that you're committing fourth degree stalking in the state of New York, which will get you sent back—it doesn't matter if you actually initiate contact. If you really care about this woman, walk away," Alyson said.

She opened the door and pushed me over the console into the passenger's seat, and climbed in. "How does she afford that house? I thought they lost all the life insurance money when the husband killed himself?"

"They did—she moved in with her mother."

She nodded that it made sense and started the vehicle. "This is a nice piece of machinery. Can I have it if you go back to jail?"

She smiled, which clashed with her nose that looked like a piece of rhubarb pie topped with two very black eyes.

"You'll have to ask Libby—she owns it now. I transferred all my belongings into her name before the feds could freeze my assets."

"How about the Ferrari?"

"It's stashed away in the barn on the Pound Ridge property. Although, rumor has it that it might be in danger of being evicted to make room for a couple of ponies."

She began driving out of the neighborhood. I watched as Jacqueline Helada got smaller in the rear-view mirror. I wished it was that easy to get her out of my life.

"Where's your car?" I asked.

"In Brooklyn."

"Then how'd you get here? And come to think of it, how did you know I'd be here?"

"That's a trade secret. But I will say that I heard you called in sick with a case of stupidity today. So this sounded like a place someone would come who was suffering with an ailment like that."

"What's *your* excuse for skipping out on work?"

"It's a tradition for me to take off the 23rd to go Christmas shopping. I used to have a boss who would send me out two days before Christmas to get gifts for the staff and clients that he completely forgot about, even though his dedicated assistant reminded him at least ten times about it."

I sighed. "So where are we going, Rudi?"

She smiled. "The North Pole."

CHAPTER 16

Libby Wainwright entered the midtown office of Wainwright-Collins & Rudingo on Monday morning. The office was still the same as when it was used by Kris Collins Esq. to impress celebrity clients, but the clientele was less glitzy these days, which suited Libby.

She was met by Joanne, the last remaining staff member from the time before Kris went to jail. He had kept a much smaller staff than most firms, worried about leaks involving his high-profile clientele. And a big reason why he could get away with being so understaffed was that Alyson often did the work of ten people.

With Christmas on Wednesday, most of the staff took the entire week off, and Alyson had taken a personal day to finish up her Christmas shopping. Libby planned to close the office around noon and surprise Joanne by taking her out to lunch. But first there was work to be done on the Morzetti case.

Before she could retreat to her office, Joanne hit her with the first surprise of the day. "Kris called in sick."

This confirmed her suspicions. He was up to something, and using history as an indicator, that wasn't a good thing.

Joanne read her confounded look. "I don't know why you look so surprised—he always comes down with a fake illness the week of your parents' party."

"But if I recall, it was usually before the party, not after."

Then came the second surprise, a much bigger one. "There's an Agent Falcone from the FBI waiting in your office—said he had some questions for you about a case he's working on. He was waiting at the door when I arrived this morning, and I got here at 5:30."

Libby checked her watch and saw that it was 7:37. If he was willing to wait two hours it must be a high priority, which meant it must have something to do with Kris.

She stepped apprehensively into her office. Agent Falcone was younger, fitter and generally more attractive than she'd expected. He was standing behind her desk, his back to her, staring out the window at the busy Avenue of the Americas.

"This is a great view," he said without turning. "You can see the ice skating rink at Rockefeller Center from here. Can't believe there were people lined up out there at six in the morning to get in."

"Some people like to get an early start on the day ... as do you, from what I gather."

He pointed at a modern glass building. "Isn't that the old Kerstman Publishing building?"

"It is, or at least was. I think a dot-com took it over last year."

"I need to get me an office with a view like this. I'll bet you didn't have one like this when you were a prosecutor."

Libby set her briefcase down. "Are you looking for a lawyer, Agent Falcone?"

He finally turned around, and their eyes met. "I'm actually looking for a billion dollars."

"And you think I can help you with that?"

"I thought your husband could, but he mysteriously called in sick today."

"I no longer have a husband, but I assume you are referring to Kris. And since there is a flu bug going around, I don't believe 'mysterious' would be a proper description of his absence."

"Maybe that was a poor choice of words on my part. I think 'unexpected' would be more appropriate, since he was out on the town last night, and seemed *very* healthy."

He moved to the other side of the desk and took a seat. His expression told her that he was both exhausted and irritated. Not unusual for this time of year, or this time of the morning, but Libby felt a certain uneasiness in his presence.

She sat at her desk, and he slid a couple photos in front of her. The first one was of Kris arriving at Temple of Duma's with Zee. The second one featured Kris and Candi Kane entering a club called Vida's.

She looked up. "I don't see why these would elicit a visit from the FBI."

Falcone handed her another photo—it was Kris and Candi locking lips inside the club. Falcone grinned broadly, which Libby found rather insensitive.

"Maybe she passed him that flu bug," he said.

"Kris is a grown man, and as far as I know a single one. So I'm not sure why these photos should be of interest to me … or you, for that matter."

"The woman kissing him is the same one who broke up your marriage, correct?"

Libby's shoulders tightened. It still hurt, no matter how much she tried to convince herself that she'd forgiven him and moved on. "It was one of numerous reasons for our split."

"You ever hear the line—once a cheater, always a cheater."

"As we've already established, Kris is free to kiss anyone he desires these days."

"I wasn't talking about your ex-husband. Candi Kane is the one who is currently in a relationship—one that she's worked very hard to keep low profile. And we both know it's not easy for Candi to keep anything low profile."

He tossed more photos in front of Libby. In these shots, Candi was getting out of a limo with a slender, older man in a sharp suit. In one photo, she was kissing him. Libby wondered if her lips ever got tired.

"I don't think I need to tell you who that is," Falcone said.

He didn't. Stone Scroggie was the man who stole more than half-a-million dollars from her father. Money that was now missing, and most observers believed Kris knew where it was.

The human Fotomat had more for her. One was of a woman who had been following Kris last night, while the other was a gruesome shot of a dead body. At least that's what she believed it to be—it was so mangled, it was hard to recognize.

Falcone explained that the first one was of a Scroggie associate named Jacqueline Helada. And since he didn't have a photo of Scroggie's assassin who called himself Gooch, he provided her an example of some of his work. The photo of the woman shocked her more than the dead body.

"You see, it's very important for everybody's sake that we find that money before Scroggie does. That way we can protect Kris. But if Scroggie gets his hands on it first, he has no reason to keep him alive, and my bosses will have no motivation to offer protection."

"Then perhaps you'd be better served by looking for this money, instead of talking to me."

"Oh, I know where the money is …"

"That's good to hear. I look forward to you recovering it, so that we can all move on with our lives."

"It's not that simple … the money is in the Bermuda Triangle."

"I have no interest in the details of your treasure hunt, other than I will be watching to make sure that it's returned to its proper owners when recovered—specifically my father. And if the FBI needs legal advice, I would suggest an international lawyer of offshore accounts. It's not my expertise."

"Maybe not, but this triangle I speak of is made up of Scroggie, your father, and your ex-husband, which puts you smack in the middle of it, whether you like it or not. And everyone knows how dangerous the Bermuda Triangle can be."

"As much as I'm enjoying your cryptic riddles, Agent Falcone, I have much to work to complete before Christmas break. So I would really appreciate if you'd get to the point of your visit."

"I need you to tell me where the money's located. And if Kris hasn't told you, then you best get the answer from him as quickly as possible."

"You know very well, as his lawyer, I cannot discuss any conversations I've had with my client."

He smiled. "I've heard that one before. I'm surprised you didn't represent Kris during his plea deal. They say only a fool would represent himself in court."

"Then I believe you've answered your own question."

"I just find it strange that he so easily agreed to spend three years in jail, without so much as a fight. He'd gotten off clients who were in much dire circumstances."

"I think it would have been difficult to win a case in such a climate of negativity. Perhaps he didn't think he had a chance, and cut his losses."

He continued smiling like he knew something she didn't. "On that note, I'd like to thank you for your time Ms. Wainwright, and I'll be on my way. I wish you and yours a merry Christmas, and hope all of you are alive to spend it together."

"And yours, Agent Falcone."

"Unfortunately, I will be working on Christmas, but I'm hoping to get New Year's off this year."

When he left, she booted up her computer. The fact that Kris has been up to something was no surprise to her. It was the reason she'd hired that private detective to follow him. And the photos the PI sent her from Kris' escapades last night were for the most part no different from Falcone's. But it did surprise her that the person she hired to follow him *was* in his photos.

Jacqueline.

Suddenly she felt the triangle closing in on her.

CHAPTER 17

Candi Kane stepped out of the Macy's flagship store in Herald Square, surrounded by flashbulbs, and high on the one drug she still indulged in—attention.

The press conference on the sixth floor was to promote tomorrow's contest to select girls for the final two spots on the *Candy Stripers* revival. And then the media followed her around the world's biggest department store as she browsed and shopped for an hour. A perfect morning.

They followed her outside like she was the Pied Piper. The sky was gunmetal gray, but to Candi it looked like a sun-filled summer day. Herald Square was bustling with Christmas shoppers, along with numerous mothers bringing their children to visit Santaland. She felt like she was experiencing her first Christmas, and in some ways she was.

Her childhood Christmases were spent in her mother's Chevy Impala, driving across the country to attend auditions. In the years that followed, starting in her teenage years, she would usually jet off to some exotic locale, where she would wake up Christmas morning in a cocaine haze, next to some stranger.

As she made her way to 34th Street, she noticed the animated window-displays outside of Macy's. She walked toward them, which seemed to catch the media off guard. It was starting to become a trend.

Their first surprise was that she showed up on time for the press conference, despite multiple reports of her being out to the wee morning hours "clubbing." That used to be code for a Candi Kane no-show, followed by a well-scripted release from her publicist about a sudden case of food poisoning or some other health related excuse.

And if that wasn't surprise enough, she really threw them for a loop with her professional attire, which included a business suit with hair tied up, and a pair of studious-looking glasses.

She set her shopping bags down and fixated on the festive animation with a childlike gaze. This year's theme was "Yes Virginia, there is a Santa Claus," based on the famed 1897 letter to the editor, in which an eight-year-old girl named Virginia O'Hanlon asked if there really was a Santa Claus. And by the time Candi witnessed the huge sign on the 34th Street side of the store that spelled out "Believe" in cursive letters, she was a firm believer that there *was* a Santa Claus. And she now understood why he took so much joy in giving to others. She couldn't wait to change some girl's life tomorrow when she selected her to become a *Candy Striper*, and she was also looking forward to her trip to Afghanistan to perform for the soldiers.

But a dark cloud ominously pulled to a stop in front of the store, eclipsing her sunny day. Without a choice, she hurried to the stretch limo and disappeared inside.

Sitting across from her was Stone Scroggie. His deep tan matched his dark suit, and his bald head was shining like an ornament on a Christmas tree. He peered at her with his beady eyes, and didn't look happy.

Sitting beside him, too engaged in his laptop to look up, was Gooch. Handsome, cold, detached, and ruthless. Just his presence scared the hell out of her.

The limo fought through traffic, heading east toward the Empire State Building, which was decked out in red and green for the holiday. They turned on Fifth Avenue, passing the many sparkly shops being attacked by swarms of holiday shoppers, until they wound their way to the front of Grand Central

Terminal. Their sudden stop was met by angry honks, but Stone Scroggie had never been a man to be pushed—he did the pushing. They waited until a woman with a short bob haircut made her way inside the vehicle.

Jacqueline took a seat beside Candi, across from Scroggie and Gooch.

"How is our friend Mr. Collins this morning?" Scroggie asked, as the vehicle began to move again.

"He seemed a little tired. He's getting a little old to be hitting the club scene," Jacqueline responded with a smirk. She then removed her wig, exposing short, spiky hair.

Scroggie held up a photo of Candi attempting to kiss Kris. "I see that you showed him a good time last night."

"You told me to make it look good."

He held up another, this one of Kris pulling away from her advance. "But I guess not good enough, since I still don't have my money."

"Our money," Candi corrected him.

Scroggie ignored her, and turned to Gooch. "Let's hear the audio."

Without looking up, Gooch hit a button on the laptop and Candi's voice filled the limo. She'd hid the listening device in the belt buckle of her Santa suit.

"Are you sure you want to go through with this, Candi?"

"I told you, sweetie—I'm dedicating myself to helping people, and by helping you, maybe I can make up a little bit for all the damage I've caused."

"Isn't that sweet," Scroggie said.

"I can't believe that sap actually bought that line … this guy is too easy," Jacqueline added.

"Only a fool would underestimate Collins at this point," Scroggie warned, as the audio file continued.

"Over the next week the treasure will be loaded into the account."

"So I won't be digging for it?"

"No—your job will be to transfer the money into different accounts around the world. Like hitting a diamond with a hammer and the pieces spraying in all different directions."

"That's beautiful ... you've always had such a way with words, Kris."

Scroggie shook his head with disgust. "You would think with all those acting lessons I paid for, I could get something resembling a professional performance."

Candi seethed. She'd been criticized for everything from her clothing to her lifestyle, and had been the butt of jokes by the late night comics for years, but go after her acting and you'd have a fight on your hands.

Gooch punched the numbers of the account that Candi had set up in Statia—the one that the treasure would be "loaded into." Right now it had just the ten thousand dollars that Candi had used to start the account. But they would be able to watch as the money rolled in.

"All I want for Christmas is you, Kris," the tape continued.

"You can't have me."

"Maybe not, but that doesn't mean I can't ask Santa for the one I love this year."

"Turn it off ... now!" Scroggie shouted.

"Don't tell me you're jealous, Stone?" Candi said. "As if all those flowers and chocolates were because you were really in love with me. All you ever wanted me for was to get to Kris."

"You would think with all I've done for you, you'd be more respectful."

"What you've done for *me?* I think you got it flipped around."

"You really think it's a coincidence that your career had such a sudden turnaround?"

"Don't you ever say that! I earned it all on my own. Maybe Kris and I will run off together, and then you'll never see your money." She tried to open the door and leap out onto Park Avenue while they idled at a stoplight, but the doors were locked.

"There is only one deal for Collins to make—return my money or end up dead … as will you, if I don't get it back. But because I'm a nice guy, I'll write off your lack of loyalty this morning as the price of doing business with a flighty child, and give you one percent. With money subtracted for acting school and your clothing allowance, of course."

"That's not out deal."

"I've changed the terms of our agreement. But perhaps I'll allow you to earn equity back if you perform certain favors for me."

Candi cringed at the thought of Scroggie's cold hands on her. "If we're done here, please just drop me off at the Waldorf … I have a very busy day."

"Not so fast," Jacqueline said. "You aren't going anywhere until you hand over the brochure."

"What are you talking about?"

"The brochure that Collins passed to you last night inside Vida's. He wrote something on it, and I want to see it."

Candi reached into her purse and pulled it out. Before she could hand it to Jacqueline, Scroggie grabbed it away.

"What's this?" he demanded.

"It marks the spot where I'm going to meet the contact on my return trip to Statia on New Year's. That's when I'll be provided the numbers of the bank accounts where they've moved the money. Or as Kris said, hitting a diamond with a hammer."

"And you didn't think to hand this over to me?"

"I wasn't keeping it from you, if that's what you're getting at. But maybe with my pay reduction my mind isn't as sharp. As they say, you get what you pay for."

"Maybe I should have you spend some time with Gooch … to jar your memory."

Just the thought sent shivers down her spine.

"What are your thoughts on the subject?" Scroggie addressed the quiet Gooch.

He finally looked up. "I would very much enjoy spending some quality time with her."

"I'm sure you would," he said with an evil chuckle, "but I was referring to your thoughts on our next move."

"It seems simple. Have Candi followed when she travels to Statia to meet the contact. I'm sure she will agree to cooperate, as will the contact, who can then lead us to the money."

Scroggie shook his head. "No, we need to speed up the process. I'm tired of these games—I want the money in our possession within forty-eight hours. Candi obviously hasn't been able to properly motivate Collins, so I will take over that aspect of the project."

Jacqueline handed her phone to Scroggie. "I took these photos this morning. He sits outside her house and just watches … he's like a lovesick puppy."

"You said you wouldn't hurt Kris. That's part of the deal," Candi called out, her voice desperate.

Scroggie held up the phone and displayed the image of a red-haired woman who was waiting for the school bus with her two children. "You're right, Candi, I did say that. And my word is good. But I never said anything about this woman."

CHAPTER 18

I held on for dear life as the helicopter descended through the morning sky. I shut my eyes, and didn't open them until we came to a soft landing in a snow-covered meadow. It wasn't actually the North Pole, but for our purposes, Harry Crawford's two-thousand-acre ranch in the White River Valley of Vermont was one and the same.

My hands were still shaking when my feet finally touched the ground. Even though Alyson constantly assured me that the Bell 206 Jet Ranger was the safest model on the market, and that she'd had hundreds of hours flying in the army, my nerves remained skeptical.

Even bundled in a heavy coat over a heavy Scottish plaid flannel, I could still feel the chill of the sharp wind cutting through me. But while the weather was not delightful, the scenery was. An orange haze of sun was beginning to peek through the cloud cover over the horizon. The view was endless—I felt like I could see all the way to the real North Pole, or at least New Hampshire.

"Why are we here again?" I asked between teeth chatters.

"Because I know you, Collins."

"You know me so well that you thought I'd like to risk my life to travel to one of the few places in the country that's actually colder than New York?"

"I remember how you would get before a big case—and you've been acting the same way the last few days. You have to feel like you're in control, double and triple checking everything until you drive everyone around you crazy. So my choice was either to bring you here for a final inspection, or kill you. I chose this."

"You're a good friend."

"Not really—the way I figured it, there's enough people out there willing to do the deed, so why risk a prison sentence."

A Jeep appeared in the distance, careening over the frozen tundra. When it pulled to a stop in front of us, Harry Crawford got out and greeted us with a big smile. But it faded when he got a look at the remodeling work done on Alyson's nose. "What happened to you, Rudi?"

"You should see the other guy, Harry."

"I'm not sure I want to," he said in his measured, easy-going style, but with obvious concern. He'd first met Alyson when she assisted me on his trial, and both he and his wife Ginny became instant fans. Harry recently hired her to be his personal pilot for his helicopter. Of course, he rarely leaves the ranch, so we were able to use it for other purposes.

If this were as close to the North Pole as I'd ever get, Harry was probably as close to Santa Claus as I would ever meet. And he had some similar physical characteristics, with his gray beard and long white hair, which he hadn't cut since Ginny died. But on the other hand, in no depiction of Santa had I ever read of him being pole-thin, or with his hair pulled back into a ponytail.

Even though he would always put on a good front, I could see the sadness behind his smile. It had been present since he lost Ginny, and I doubted that it would ever change. He would also occasionally stare off into the distance with a look of stunned disbelief. It was as if he still couldn't believe she was gone.

We piled into the Jeep and headed across the property. The place was technically a farm, but I'd never seen any agriculture, dairy, or grazing animals. The only thing I remembered him growing was a few acres of marijuana, which was the reason our lives crossed.

When the drones discovered the illegal substance growing on his property, Harry claimed it must be growing wild, and that he was unaware of it. But when the search warrant revealed a treasure chest of paraphernalia used for cultivating and smoking, Harry needed a lawyer, and since his novels had made him a celebrity, albeit a reluctant and reclusive one, he called the lawyer to the stars.

The truth was, Ginny and Harry were a couple of Deadheads who happened to like smoking marijuana in the privacy of their secluded ranch. This put them in violation of the laws of the state of Vermont. But Harry's lawyer played on the heartstrings of jurors, even putting Ginny—then a gaunt woman of seventy-five pounds who wore a bandana over her bald head—on the stand, claiming that she used it to "ease her pain" in dealing with her disease. It was her idea, and I'm doubtful that the jury bought it, but they liked Harry, and they loved Ginny, and in the end they chose not to do what the cancer would eventually do, which was to break them apart.

We passed by tapped sugar bush, an apple orchard that was taking a long winter's nap, and the frozen trout pond where Harry spent much of his time during the lazy days of summer. And of course, I spotted the customary wild animals—this time it was a white-tailed deer and a moose. On one trip we came in contact with a black bear, which reminded me how happy I was that Alyson and her gun were along for the ride.

Harry's home was not the gaudy mansion that one might expect from a man who'd sold more than three hundred million books. It was a simple cape house that was tucked into a snowy hillside.

When we entered, the heat started to bring my limbs back to life. But before we got down to business, tradition won out. A visit to the ranch always began with a hearty plate of pancakes. It was really Ginny's tradition—she always said that no day that began with a plate of pancakes could be a bad day. And who could argue with that?

After breakfast, Harry took us to his study, which he used as his office back before he retired from writing—he stopped writing when Ginny died, ending the popular Gin Rumy fiction series that was based on her. In his calm, introspective style, he walked us through updates of each part of the preparations, step by step, as if it were an outline for one of his novels. He then led us down a set of creaky stairs and into the musty tunnels.

Much of the property was connected by tunnels, which had been put in by long-ago owners who were part of the Underground Railroad for escaped slaves. Harry often mentioned proudly that Vermont was the first state in the union to outlaw slavery, way back in 1777, almost ninety years before the Civil War. And when Harry felt that those police drones had invaded his privacy, he spent a mini-fortune to reconstruct the tunnels into a modern underground city, shielding him from any Orwellian influence. I liked them because whenever I stayed here in the winter I could walk to the guesthouse without leaving the warmth of inside.

The first room we entered was filled with so many technological gadgets it could have seconded as a NASA control center. There was one man present, madly typing away on a computer. His accommodations had improved since the time we were roommates—in jail.

When he finally noticed the intruders, he got up and ran to me like I was his lost love (fill in your own prison joke) and pulled me into a bear hug. "How you been, you son of a bitch?"

To answer his question, I was doing a lot better knowing that Marcus Hacker was on our side. The feds had sent him away for an extended vacation for hacking into a government computer that allegedly had some sensitive material on it. And if Candi Kane grew up to be a *Candy Striper*, and Marcus Hacker a computer hacker, I sure hoped that I'd never meet a Joe Murderer. I already had too many people trying to kill me.

"I've got into almost all the current email accounts and bank accounts," he said, handing me a thick bound document. "I made a list for each Kerstman family with the information you wanted—and account numbers. It also includes their up-to-date plans for Christmas Eve, so we can target which ones will need to be lured out."

I nodded, even if I didn't feel good about it. But it had to be done, and it was too late to turn back now.

"Let's go see the elves," Harry said, and walked us to our final stop—a warehouse-like room that was situated underneath one of the barns on the property. It was filled with merchandise, which would rightfully make Agent Falcone very suspicious. Men, many of whom looked like they'd just arrived from the 1960s, were working diligently to box the items, and load them onto an eighteen-wheel truck that was parked in the middle of the cavernous room.

Well, a couple of them were working, but most of the workers were goofing around. Some were dancing on bubble-wrap, while others were sucking on helium, and singing along to the Grateful Dead's version of "Run Run Rudolph," in high-pitched voices. And to show they were in the Christmas spirit, they were passing around a corncob pipe.

I felt queasy, and not just from the heavy marijuana smell. We had less than forty-eight hours to go, and I realized that my fate was connected to a bunch of sixty-something, tie-dyed relics who called themselves the Puff Daddies. Not to mention, they seemed more interested in getting stoned than saving me from the clutches of Stone Scroggie. But Harry had known these guys since they were kids in the Bay Area, and he swore by them. When it came to his inner circle, Harry was the most loyal man I'd ever met. The ironic thing was that if Kerstman would have just gone to Harry for a loan in the first place, all of this could have been avoided. But his ego led him to try to prove that his company could thrive without Harry Crawford.

I wasn't sure that this trip eased my concerns, or my fears about my inability to control the outcome. But if Harry Crawford, one of the great storytellers of his generation, couldn't write the ending he wanted in life—having his happily-ever-after ripped away from him—then surely Kris Collins couldn't either. Like it or not, I was at the mercy of the muses ... and the Puff Daddies.

CHAPTER 19

"I love a man in uniform," the woman purred.

"What do you say I show Mrs. Claus my North Pole?" the mall Santa responded with a lustful look.

"It must be your lucky day," she said, pulling him into the changing room in the bowels of the Yonkers Mall. The man was all smiles … until he ran into a three-hundred-pound brick wall.

"It really is your lucky day," the large man boomed. "Because I'm gonna relieve you of your duties, Santa."

The man looked perplexed. "Hey, you're Justin Duma."

His confusion then grew when he was offered double the pay he would have received for spending his day bouncing little kids on his knee and granting bullshit wishes that he couldn't deliver on. He accepted gladly—not that he had much of a choice—and was on his way.

Duma looked at Wintry with a smile. "Mrs. Claus is lookin' good. I guess two hundred is the new thirty."

"Why don't you save the charm for the kids, Santa. Speaking of which, you're gonna be late."

He stepped toward her, the gray wig and the granny glasses strangely a turn on. "I think Mrs. Claus should give Santa a little something for Christmas. He gets tired of being the one who's doing all the giving."

Her face wasn't exactly screaming 'come hither.' "It's Miss Claus to you ... I don't see no ring on this finger, Santa."

He smiled. "I told you, baby, the reindeer will get jealous."

"All I'm saying is it might get real cold up at the North Pole." She patted his midsection. "Good thing you got that big Santa-belly."

Since Santa was all knowing, he knew this wasn't going to work out well for him, so he finished putting on his red uniform and itchy beard, and they headed out on their reconnaissance mission.

"You got the list?" Duma asked.

"Of course I do."

"Can you just double check?"

She reached into her purse with annoyance and pulled out the folder. It had all the Kerstman families listed alphabetically, including all the pertinent information and pictures. She handed it to him.

"This is good ... really organized," he said, leafing through it.

"You sound surprised. Do you think it's a coincidence that Temple of Duma's has gone to another level since you put me in charge of the talent?"

He continued to review the file as they walked. "I weep for these Kerstman people. I guess they had to downgrade from a Mercedes to a Honda Accord."

"Not everybody who worked there was rich."

"But they weren't poor, either."

"I forgot—Justin Duma grew up dirt poor so now everybody else has to feel his pain. You're not suffering unless he says so."

"Hey, life ain't fair—do you think they'd be having all these fund raisers for these Kerstman kids if it was a bunch of black families from Newark?"

"I have no idea. All I know is I feel sorry for these people. It's not just the money—every night in the club I meet rich guys who're poor, just like there are a lot of people with no money who are rich. They've had their lives ripped away—they probably will never trust anyone or anything ever again."

"Yet they're about to have their kid sit on the lap of a total stranger, completely clueless that he's been tracking them. Talk about naïve."

Wintry shook her head with disgust, which meant the conversation was over.

They reached the festive center of the mall, where a line of eager children and their parents had already formed to see Santa Claus. Flyers had been mailed to all former Kerstman employees, offering them a hundred dollar voucher to be used in the mall if they stopped by to see Santa. It said the gift was courtesy of the Yonkers Mall, but the vouchers were really purchased by Kris Collins, with hopes of getting some needed information. If they were as poverty-stricken as Wintry made them out to be, it would be a good showing—Duma knew that a hundred bucks was like a million when you've got no money.

They put their spat aside for business purposes, and worked out a system in which Wintry would signal that a Kerstman kid was approaching by removing her granny glasses.

He played his part with ho-ho-hos and belly laughs. He was able to extract the necessary information, all while keeping his identity hidden and the line moving—although one five-year-old informed him that Santa wasn't black, which caused his embarrassed mother to spend five minutes apologizing, slowing things down.

After promising another child an Xbox—*did any of these kids ever leave the house?*—a little girl marched toward him like she had important business with Santa. Wintry removed her glasses.

The girl took a seat on his lap. "Hello, Santa."

"Ho, ho, ho … Merry Christmas! And what's your name?"

"You're Santa—I thought you knew everything?"

He glanced in Wintry's direction. She looked like she wanted to hang him out to dry, but played nice, holding up the folder for him to see. "Santa knows that you are Susie Woods, six years old, from Harrison, New York."

"We actually live in our car now. My mom and dad tell us to keep it a secret, so maybe nobody told you."

The response took Duma back to when he was her age. He lived with his mother and five siblings in a Caprice Classic. But it wasn't a car that you could drive. It had been stolen, stripped, and left to die by the side of the street in their neighborhood. And like most things that were left to die in Oakland, it had a few bullet holes in it.

"I have a secret for you, Susie," he whispered. "When I was your age I lived in a car, too."

"Why didn't you live in your sleigh?"

"That's a good question—you're very smart. So what does such a smart girl want for Christmas this year?"

"Can I ask for gifts for more people than just me?"

He shrugged his big shoulders. "It never hurts to ask."

"Then for my mom and dad, I want them to get their wallets back."

"What happened to their wallets?"

"We were robbed last night. But the guy seemed nice, so I think if Santa asked him to give them back, he would."

"If he doesn't, then he'll be on Santa's naughty list … and nobody wants that, ho, ho, ho."

"Santa knows all about being on the naughty list," Wintry muttered, just loud enough for him to hear.

"And for me, I'd like a house to live in," Susie continued. "If you could get us our old one back that would be my first choice. But if not, I'd take one with a yard with tall trees in it. I love climbing trees! And a big chimney, so that you can fit down it with your big belly."

He patted his gut and let out a laugh. "You don't mess around with the small stuff, do ya? Were you a good girl this year? You'd have to be a really good girl to get a house."

"I thought you had a list that told you stuff like that?" She pointed at Wintry. "Maybe your helper can tell you."

Wintry played along, browsing through the file. "Let me see … oh, here it is, Susie Woods. Yes for sure, Susie is on the good list. Let me just double check … yep, good list it is."

"Sounds like you're in business this year, Susie," Santa said.

She let out a huge sigh of relief. "Phew … I was worried that I might not get my wish this year."

"Why did you think that?"

"Because you made my wish come true last year. I didn't know if it was fair to get it two years in a row."

"What did I bring you last year?"

She looked skeptically at him.

"Santa's getting a little old … and forgetful. Maybe you can help him out, Susie," Wintry said.

"I asked you to make my brother's cancer go away, and you did. I thought you'd remember that—it was kinda a big deal."

Duma felt a lump form in his throat, and fought back a tear. He gathered himself, and said, "Thank you visiting me today, Susie … Merry Christmas to you."

She looked up at him with optimistic eyes. "It will be if you get me that house!"

CHAPTER 20

"And you say I never take you out to any nice restaurants," Duma said with a sly grin, as they ate in the food court during Santa's allotted fifteen-minute break.

But Wintry wasn't listening. She was viewing the girl off in the distance, who was staring at the poster that was promoting tomorrow's *Candy Stripers* auditions at the Macy's in Herald Square. Wintry checked the file and matched the girl as fourteen-year-old Hope Roberts.

"I'll be back," she said, and headed toward the girl. Duma looked momentarily surprised by the sudden departure, before returning his attention to his pile of fries.

She eased up next to the gangly teenager with sandy colored hair tied in a ponytail. It seemed like yesterday when she was that age, when her long legs felt too big for her body and her metal-filled mouth made her not want to speak.

"I can't believe they're bringing back *Candi Kane & the Candy Stripers*, it used to be my favorite show," Wintry said.

The girl grew enthusiastic. "And this version is going to be more than a teen soap. It's going to have singing and dancing … kind of like *Glee*!" She paused for a moment, and added, "My name is Hope, by the way."

"A perfect name for this time of year. I'm Mrs. Claus."

"Yeah, if Santa were married to Rihanna you are."

"He'd probably be too dense to appreciate it, even if I was." She pointed to the poster. "Are you thinking about auditioning?"

"Me?"

"No, the other person I'm talking to … if you stare at the poster any harder you're gonna burn a hole in it."

"Um … I wouldn't be able to. And besides, there's gonna be like hundreds of girls there … I would never get picked."

"You sure as hell aren't going to get picked if you don't show up."

"I have a job over Christmas break, so I gotta work."

"Trust me, you'll have plenty of time to work when you're grown up."

"My mom lost her job a couple years ago and I'm trying to help out with the bills. She worked at Kerstman."

"That's the dude who stole all his employees' money, right? Then he ran off and hid the loot, or something like that?"

"That's my life. But it's pretty much going to be over soon, anyway."

Wintry looked to the girl with concern. "Don't you even think like that."

Hope seemed surprised by the reaction. "Oh, I didn't mean it that way. I meant that when my mom finds out I skipped school today, she's gonna ground me for like a year."

"I remember those days … blowing off school to hang out with my friends."

"I don't really have any friends at my new school. After we lost our house, we moved to an apartment in Elmsford. I hate it there, and I don't really know anybody."

"Well, they're all gonna want to be your friend when you become one of the *Candy Stripers*. Is your dad in the picture … maybe he can help convince your mom to let you audition?"

"He's in the military. He's basically been over in Afghanistan since I was little, so it's really just been my mom and me. He won't be making it home for Christmas … again."

"You must be very proud of him."

"I am—I just wish he was around once in awhile so I could tell him."

"If it makes you feel any better, my dad was stationed at Fort Wherever I'm Not. He took off when I was five, never saw him again." Wintry motioned to the part of the poster promoting that the new cast would be joining Candi Kane on a Christmas trip to entertain the troops. "Maybe *when* you get the part, you can get to see him. If he can't get to you, go to him. I'm sure he'd love to see his little girl perform."

"Thanks for what you're doing, but even if I wanted to, I couldn't afford the entrance fee."

Wintry pulled out a couple of vouchers and handed them to her. "I'm giving you two hundred dollars worth to put toward your audition tomorrow, courtesy of Santa."

Hope studied them. "But it says the money can only be used in the Yonkers Mall."

"If they're advertising the *Candy Stripers* audition in the mall, then it counts. If anyone questions you, tell them that Mrs. Claus said so."

She continued to stare at the voucher. "Thanks for trying to help, but I just don't think I can."

"Listen, I would love to audition for this, but I'm too late. I didn't chase my dreams as hard as I should have, and I'll always regret it."

"Yeah, but you got to marry Santa Claus," Hope replied with a smile.

"Don't get me wrong, I have a great guy, two adorable little monsters, and an amazing job at a hot club in the city. But I always wanted to be on Broadway. And as you get older, the excuses fade away and the only thing you're left with is the fact that you didn't go for it."

"Thanks for the pep talk, I appreciate it, but when my mom …"

"This isn't about your mom, this is about Hope. I think the problem is you really don't have the talent."

A determined look came over her face. "I'm good."

"Prove it to me."

"What?"

"Look at these people—they're like a bunch of shopping zombies. Let's wake 'em up."

"You want me to sing and dance in the mall?"

"I knew you didn't have the guts."

"I didn't say that."

"Do you remember the 'Jingle Bell Rock' scene in *Mean Girls*?"

"You want to do that here? We don't even have any music."

"You said you could sing," Wintry said and then sung out like she was on Broadway, "What a bright time, it's the right time to rock the night away."

Hope hesitantly joined her, "Jingle bell time is a swell time to go riding in a one horse sleigh."

She found her confidence, and together, their voices grew powerful. And when they added the dance number, they had the crowd in the palm of their hands. It was exhilarating. Wintry had forgotten what a rush it was to perform in front of an audience.

When they finished, the mall crowd gave them a rousing ovation, and someone shouted out, "Encore!"

"I can't believe we just did that!" Hope gushed, her self-esteem now bouncing off the third floor.

"You up for another?"

"What do you have in mind?"

Wintry searched the crowd to find Duma in the back near the food court, sporting a proud smile on his face. "Do you like Beyonce?"

"Who doesn't?"

Wintry grinned. "I say we do the one where she sings about 'if you liked it you should have put a ring on it'."

CHAPTER 21

Zee Thomas got emotional, just as he always did when he got to this part of his presentation.

But he couldn't detail the actual low point that drugs had led him to, because he couldn't even remember the incident that left two people dead. So he told the seventh and eighth graders at the assembly about the children who survived—they were just a few years younger than those in the audience at the time, and he described what it meant to grow up without a mother and father. As he spoke, he clasped the locket around his neck—it contained a picture of the family.

Zee always felt like he was having an out-of-body experience when he gave these speeches. He normally struggled to talk to one person, much less this packed auditorium at Tarrytown Middle School. When he attended school here a few lifetimes ago, Kris would do all the talking for him. Just as he had at his trial. He was indebted to him for the rest of his life, which might not be that long if this latest stunt didn't go well.

When Zee finished the prepared talk, he opened it up to questions from the audience. There were none—just blank looks. He wanted to think that these presentations were making a difference in the kids' lives, and steering them toward the right path, but he knew they were more about himself and his own recovery. Most of the students were too young to remember him from his playing days, anyway. He was just another guy to them.

On the flip side, the teachers and principal very much remembered Zee Thomas. Not just from that magical summer in the Bronx, but from his days growing up in Tarrytown. He mingled with them afterward, but once the speech ended so did his superpowers. When the conversations grew into a painful struggle for him, he excused himself and made his way out.

As he did, he spotted the student he was looking for. But not until Bailey Reed had already noticed him, and was heading in his direction. This was unexpected, but would make things easier.

The shaggy-haired kid appeared nervous. He reminded Zee of himself at that age. "Nice to meet you, Mr. Thomas, my name is Bailey."

"It's nice to meet you, Bailey."

"I think your tattoos are cool."

Zee didn't think so. A couple from recent years were special to him, but he couldn't even remember getting most of them. They were a daily reminder of those wasted drug-filled years.

"My dad is your biggest fan. Do you think it would be possible that you could meet him sometime—he's been really sad lately, and I think if he got to meet you, he'd feel a lot better."

"I'll see what I can do. Why is he sad?"

"He lost his job a couple years ago—the Kerstman thing—and hasn't been able to find another one."

Zee just nodded.

"You know how you said at the assembly that you started playing baseball because you would have a catch with your father every morning before school?"

"I do."

"Me and my dad used to do the same thing, but lately he always wants to be alone. He never wants to have a catch anymore."

The mention of the baseball catch was like a gut punch for Zee. "Have you talked to your mom about this?"

"She's mad at him all the time. And when she yells at him, he just says he wants to be alone and wanders off."

When Zee got to high school age, the catches with his father became few and far between. His father would say he was too busy with work, and Zee was focused on hanging around with Kris and partaking in typical teenage hijinks. But he also remembered his father wandering off and wanting to be alone, and the fighting with his mother. It was an all too familiar story. As illogical as it was, Zee thought if he could have forced his father to have a catch on that fateful morning, he could have prevented what had happened.

"How about I drive you home, Bailey? Maybe we can surprise your dad."

"You mean it?" he said with excitement.

The boy followed Zee to the parking lot, where Sophie was waiting for him. When Bailey laid eyes on her he started to hyperventilate, and suddenly lost his ability to speak. "I see you two have a lot in common," she said with a brilliant smile.

Sophie drove her red 1947 Chevy pickup truck to the Reeds' house, with Bailey sitting nervously between them in the front seat. Zee couldn't believe that the boy lived on the same street that he and Kris grew up on. They parked in front of a modest house, only a couple lots down from Zee's childhood home, and he fought off the memories. There was too much at stake to lose focus.

Sophie waited in the truck as Zee walked Bailey in. The door was locked, and there was no answer when they rang the bell. "I guess my dad's not here," Bailey said. "Some days he says he's out looking for a job, but my mom says he goes to Starbucks and drinks coffee and reads the paper all day."

"Where is your mom?"

"She's a waitress at Shea Polo's. She'll be home around four-thirty."

Zee knew the place well; it was his favorite restaurant growing up here—best pizza in Tarrytown—and he remembered his father taking their entire Little League team there after big wins ... and losses. It was always a winning game if they ended up with a slice of Shea Polo's pizza.

Bailey wasn't tall enough to reach into the hanging plant on the porch and retrieve the spare key, so Zee helped him out. When they entered the house the boy excused himself and ran to his room. Zee took the time to case the downstairs and gather some of the information he came for.

The boy soon returned, holding a baseball glove. He handed it to Zee. "I bought it for my dad for Christmas. I'm hoping it will make him want to start having those catches again. And if you could sign it I think it would make him really happy."

CHAPTER 22

It was late afternoon when Alyson dropped me off in front of the apartment building in Brooklyn Heights, and it was already starting to get dark.

Alyson was heading back to the office for a few hours to catch up on a couple of cases, and hinted that it would be nice if I prepared dinner for her when she returned, adding, "That is, if you don't have plans with any washed-up teen stars tonight."

Obviously she wasn't up to speed on Candi's comeback. But I promised to cook her the best meal of her life, which she knew was Collins-speak for I would order takeout.

Before I exited the vehicle, she handed me a Christmas gift—a Beretta 92FS pistol. I tried to hand it back to her.

"What are you going to do if Gooch comes back with a tray of Christmas cookies? I can't be saving your ass 24/7."

She had a point, even if I was more likely to shoot myself by accident than protect myself from an intruder. But I agreed to take it.

As I headed for the building, I turned back and said, "If I haven't mentioned it, thanks for sticking your neck out for me last night ... or should I say your nose."

"Which reminds me, since you were the cause of the bloodstains that ruined my living room floor, you're not getting your security deposit back."

Sounded like a fair trade, but that didn't mean I wasn't going to debate it. "Technically, it was your blood."

"Just try not to add any more to it tonight, okay?"

Proving that a middle-aged dog can learn new tricks, I entered through the fire escape to avoid inciting the pugs. The moment I set foot in the apartment, something didn't feel right. I froze, counting to ten before taking my next breath. If I reached ten without hearing a sound, it would mean that I was just being paranoid. That's how all the legendary bad-asses roll.

When I got to eight-and-a-half I heard a clicking noise coming from the spare room where I stored my things, and had my computer set up. My first instinct was to make a run for it, but I realized this needed to end, one way or the other, and the next encounter I might not be packing a gun, or have the element of surprise on my side.

I took off my shoes and skated across the floor. I positioned myself next to the door, and wrapped my perspiring hand tightly around the gun. I counted the final second-and-a-half and bolted into the room. I flipped on the light, hoping to startle the intruder. "Freeze!" I yelled like I was starring in a bad cop show.

But the sudden flash of light disorientated me more than the intruder, and I didn't see the kick heading right toward my midsection. I fell to the floor, and this time the toe of the shoe connected with my ribs. The next one hit my wrist, dislodging the gun.

My attacker swooped up the gun and pointed it at me. But when we realized who each other was, we both screamed.

"Libby—what the hell are you doing here!?"

"I could ask you the same question."

"I live here! You're the one who's breaking and entering."

She looked like a rabid animal. It was always strange to see her not under control, but she was greatly affected when she was attacked in college while jogging in the park. Prior to that, she believed in the good of all people, which was the main reason the Amigos ended up in the Lake House instead of the Big House. The attack changed her view, and was the driving force behind her becoming a prosecutor—so that she could put away the bad guys who had the nerve to harm her idyllic vision of the world. She showed a similar pragmatic side toward me when I ruined her vision of our perfect marriage.

So sneak up behind her at your own risk. And besides changing her career course, the attack also caused her to take martial arts self-defense classes to protect herself ... or knock the crap out of her ex-husband when he entered his own office.

She realized that she was still pointing the gun at me, and changed from The Incredible Hulk back into Libby. She dropped the gun on the floor as if she didn't know how it got in her hands and helped me to my feet. We both took deep breaths, and I said, "Let's start again, Libby ... why are you robbing my apartment?"

"I wasn't robbing anything."

"Then what are you doing here?"

"It became clear to me that you're up to something, so I decided to find out for myself."

I noticed that she had been going through my desk files, and the electronic ones on my computer. I also took note of her designer business suit. "FYI—next time you break in here, you should use the fire escape. Alyson's dogs get riled up when someone comes through the front door."

She looked at the rips in her pants, noticing them for the first time. "Thank you for the tip, but to repeat my earlier statement, I didn't break in— Rudi left a spare key with me."

"Did she also give you access to my computer?"

"No, but you always leave the passwords in the top drawer of your desk—you're a creature of habit. I have a duty to protect our children."

"That's all you have to say for yourself?"

"No—I also want to say that you need to give the money back, Kris."

"Stay out of it, Libby."

"You already dragged me in … and our children. The FBI came by for a visit today—he told me about this guy, the Grinch."

"When you've tried enough cases as a defense lawyer, Libby, you'll learn that the FBI's definition of the truth is whatever helps them meet their agenda. And it's Gooch. The Grinch had more Christmas spirit."

"That doesn't exactly make me feel better. And these people can get to you anywhere, anytime, anyplace."

"As can my ex-wife, it seems."

"Even the private investigator I hired to follow you is one of them—Jacqueline, if that's really her name. You always think you can charm your way out of these matters, but these people aren't playing around."

It took a couple seconds for what she said to fully sink in. "Whoa, whoa, whoa … did you just say that you hired a PI to follow me?"

"Do you ever listen? She wasn't a PI, she was working undercover for Stone Scroggie."

"That's not the point, Libby—you owe me an apology."

"You're the one who pulled a gun on me, and brought this Scroggie character into our lives."

No, that was actually her father. "Fine, I'll be the bigger person. I'm sorry, Libby … I apologize."

I waited. And waited. "Well …"

"Well what?"

"It's your turn." Getting an apology from Libby Wainwright was like trying to get a slice of pizza away from Duma.

"I will use my turn to tell you that you are suspended without pay from Wainwright-Collins & Rudingo until further notice."

"That's your apology?"

"And while on suspension, you will be in charge of watching our children during their holiday break from school."

"I thought I was the one bringing 'danger' into their lives?"

"You are less likely to try to pull off any shenanigans with them around. You love them too much to place them in harm's way."

Before I could argue, or threaten to call the cops on her burglar ways, her phone rang.

The call was brief.

"It was Alex," she said.

"Is he okay?"

"Yes, but Zee isn't. He's been arrested."

CHAPTER 23

Upon my boss's request, I changed into a more professional look of an Oxford and khakis with a sport jacket. But because I was now suspended, I refused to wear a tie.

I left a note for Alyson, explaining that I'd gotten an offer from another washed-up teen idol … this time Zee Thomas.

Since Alyson had the Volvo, Libby did what Wainwrights do, and called her car service. Fifteen minutes later a large black SUV that looked like something the president would travel in, arrived outside the apartment.

It drove us to police headquarters at One Depot Plaza. I knew many of the Tarrytown PD, which I thought might be helpful in resolving this matter. But upon our arrival, it was clear that the local police had been pushed aside by the FBI.

I followed Libby into the interrogation room, where Zee was being double teamed by my good friends Agents Falcone and Boersch.

"And what exactly are you holding my client on?" Libby said, her eyes locked on Falcone.

"A Mrs. Mary Reed filed a complaint, claiming that a valuable necklace was taken from her home today. An investigation revealed that Zee Thomas had been in the house earlier in the afternoon. In fact, he was the only one in the house besides the Reeds' thirteen-year-old son. So we brought him in for questioning."

"So he hasn't been arrested?"

"Not yet."

It seemed that Alex had mixed up the legal terms, which gave me hope that one of our children would break the bad family history of becoming lawyers.

Libby looked to her client, who was sitting stoically at a metal table. "What really happened, Zee?"

I could tell that he'd completely shut down—he wasn't talking to anybody. Libby knew the drill, and asked for a piece of paper and a pen. When she was obliged, Zee wrote down his account. Not only did he explain his side of the story, but he counter-charged that the FBI had stolen his necklace.

Libby again glared at Falcone. "Why did you take his necklace?"

"We had to be sure it wasn't the stolen item."

"I can assure you it's not, now please return it to my client."

"He'll get it back when we're done here."

"No, you'll give it back now, or we *are* done."

We all knew how sacred that necklace was to Zee. Falcone finally figured out that it was a deal-killer and relented. But before he handed it over, he made another error … he opened the locket.

His face crinkled in surprise. "You keep a photo of the family you were accused of murdering? You're not hooked up right, Thomas."

Libby grabbed the locket away from Falcone and handed it back to Zee, which seemed to calm him.

But Falcone wouldn't let up, "I guess it shouldn't surprise me—breaking into homes seems to be your thing. I guess it's a good thing that it was only a necklace this time."

The night of the home invasion, Zee traveled with a couple of addicts he'd met just hours earlier in a shady club, to a house in Mount Kisco with the intention of stealing money to purchase drugs. In the process, one of the men shot and killed the owners—a husband and wife, leaving behind three young children—dead on Christmas Eve. Zee was arrested as an accomplice to the murder, which was legally the same as if he pulled the trigger.

The law was not on our side, and no matter what the public thought of Zee Thomas the baseball player, this was a brutal crime. And Zee couldn't make a case to defend himself, since he was too whacked on drugs to remember anything.

Things weren't looking good for us, to say the least. But just when it appeared imminent that Zee would be spending the rest of his life in prison, credible witnesses came forward to testify that not only was Zee comatose in the car during the invasion, but that he'd lost consciousness at the club and was dragged to the crime scene by the assailants, like a scapegoat to slaughter. He hadn't gone with them of his own free volition. But the verdict that cleared Zee didn't stop people like Falcone from holding the past against him.

"So does the FBI normally investigate local thefts?" Libby asked the FBI agent.

"We have reason to believe that this case might be connected to another one we're investigating."

"What you don't have is a shred of evidence that my client took a necklace from the Reed house. And for the record, he didn't break in, he was invited in."

The similarities from our earlier confrontation popped into my head, but since I was suspended I decided to keep my mouth shut.

Falcone leaned back in his chair and rubbed his temples. He appeared to be tired of the gamesmanship. "Don't you find it interesting that the Reeds are a Kerstman family? The ones whose money is being held captive by your glorified assistant over there." He pointed at me. "And his best friend just happens to end up inside their house, and accused of stealing. This is all connected, and you know it, Collins."

Libby was also my lawyer, and spoke for me, "Many Kerstman families were hurt financially. How do you know that once Mrs. Reed found out that her son had brought Zee Thomas home, she didn't devise a plan to help their financial situation?"

"That's what I'm trying to find out."

"No, you're making a desperate attempt to connect me to some grand conspiracy, and you're holding my friend on some bullshit charge as leverage," I chimed in, and Libby didn't look happy about it. A chatty client is the worst kind.

"I'm glad you've got your energy back after your apparent illness this morning," he retorted, and as a friendly reminder that they were following me, he added, "They must have some magical cures up in Vermont."

"I smoked some pot with a bunch of elves and now I feel great. I'm surprised you couldn't get Boersch in, he did such an elfy good job at the Wainwright party."

"The smell had already given you away," Boersch asserted.

Libby nodded. "He's right, you do smell like marijuana, Kris."

If she was the one representing me, I'd hate to see the lawyer who was against me.

"Which puts you in violation of your parole, Collins," Falcone said.

"Don't answer that," my lawyer said, back on my side.

I chose not to take her advice. "I would love to go back to jail—it would keep me safe from the FBI. But to clear things up, I'd be willing to take a drug test right here, right now. All I need is the cup to pee into." I grabbed his coffee mug and began to unzip my pants.

"Kris!" Libby called out. Her look said: *if you thought the kick to the ribs was painful, wait until I kick the next thing that comes out of your pants.*

A knock on the door saved me—and likely all parties present. A Tarrytown police officer entered. He brought with him a man about my age and a young boy.

"This is Stu Reed, and I think he can shed some light on this situation," the police officer stated.

Mr. Reed cleared his throat and said, "Our family has gone through some tough financial times the last few years. So I'm the one who took my wife's necklace—I sold it to make the mortgage payment this month. I never told her, which is why she assumed that Zee Thomas was responsible for it being gone."

He looked like a beaten man, as did Falcone.

Mr. Reed looked at Zee. "I'm sorry about all of this—I've always been a big fan of yours, and Bailey told me about signing the glove … I appreciate it. Can I do anything to make it up to you?"

"Yes," Zee surprisingly spoke up. "I want you to use that glove to have a catch with your son every morning before he goes to school."

CHAPTER 24

The pounding on her bedroom door startled Hope Roberts awake. Before she had a chance to respond her mother had barged in with her angry face, waving a piece of paper at her.

"What is this!?"

"Oh, crap," Hope muttered. She'd left the flyer for the *Candy Stripers* audition on the kitchen table.

"Don't oh crap me—answer my question, young lady."

She took out her earbud headphones, even if she was tempted to turn up the volume.

"I think it's a flyer for tomorrow's audition for the new *Candi Kane & the Candy Stripers* show. It says it right on there."

"You better not be planning on going to this."

"I haven't decided yet."

"It wasn't a question—you're not going. And where did you get this money?" Now she was waving two crisp hundred-dollar bills.

"What do you think, I stole it?"

"You don't make that kind of money at the Christmas tree lot. And I know Santa certainly didn't come early this year."

"I got it from his wife."

Her mother looked confused. "Whose wife?"

"Santa Claus."

"I'm not messing around, Hope."

"I told you," her voice raised. "I got it from Mrs. Claus!"

Her mother shook her head in disgust. "Then I'm going to need a phone number so I can validate that this person gave you the money."

"I guess she's from the North Pole, so you can try there. But she also looked like Rihanna, so maybe try calling MTV or something."

Her mother glared at her. Hope knew she'd pushed as far as she could. "Fine, I was in the mall today and looking at an ad for the auditions. And the woman who was helping out the mall Santa convinced me that I should go for it. I told her that I couldn't afford the entrance fee, but she and Santa were giving out mall vouchers for Kerstman people, since they feel sorry for us or something, and she was able to turn it in for me and get the money. End of story."

Her mother's face reddened. "You skipped school today!?"

"Oh, crap," Hope muttered again. She got suckered into that one. "It's not like we do anything on the last day before Christmas break, anyway."

"That's not the point. You have to stop living in this fantasy world. You need to focus on things that are realistic. College is a reachable goal." She held up the flyer. "This isn't."

"Like we can afford college. Talk about unrealistic. And since I have no friends in Elmsford, it's not like I won't have plenty of time for studying on the weekend."

"Your father says the military offers a lot of plans to pay for college."

"But then I'd have to be in the military and spend Christmas in Afghanistan like Dad. No thanks."

"Honey, your father and I learned stuff the hard way, in hopes that you wouldn't have to. We've always been at the mercy of others. I started out in the warehouse at Kerstman, and had to bust my rear to make it up to bookseller. But when they took that away, I had nothing to fall back on. And your father—do you think he really likes spending his Christmases so far away?"

"I don't know, he's never here for me to ask him."

"You Skype a couple times a week."

"Yeah, that's totally the same."

"I understand your frustration Hope. But we're all frustrated—you, me, your dad. It's just very important that we pull together as a family right now, and that you listen to me. I'm not trying to hurt you, I'm doing what I think is best."

"Maybe you should have done what was best for yourself."

"What's that supposed to mean?"

"You wanted to be a singer and you never did it. I think you wish you would've gone to some audition when your mother told you not to. I think you regret it."

"I made my choices—I have no regrets."

"You probably weren't good enough. I think your just jealous because I'm more talented than you ever were."

"I was plenty good enough, I just …" She caught herself.

"Go ahead, say it … you had me."

"That's not what I meant, Hope."

"You mean it's not what you *meant* to come out."

"I said it's not what I meant. When I mean something you'll know it." She held up the flyer. "And if you defy me on this, you're going to find out the hard way."

After her mother slammed her door shut, Hope put her earbuds back in and Beyonce sung her to sleep. She dreamed that she was on stage at the base in Afghanistan, performing with *Candi Kane & the Candy Stripers*. Her father was in the audience, smiling proudly at her. She smiled back at him, and mouthed, "Merry Christmas, Dad … I miss you."

And he mouthed back, "Never give up on your dreams, baby girl."

CHAPTER 25

I did a double-take when Libby suggested that the car service drop me and Zee off at Temple of Duma's. Especially when she added that Zee "deserved some fun" after his tumultuous experience at the police station.

But then I remembered that tonight was Duma's annual hunger drive, which was more along Libby's idea of fun—a black-tie party and helping poor people. She gave me a sealed envelope that included a donation from the Wainwright family. If she had a sense of humor, she would have warned me not to sail off with it.

I did agree with her on one thing—today's events had shaken Zee. He might not show much emotion, but his comment to Stu Reed about having a catch with his son was Zee's version of wailing in pain.

After Libby dropped us off, we stopped at a Food Emporium in Times Square to obtain the admission to the party, as listed on the invitation—ten cans of food. Of course, most of the high rollers at the party dropped much more than that at the auction that's held during the event. Last year they raised over three million dollars to fight hunger.

Before we entered the club, Zee slipped me a key. He didn't say anything, but I knew it was the key to the Reed home.

We stepped inside, looking very under-dressed. I was still in my sport-coat and khakis, while Zee was wearing a black T-shirt and jeans with a leather jacket. I'd grown quite paranoid about my recent entrance music, and it just happened that the house band was rocking out a version of The Ramones' "Merry Christmas (I Don't Want to Fight Tonight)". I could only hope that this would be a more peaceful visit than my last trip here.

It was always strange for me to see Temple of Duma's transform each year from a strip club, albeit a high-end one, into something along the lines of the ballroom at Wainwright Manor. But while there were no naked pole dancers present, there was certainly plenty of eye candy. It was a who's who of celebrities, awkwardly mixing with the many homeless folks that Duma invited to the event each year.

We made our way through the crowd, and I kept running into former clients. I had maintained good relationships with most of them over the years—mainly because I had kept them out of jail—and I never took offense that not one of them supported me during my own troubles. I understood that being linked to me at that time would not be perceived well by the public. If I was still their lawyer, I would have advised them to stay a couple states away from me at all times.

The first one to greet me was Hollywood bad boy Brett Modino. His penchant for bar fights had kept me gainfully employed for many years. I could tell that his publicist was working with tennis star Natasha Kushka's people to keep the former explosive couple nicknamed Bretasha, away from each other.

The room was also full of many famous athletes like Yankees second baseman Juan Azocar, along with many of the New York Jets, past and present, including the other members of the feared defensive line that Duma anchored, called "Dume & Gloom."

But some of the brightest stars in the room came from the music world. I was introduced to my daughter's favorite pop star, Natalie Gold, who didn't seem to care that her music mogul husband Nick Zellen appeared more interested in her arch rival in the pop world, Maria DeMaio. I got a picture taken with Natalie to give to Taylor. How cool was Dad now?

Zee did briefly chat with former professional wrestler Coldblooded Carter. But he really only had eyes for one person in the room—Sophie—even if they went out of their way not to be seen together.

Zee and I made our way through the crowd, and up to Duma's office. We found him with Wintry. Their sons, Jarren and Terrance, were also there, wearing miniature tuxes. I could tell that we'd just interrupted a fight. And when he sent Wintry and the kids away, it seemed to make things even wintrier.

We didn't have much time, so I quickly detailed the events that occurred since I'd left this office last night—an unpleasant ride with the FBI, an even more unpleasant visit from Gooch, a trip to the North Pole, and Zee being taken in for questioning.

Duma then summarized his day at the mall, which went off without a hitch. He did mention that he preferred the Santa suit to the tux he was forced to wear tonight.

There was really nothing left to say. In football terms, we were 24-hours away from kickoff and the game was a toss-up. Duma stood to signal the end of the meeting and said, "I'm putting you two at the head table."

And that was before I handed him the Wainwright donation. When I did, he made the expected joke about being surprised I didn't try to sail away with it. Then he let us know the reason for our prime seating was to best keep us out of trouble. We all knew that would be easier said than done.

Prior to dinner, Duma briefly addressed his guests. It wasn't the preachy speech you normally get at charity events. He spoke from the heart, focusing on his own childhood, and how hard his mother had to scratch and claw just to feed her children each night. When he finished there wasn't a dry eye in the strip club, and more importantly, checkbooks were out. When he trotted out his closers, Jarren and Terrance, I was confident that the cuteness factor would add an extra zero to each contribution.

Our table featured Duma, Wintry and their family, along with Duma's mother. The mayor of New York—who unlike the last mayor, was a big supporter of Temple of Duma's—was also present, along with a couple of select homeless invitees. The mayor couldn't take enough photos with the homeless, but stayed as far away from me as possible. It was good for business to be seen supporting the downtrodden, but not with the man who'd become synonymous with enabling corporate greed.

After dinner, the band began to play and the party started to heat up. At one point, Maria DeMaio and Natalie Gold joined them onstage in an up-tempo version of "Little Drummer Boy." But everyone's attention was hijacked by a curvy blonde who'd begun dancing on one of the stages like she hadn't got the memo that it wasn't business as usual tonight. She was going for the naughty librarian look, wearing a professional business suit with glasses, her hair tied up. But in a flash, the clip came out of the hair and it fell to her shoulders. Then the jacket came off, followed by the skirt.

A murmur could be heard throughout the room. At first I'd thought it was one of the dancers from the club who'd had one too many, but then I realized who it was. As did the rest of the room. The dancer, who was down to nothing but a skimpy bra and panties, was Candi Kane. And with each shake of her bottom she was putting new meaning in *pa rum pa pum pum.*

Sadly, most people in the room had seen this act before. Candi's attention-seeking, often drug-fueled antics had become too common of a sight in the Hollywood scene. The incident that got her banned from the Chateau Marmont Hotel had become a thing of legend. Judging by the looks of those around me, all this latest incident did was confirm their belief that Candi's comeback was nothing but a farce. The crowd was so uninterested that nobody attempted to stop her, and the band played on like they were on the Titanic.

Duma shot me an "I told you so" look for including her. When security asked if they should remove her, he told them to wait until she finished and then remove her as quietly as possible. But Candi was a long way from finished.

She hopped off the elevated stage—not easy to do in six-inch heels—and moved in our direction. Wintry held her hands over her boys' eyes to shield them from the scene. The mayor looked horrified, while a couple of the homeless guys seemed to like the idea. But I knew she was coming for me, and I braced.

"I told you all I wanted for Christmas was you, Kris Collins," she whispered in my ear. When I tried to move, she held me down.

She kicked off her pumps and did a long, seductive production of unhooking her garter and rolling her black stocking down one leg. She danced around with it, before hooking it around the back of my neck and pulling me toward her for a kiss. She left it there like a scarf, before repeating the process with the other leg. Then the remainder of the clothes began to come off.

Once the bra was removed, she'd crossed the red line, and security moved in. She fought them as they dragged her away. Just another in a long line of sad and destructive Candi Kane moments. It's what the crowd thought, and it's what I was thinking.

Until I found the note in her stocking.

CHAPTER 26

Zee and Sophie returned to his apartment and locked the door behind them.

Sophie pulled him into an embrace. "You've had a long day, ZT, why don't you go take a shower. And then I'll give you what you really want ... a burrito."

He grinned, and headed to the bathroom.

He soaked in the hot shower for twenty minutes—trying to wash off the stress of the day. But it seemed like every day was a battle against the demons for him. Today was no different.

He returned to the living room, wearing just a towel. But to his surprise there was no Sophie, and no burrito ... except for the one Agent Boersch was munching on as he sat on his couch.

"Hey, ZT—your girlfriend can really cook her hot ass off," he greeted him, and took another bite.

"Wow—look at those abs. If I had a girlfriend who could cook like that, I'd be three-hundred pounds," Falcone said with a wise-ass look. "Of course, I'm sure you two figure out a way to burn off the calories."

"I doubt he's dating a stripper for the conversation."

"I admire it, Boersch. They don't waste time on frivolous things like talking. They get right to the important stuff like eating, sex ... and helping Kris Collins steal money."

Zee just stared at them, trying to figure out where this was headed.

"Since you don't like to waste your energy on talking, ZT, let me answer your questions for you. Sophie let us in, and when she realized that we needed some alone time, she went out for a walk ... it's a beautiful night for it."

"But she's still with us in spirit ... or at least on video. Why don't you come over here and take a look?" Boersch said.

Zee reluctantly joined them on his couch, his eyes fixated on the television screen. Playing was a black and white surveillance video, featuring a man and woman in a hotel room.

"I hardly recognize her as a brunette, and how can I put this ... she wasn't as filled out back then," Falcone said.

"And here I thought those were real ... it's very disappointing," Boersch added.

"We took some amateur video the other night at Duma's when those girls got into a scrap over you."

"I need your life, ZT. Beautiful women fighting over you. Sure would hate to see you go to prison and screw that up."

Falcone continued, "And we have this really cool technology at the Bureau, called Face Recognition. When we ran the video through, guess who came up as a match?"

When Zee didn't answer, Boersch said, "It turns out that Sophie isn't her real name. It's Gertrude, which is unfortunate, as is the fact that she was born and raised in a trailer park in Ohio—abusive father, alcoholic mother, yada, yada, yada. Seems that little Trudy left her broken home to move to LA when she was just fifteen, and by seventeen she was working as an escort."

Zee remained stoic. None of this was new information to him.

"And the agency she worked for only 'escorted' upper-echelon clients. CEOs, professional athletes, actors, and I know this one is hard to believe … politicians," Falcone said.

"The problem, besides the obvious, was that this agency catered to clients who had a thing for underage girls," Boersch added.

"But I have to hand it to your Sophie—even though she got herself in a bad situation, she ended up doing the right thing. She cooperated with the FBI to bring down the entire operation, which is why we have her on file."

"And because she was underage, her identity was never revealed. She was able to move across the country, dye her hair, change her name, and get out of the adult entertainment industry … well, she dyed her hair and changed her name, anyway."

"It would have been a big problem for her if the Madam figured out who was responsible for their prison sentences. Good thing they never learned what sweet little Gertrude did … or where she is today."

"And by Madam, we don't mean a Heidi Fleiss wannabe, or some aging beauty queen. The agency was run by the Tamarez crime syndicate, which is best known for their expertise in human trafficking and murder."

"They make Stone Scroggie seem like a pussycat."

Zee tensed. He wanted to lash out at them for threatening Sophie, but he knew he had to keep his cool.

"It's time for you to follow your girlfriend's lead, ZT, and do the right thing."

"Collins was there for you when you were at your lowest point. Now it's your turn to help him. If Scroggie finds that money before we do, your friend is going to be expendable. You'll be saving his life by helping us."

"And when we get the money back, and put Scroggie away, we'll have more time to dedicate to making sure that Sophie's file isn't accidentally leaked. You know how accidents can happen when people aren't paying attention."

Zee's stare met Falcone's, neither backing down. He also noticed that Falcone was twirling the locket in his hands, which he'd left on the table before entering the bathroom. It was as if he was gloating in the fact that he had the upper hand ... mocking him.

"We need you to wear a wire for us, and be our eyes and ears, ZT. And we got a few bugs for you to drop up at the ranch in Vermont. We need access on the inside, and you're our ticket."

Zee looked straight ahead, but he knew he didn't really have a choice. He nodded that he would.

As Falcone headed for the door, he tossed his necklace back to him. "You made the right decision, ZT."

CHAPTER 27

The power cord fell out of the cigarette lighter and the computer screen went blank. As did the editing project Dora Woods was working on.

She'd been doing freelance work for almost a year now. The work was sporadic, and it sure wasn't enough to save their home, but with the price of gas these days it wasn't exactly cheap to be living in your car. Every little bit counted.

"This thing is a lemon, I'm going back there tomorrow and demand a new one," she bristled, jiggling the power cord they purchased at the mall with the voucher money that they'd received for Susie's visit to Santa.

"It's not the cord, Dora—it's the outlet," Edmund said, maintaining a calm voice.

She slammed her fist into the dashboard. It felt cathartic, so she did it again. "I hate this goddamn car!"

"Shh—you're going to wake the kids."

"I wish somebody would wake me up from this nightmare!"

"We're already awake," Susie belted out enthusiastically from the backseat.

"Speak for yourself, kid," Payne followed in a groggy voice.

"I don't know how you can sleep, Payne—Christmas is only *one* day away!" his sister exclaimed.

Dora snapped, "Susie—I told you there isn't going to be a Christmas this year. It's going to be like every other day—crammed in here, riding around with no place to go, and nothing will work."

Edmund countered, "There will be a Christmas, Susie … it just might not be like it was in past years. But Christmas is about family, and as long as our family is together there will be Christmas."

"Will you stop telling her lies—you're just setting her up for a big disappointment."

"Don't worry, Mom … I asked Santa to bring us a house. He'll come through, I just know it."

Dora blew out a frustrated breath. "Susie—that wasn't a real Santa Claus in the mall."

"Dad says the ones in the store are Santa's helpers. I'm sure he'll tell him what I said."

"Santa's helpers don't have the authority to make decisions on gifts. So I'm sorry that your father got your hopes up, but there isn't going to be Christmas this year, or a house. But at least we still have this lovely three-bedroom with central air and a great stereo system." She cranked the radio to full blast to make her point, and John Lennon's "Happy Xmas (War is Over)" shook the vehicle. Obviously Lennon wasn't referring to them.

"I asked him for a bigger gift last year and he came through."

"A lot of things were different last year."

"What did you ask for that was bigger than a house?" her father asked, inquisitively.

"I can't tell you," she said, looking at Payne.

"For the last time, there isn't going to be a Christmas!" Dora shouted with exasperation.

"If Susie says there is, then there is," Payne challenged.

"Keep your voice down."

"Why—will yelling make my cancer come back?"

"Dad—will you *please* tell Mom that Santa is coming?" Susie whined.

Edmund cleared his throat. "There was one year when they didn't think Santa would come, sweet pea. It was really foggy and he didn't think his sleigh would be able to fly."

Payne picked up where his father left off, "Then one foggy Christmas Eve, Santa came to say, Rudolph with your nose so bright, won't you guide my sleigh tonight?"

Father and son began to sing, "Rudolph the red nosed reindeer, had a very shiny nose …"

Susie added backup vocals, "Like a light bulb!"

"And if you ever saw it."

"Saw it!"

"You would even say it glows."

When they finished, Dora responded by opening the window and lighting a cigarette.

"When did you start smoking, Mom?" Payne asked.

"In college, but I took a twenty year break."

"Icky!" Susie said, holding her nose.

Dora held the cigarette out the window, its orange tip glowing in the dark night.

And then it was gone.

When Dora looked up, she saw a large man in a ski mask holding her cigarette. It was the same guy as last night.

He took a drag, before tossing it on the ground, and rubbing it out with his foot. "These things will kill you," he said with a cryptic smile.

"Didn't you take enough from us last night?" Dora asked.

"I thought I told you to stay out of my neighborhood?"

"We're not even in the same city," Edmund spoke up. "How'd you find us?"

"It wasn't hard, I just followed the bad vibes and they brought me here."

He looked in the backseat and smiled. "We meet again, Susie."

She looked happy to see him. "Did Santa come talk to you? He told me he was going to."

"He did … he told me I better give them back or I'm going to end up on the naughty list."

Her face lit up. "I told you, Mom!"

Dora threw her hands up in defeat. "I can't believe my daughter is listening to some criminal over her own mother."

The man's attention switched to Payne. "How's that stomach doing, fighter?"

"Much better … thanks."

"Stop talking to my children," Dora cried out. "Take whatever you came for and get the hell out of here!"

"I've been looking for one of these," he said, and grabbed the power cord. "Merry Christmas to all, and to all a good night."

He disappeared into the darkness.

She turned to Edmund. "If you don't go after him this time, I will."

"It's not worth dying over a power cord, Dora."

Wrong answer. She flung the door open, and marched off. "Dora, get back here," Edmund feebly shouted, but she was done listening to him.

She followed the large footprints in the snow like she was tracking Bigfoot. The prints took her a couple blocks until they suddenly stopped. As she pondered this development, a large hand grabbed her by the hood of her jacket and pulled her into an alleyway. She tried to scream, but an enormous hand covered her mouth.

"Big mistake," the man said. He forcefully turned her around and tied her hands with the power cord. He pushed her up against the wall and pressed his body against hers. "It doesn't seem like your husband is putting you in the Christmas spirit, so maybe I'll have to do the job for him."

"Please no …" Dora whimpered.

She could feel his hot breath on her neck, and felt his hands roam to the back of her jeans.

Footsteps momentarily stole his attention. Edmund had dashed into the alley. "You leave my wife alone."

"Are you willing to die for her?"

"Damn right I am … but you're the one who's going down!"

The man laughed at Edmund, who was half his size. But when he showed no fear and rushed at him, the man bolted. They could hear his footsteps running down the sidewalk, getting further and further away. The bully ran away like a coward.

Dora fell to the ground in a daze. Edmund hurried to her and untied the power cord. When she regained her senses, he slowly walked her back to the Range Rover. "Are you okay?" he asked.

She just nodded.

"Did he hurt you?"

"I'm fine."

"I'm going to get the First-Aid kit out of the back, just to make sure."

"Mom—are you alright?" Payne and Susie asked simultaneously as she entered the vehicle.

"I am now," she said, and forced a smile at them.

When she took her usual seat on the passenger's side, she felt something. She reached into her back pocket and pulled out their wallets. He must have returned them when he had her pushed up against the wall. Weird.

She checked through the wallets to find that everything was still there— money, credit cards, driver's license. But Edmund's wallet had something else in it—a newspaper clipping of their wedding engagement.

And when she read the words he had scribbled on it, the tears began to stream down her face. It said *I miss you Dora.*

TUESDAY DECEMBER 24

CHRISTMAS EVE

CHAPTER 28

Tomás peered out over the dark yard. Not a creature was stirring, not even … suddenly a clatter arose from the lawn.

He saw the two figures exit the home and make their way in his direction. Even if the quiet street hadn't fast asleep in this pre-dawn hour, the men would still have been virtually undetectable in their black scuba suits, but this didn't lessen Tomás' concern.

Gustavo and Berto always referred to him as Señor Nervioso for his constant worries—in turn, he wished they would worry a little more. While this was only a trial run, they would still end up in a very real prison if they were caught. They couldn't afford any mistakes.

Gustavo and Berto piled into the van, and they were off to the next house.

"When you got it, you got it," Gustavo beamed, removing his ski mask to reveal an ear-to-ear smile.

"For those who said we're washed up, may I suggest a better alarm system, and *un perro guardián*," Berto added with laughter, while adjusting the snowshoes they wore to avoid leaving footprints.

Tomás knew this was an action business, and words were empty. He took notice of Berto's heavy breathing, and feared his below-standard conditioning could be a weak spot for them tonight when the money was on the table. The Amigos had never attempted to hit so many houses in one night, not even close—it would be a test of endurance for them. And they were hardly in their prime.

Berto studied his diving watch, and a confident grin came over his face. "Three minutes and thirty-six seconds, in and out."

"That's a new Olympic record," Gustavo said and they slapped high fives.

"This is just a test run," Tomás cautioned. "When the real objects are moved tonight, is when the records will be kept."

"It will be easier," Gustavo responded. "Most people will be out tonight. Although, I do enjoy the challenge when I know they're sleeping in the next room."

"I don't doubt your talent—the one thing that can bring us down is overconfidence. If I remember correctly, it only took one slip to bring down the whole group."

"But that worked out well for us, no?" Gustavo said.

"Maybe if we're captured this time we'll get to live in a castle," Berto added.

"The only place we will end up is a six-by-nine cell with steel bars."

Tomás thought back to when they were captured by the Wainwright's security force. They were too arrogant back then to prepare for worst-case scenarios. But he was older and wiser this time, and would make sure they were ready for anything, even if his teammates were still chasing childish glory. He thought of what Kris had said at the party—they did have much more to lose this time.

They arrived at the final house—a large colonial in Sleepy Hollow. As they entered the neighborhood, Gustavo and Berto put on their ski masks and gloves. Gustavo placed his earpiece in, and both men made sure their equipment and weapons were secure.

The van slowed to a crawl and the two men dove out onto the lawn with a roll. Never stopping, Tomás kept driving around the block. He would time his return just as they exited the house.

Gustavo and Berto used a heavy row of pine trees to shield them. They'd already been in and out of several apartment complexes, so they figured this secluded house would be a piece of cake.

There were no trees in their yard growing up, or large houses for that matter. They often wondered if their own children had grown up too soft and naïve, unprepared to survive the lightning bolts that life would inevitably throw their way. The Kerstman victims were perfect examples. And based on the ease with which they'd broken into their homes tonight, they were no more prepared to deal with predators than last time.

Within moments, they were at the back entrance of the soon-to-be foreclosed home of former Kerstman Publishing executive Jeffrey Yu, which he shared with his wife and their three kids.

Berto punched in the alarm code, quickly disarming it. The Hacker guy that Collins had found in prison was worth his weight in gold—literally—and if they had him at their disposal back in the day, they would've been retired in the Caribbean by now.

Gustavo had Hacker's voice in his earpiece, just as he'd had all night. He walked him through the floor plan, and the other important spots they needed to hit within the house. He would also be able to guide them in the dark, using the hidden cameras the Amigos had installed earlier this month on a similar run-through.

Hacker guided them to where the spare key was "hidden," and they entered with guns drawn. They faced no resistance—there hadn't been any all night, so it wasn't unexpected. They moved into the living room area where a Christmas tree stood proudly—once again showing these people's devotion to the ideal over reality.

They scouted the downstairs area, and made notes for when they'd return for real in twenty-four hours. And after waiting the minimum three minutes that would be needed to accomplish their goals tonight, it was time to head back to the van.

That's when they heard the footsteps upstairs.

CHAPTER 29

"Jeffrey Yu has entered the bathroom. All other family members remain sleeping," Hacker informed them.

Minutes later, they heard a flush, and Mr. Yu retraced his steps back to bed. Part of them was disappointed that there would be no confrontation—they really missed the action.

Back on task, Berto began counting down the seconds in a throaty whisper. When it was time, he nodded to Gustavo, and they were on the move again.

The morning sun was beginning to peek through the darkness, but it was still too faint to help guide them. They retraced their steps through the trees, keeping one eye on the van as it came to a stop at the curb. The only sign of life was an early riser out walking his dog on the otherwise deserted street. But he wouldn't be a problem.

It seemed like another easy return ... until the van drove away. "What the ..." Berto whispered. That wasn't part of the plan—Tomás never went off script unless there was a good reason.

They felt naked, and then things got really complicated. The dog began barking, which sent the owner's attention their way.

"Is somebody there!?" he shouted out.

Always calm, Gustavo grabbed Berto and guided him through the pine trees into a wooded area that separated the Yu's home from their neighbors. They could hear the man's footsteps moving in their direction, and the dog's bark grew louder.

Gustavo scouted out a large oak tree, its leafless branches covered in snow. He climbed it like a cat.

The dog owner called out again, "Who's there!?"

Gustavo couldn't believe they encountered the one guy left on the planet with a sense of community. It seemed like people would walk silently by a murder these days if it would slow down their schedule. The steps moved closer.

There was no way that Berto could get up the tree, carrying those extra thirty pounds, and he began to panic. So Gustavo draped his legs over the branch and hung himself upside down like a bat. He then grabbed Berto by both arms and pulled him up to him. They dangled like a branch, as still as could be.

Gustavo held on for dear life as the dog owner crossed beneath them, without even looking up. The dog was another story. But Rover must have understood what it was like to be incarcerated, because he chose to remain silent, and tugged the owner in another direction.

The owner shrugged and mumbled something about how he must be hearing things. Having done his neighborly deed, he continued on with his walk. When the coast was clear, Gustavo and Berto headed out of the Yu's yard, unsure what to do next. Nothing like this had ever happened before.

As the sun began to brighten over the winter sky, the van pulled up behind them. They scrambled inside, more angry than relieved.

Tomás smiled at them. "I wanted to see how you'd respond to a chaotic situation. As we know too well, no plan ever goes as expected. It's important to be able to respond to sudden changes tonight."

CHAPTER 30

I got the phone call I'd been waiting for. It was Tomás with the news that the final dress rehearsal went off without a hitch. It was good news, but my bigger problem was straight ahead of me.

I'd been camped out across the street from Nicole's residence since last night. The minute I received the note from Candi, informing me that Scroggie planned to harm Nicole and her children as a way to get to me, I made up an excuse to leave the charity event and head to Ossining.

Candi risked her cover to get me the information, but a drunken Candi Kane meltdown was not out of the ordinary, and for those who knock her acting skills, it was very believable. And even if Scroggie was on to her, she would be at the *Candy Stripers* auditions today in one of the most crowded shopping areas in the world, so I was confident that she'd be safe … for now.

Up until this point, Scroggie had been playing on my terms, likely thinking that I'd eventually cave in and hand him what he wanted on a silver platter. The fake paparazzi and visits from Gooch were meant to rattle me, but for the most part he'd remained patient. But that strategy had changed, and he was now taking a more direct route. And because of my stupidity, I'd offered up Nicole as a way to do so.

I returned my attention to her mother's house—still no movement. I wasn't sure if that was a good sign or not.

My vehicle was situated in the driveway of a neighbor's house. On my last stalking trip I witnessed them leave with their children and a car packed with gifts. Wherever they were headed, over the hills or to grandmother's house, it appeared that they planned to stay through the holiday.

The neighborhood was silent over the next half hour, until a snowplow arrived and began clearing a neighbor's driveway across the street. With my paranoia-meter now off the charts, I studied the plowman from afar. He had a beard and wore a baseball cap. He had a slight frame, definitely not Gooch.

Distracted by the plow, I didn't even notice the woman step out of the house and march down her driveway. Her bathrobe hung from underneath her winter coat, and even without makeup and with a knit cap pulled over her long red hair, I was still taken by Nicole's natural beauty. So much so that I didn't realize that she was walking directly toward me, until it was too late.

I thought to make a run for it, but since I was allegedly protecting her—from a danger I created—it didn't strike me as the most chivalrous of maneuvers. So my plan was that when she knocked on my window, I would act like she wasn't there. By the third knock, it was pretty obvious that it wasn't a very effective strategy.

I rolled down the window, and she looked suspiciously at me. "Hello—I noticed that you're parked in the McCarty's driveway. I'm watching their house while they're on vacation, so I'm going to have to ask you to leave."

Her words were firm, but her tone was friendly. The noise of the plow scraping the ice off the neighboring driveway gave me a moment to come up with a lie. But I couldn't—I was much better at it in court. I just stared at her.

She focused on my face, and something registered with her—her face twitched in anger. "You!"

"My friends call me Kris," I responded nervously.

"I'm not your friend! What are you doing here!?"

Once again I couldn't find the words. But luckily she had plenty to say, so the conversation didn't lag. "Haven't you taken enough from our family!?"

"I come in peace."

"Because of that snake you represented, there will never be any peace for my family."

"I didn't mean to bring up any bad memories, but ..."

"Bring up bad memories? This must be some kind of cruel joke. If you've come to take anything else from us, we're all out—you can't take blood from a stone!"

"I'm not here to cause you or your children any harm."

"You leave my children out of this!"

"You're in danger. I'm here to protect you ... and them." It sounded okay when I said it in my head, but hearing it out loud the statement was laughable.

"That's a good one—the person we need protection from is you."

She began stomping away. As she did, she turned back to me. "If you're still here when I get in the house, I'm calling the police."

I got out of the car and chased after her. It was a dumb move, but not as idiotic as when I grabbed her arm, attempting to stop her. "You have to listen to me ... please," I pleaded.

When she finished swinging her arms wildly, causing me to let go, she slapped me across the cheek. It stung like nothing I'd ever felt before. "You have some nerve," she said, and began walking away again.

I called after her, "I don't have time to explain, but please don't send your kids to school today. And please *do* call the police—say I threatened you—that way they'll at least have to patrol the neighborhood."

She stopped, shaking her head with disgust. "Not that it's any of your business, but there is no school today. So we're going to do what we always do on Christmas Eve—take the kids to Santaland. Their father used to take them, but he's no longer here to do it!"

The point was clear. Nothing had changed since that day in court. Murderer. Blood money.

She turned and stormed back to her house. The shouting had attracted the watchful eyes of a few neighbors, and her mother was now standing on their porch, looking concerned.

I put my tail between my legs and walked back to my vehicle. The plow drove by and the driver gave me a thumbs-up and a wise-ass smile. I gave him the finger.

When I got back in the Volvo, I was greeted by a phone call. It was Libby.

"Where are you?"

I was confused. "I had some business to take care of in Ossining. Why?"

"I tried to get you at home last night, but you weren't there."

"The charity event ran late so I slept at a friend's house. And my cell was off." Because I was paranoid that the FBI was using technology to track me, but I kept that part to myself. "Why were you trying to reach me?"

"To make sure you were here to pick up the kids this morning. That was the agreement as part of our new guidelines, which I see you either didn't remember, or failed to take seriously."

"I didn't forget—I thought there was school today. Give me an hour and I'll be there."

CHAPTER 31

The snowplow pulled into a parking space at the Ossining train station. The driver got out and entered the stretch limousine parked beside it.

She took a seat across from Stone Scroggie and pulled off the fake beard. Gooch was in his familiar seat next to Scroggie, his eyes never leaving his laptop.

Jacqueline got right to the point, "Just like you predicted, Collins tried to warn Nicole Closs of an impending 'danger' to her. He spent half the night stationed across from her mother's house, and they eventually got into a public confrontation. It seems she still holds him responsible for the sins of Diedrich Kerstman."

"An interesting dynamic between these two, no doubt. He is obsessed with her, and she finds him vile. It sounds like my first marriage," Scroggie said, and laughed at his attempt at humor.

Gooch joined the laughter. "My favorite part was that he thought he was the one who could save her from this danger."

The comment turned Scroggie serious. "Collins has a big set of silver bells, I'll give him that. Hopefully we've learned our lesson about underestimating him. Any ideas how he learned that Ms. Closs might be in danger?"

Jacqueline spoke up, "Candi Kane made an appearance at a charity event last night at Temple of Duma's. She made a fool out of herself, stripping down and providing a private dance for Collins, before being thrown out."

"What she was doing was trying to make a fool out of *us.* A perfect opportunity to transfer the Closs information to him," Gooch said.

"I'm getting the idea that my girlfriend isn't as loyal as she claims," Scroggie said with a sardonic grin.

"It's likely that they've been conspiring together for the entire time. I would be suspect of all the interactions we taped between them," Gooch added.

"It never seems to work out well for Collins when he collaborates with Candi Kane," Scroggie said. "But I'm more interested in his relationship with this Closs woman. I think I will have them over to my house for Christmas Eve and see if any sparks fly. It's the least I can do for Collins, since he's been so nice to hold onto my money for me these past few years."

Jacqueline nodded. "Nicole Closs stated that she would be taking her children to Santaland today, we can pick them up there."

Scroggie laughed devilishly. "Looks like both of Kris Collins' girlfriends will be at Macy's today. Talk about killing two birds with one stone."

"What about Candi Kane?" Gooch inquired, sounding bored.

"She has worked very hard trying to deceive me, so I think she's earned a long vacation. I'll leave you in charge of that, Gooch."

"How long do you suggest it be?"

"Permanent," he replied coldly.

Stone Scroggie looked out the window and couldn't hold back a smile. "I think it's going to be the merriest of Christmases this year."

CHAPTER 32

Hope Roberts stepped out of the taxi at Herald Square. She felt like she was standing at the center of the Christmas universe. Swarms of last minute shoppers raced by her, the smell of roasting chestnuts drifted from pushcarts, and the Salvation Army rang their bells.

In front of her stood Macy's, with its large sign reading *Believe*. She didn't exactly believe that she would get one of the final two spots for the new *Candy Stripers,* but like her name, she did have some hope.

Not to say it wouldn't be the long shot of all long shots. And noticing the many power-shopping women gliding by her in their stylish outfits, gripping their giant shopping bags, she realized how over her head she was. She was anything but stylish in her heavy parka that covered her flannel shirt and jeans, with her hair worn in a ponytail. It was the outfit she wore for her job at the Christmas tree lot, which she cut out of early this morning, claiming she was suffering from "female issues"—an excuse that never failed to work on her male boss. She then raced to the train, and an hour later here she was.

She rushed into the revolving doors of the Seventh Avenue entrance. Maybe too fast. Her backpack got stuck as the door rotated and she fell, the bag remaining lodged in the door and dragging her. A security guard saved her from being trampled to death, but not from embarrassment.

She had no more time to waste—it would truly be a Miracle on 34th Street for her to make it to the audition on time. She secured her bag and ran past the dirty looks of the shoppers she'd held up, and into the block-long main floor. Her focus was grabbed by the decorated display cases and the model-looking women offering samples of the latest perfume, which caused her to run right into … Mrs. Claus.

Hope began to apologize, but then she realized who it was. She was stunned. "Oh my God, what are you doing here!?"

"I work here. Santa and I are doing some meet and greets on the fifth floor. I think the real question is—what suddenly got into you?"

"I'm … um … I thought about what you said and ..."

Mrs. Claus grinned. "About time you decided to take my advice."

"About time? I just met you yesterday."

"Better late than never. But too bad you're not gonna get the part."

"Then why did you convince me to come here?"

"I didn't convince you of anything—you're here because you want to be here. I meant you're not going to become a *Candy Striper* in that outfit. Where do you live, in the woods?" She brushed pine needles off Hope's shoulder.

"I had to go to my job at the Christmas tree lot to fake out my mom. I brought my hair and makeup stuff." She held up the backpack as proof. "And I read that they provide the wardrobe for the contestants."

"Why are you talking to me?"

"What? You asked me a question."

"You didn't come here to be interviewed by me, you came to win that spot. So don't let anybody trash-talk you out of your dreams, especially some Mrs. Claus impersonator who took the easy way out. Now get your ass to that audition before it's too late!"

"I think I may already be too late—look at that line for registration. I'm never going to make it."

Mrs. Claus eyed the endless line of hopefuls. She then turned back to Hope and handed her a sheet of paper.

"What's this?"

"It's your registration—I filled it out and paid for you. All you gotta do is sign it. Think of it as your EZ Pass to destiny."

Hope couldn't believe it. How did she know that she would even show up? "Are you following me or something?"

"The only thing anyone should be following is their dreams. Now get going!"

She didn't have to say it twice. Hope practically ran to the wooden escalators that took her to the sixth floor. She handed in her registration and was taken to a fitting room to prepare. And there it was.

Hanging up was the uniform she'd dreamed of wearing since she was a little girl. The iconic red and white *Candy Striper* uniform, with its short skirt and white boots.

She got ready in record time and was taken to a large cattle-call room with all the others. All tall and gorgeous, and probably with professional experience. Each contestant was given a short script to memorize, and lyrics to the song they were to sing. When Hope saw what the song was, she felt for the first time that Mrs. Claus might be right—maybe it was destiny.

The first test was the interview. They would be taken in front of the judges and asked about themselves. It wasn't so much about the answers, but to see if they had the charisma and presence to be a *Candy Striper*. The "it" factor.

When she was called, Hope stepped into a room that featured a large window that looked out onto Broadway, with a direct view of the Empire State Building. But the skyscraper wasn't half as intimidating as the sight before her. Candi Kane was sitting at the center of the judge's table and staring right at her.

CHAPTER 33

I stepped off the elevator on the eighth floor. Beside me were Taylor and Alex, each pushing a stroller.

"Aren't they too old to be in a stroller?" I asked.

Taylor rolled her eyes. "You've been out of the parenting game too long. When their legs get tired and you're stuck dragging two cranky kids through Manhattan on Christmas Eve, you'll be thanking me."

I assumed she was basing this on her vast parenting experience. Or maybe she'd seen her father screw up enough that she was an expert on what not to do.

Franny looked up at me and exclaimed, "Put your antlers on, Daddy."

"You promised," Zooey seconded.

"Oh, they must have slipped off," I said, as Alex handed me the plastic reindeer antlers. I placed them on my head to match the twins. I thought they might be overkill, since I was already wearing the reindeer sweater that my mother had knitted for me, matching the ones that Franny and Zooey wore. They refused to leave for the city this morning until I agreed to wear it. I didn't have time to argue, since I was desperate to get to Macy's before it was too late.

Taylor looked like she might be ill. "Could you be any more embarrassing, Dad?"

I wasn't sure if she was referring to the antlers or the sweater, but I assumed the question was rhetorical, so I left it alone. I love my mother, but I much prefer her cookies to these hideous sweaters she knits. Taylor cut hers up and used it as covers for her lacrosse sticks.

She wasn't finished with her gripes. "I can't believe you're taking us to Santaland on our day off. What are we like, six?"

"You know what they say—the family that sits on Santa's lap together, stays together."

"Gross. "

"And if you haven't forgotten, your sisters *are six,* and this will be their first time. But I believe in democracy—raise your hand if you want to go to Santaland."

Franny and Zooey's hands shot up, as did their antler-wearing dad. I looked to Alex and he grunted, "IDC."

I turned to Taylor, who translated. "It means 'I don't care'."

"Well, it looks like it's three for, one against, and one abstained. Santaland it is."

Taylor didn't look happy about this development. I tried to make peace before she became the cranky kid I was dragging through Manhattan. "C'mon Taylor, can you be a kid for five more minutes before you go off to college?"

"It's just weird that you suddenly got the urge to have a family day. I think you're up to something."

Like mother, like daughter. I needed to change the subject before her inquisitive mind began to further explore my motives. But luckily Franny did it for me. "Look, Daddy—it's Santa Claus."

"And Mrs. Claus!" Zooey followed up with a point in the direction of the Christmas power couple.

It was one of the many Santa impersonators that were roaming around the store, and confusing kids as to which one had the ability to deliver on their gift requests. But I recognized this one.

"That Santa and Mrs. Claus look a lot like Uncle Justin and Aunt Wintry," Taylor said, adding to my fears.

Duma winked at me as he began walking in the opposite direction. I laughed. "That's a good one, Taylor. I'd love to see the day when Justin Duma wakes up this early ... or works for scale."

"I said it looked like him—I didn't really think it *was* him."

I exhaled with relief and asked, "Can you do me a favor?"

"As long as it has nothing to do with me wearing reindeer antlers."

"If you ever plan on referring to them as Uncle Justin and Aunt Wintry around your grandparents, can you please make a pre-emptive call for an ambulance." Or on *second thought* ...

Even Alex laughed at that one.

As we moved closer to Santaland, and the crowds grew thicker, Taylor pulled out her phone and began typing. I had declared that nobody was allowed to bring their phones on our trip, claiming that I didn't want any interruptions to our bonding time. But my true intention was the same reason I turned mine off last night. And right on cue, I noticed an elf that looked too much like Agent Boersch. He must have splurged for the multi-day rental on the outfit. It also meant that Falcone wasn't far behind.

"I thought I said no phones."

"I just needed to tweet that my dorky dad took me to see Santa."

"Delete it ... now!" I erupted. We had enough people chasing us without posting our location on the internet.

She looked surprised. My outburst was out of character. "If it will make you less of a psycho ... then fine," she replied and deleted it. At least she pushed some buttons. For all I knew she could have sent another one. Sometimes I forgot that she was still a teenage girl and came with all the dramatic mood swings to prove it. Teenage boys might have the same issues, but Alex was my only experience with that species, and he never changed his mood. I wasn't even sure he had a mood.

And just when I thought I'd be spending the rest of my day with an angst-filled seventeen-year-old, she changed again, this time into someone wise beyond her years. As we stood in the long line to enter Santaland, she observed, "Look at this mob scene. How did Christmas ever get from a baby in a manger to 'step on thy neighbor' to get the latest Xbox?"

"You are a Wainwright, aren't you?" I asked with a smile.

She didn't see the humor. "Dad!"

"Just checking."

"When I get access to my trust fund, I'm going to use it to help people. I'm not saying I'm going to go all granola or join the Peace Corps, but at least I'm gonna remember what Christmas is really about."

I doubted that the poverty-stricken were going to shed any tears for poor-little-Taylor and her trust fund. But her words were about as close to Mother Teresa as a Wainwright would ever get, and I was proud of her. I just hoped that Alexander and Beatrice wouldn't get word of such "crazy talk" and disown her.

She continued on her soapbox, but my attention drifted. Part of it was on Boersch, who was pretending that he wasn't watching us. But the majority of my focus was on Nicole Closs, who was about ten spots ahead of us in line, standing with her two children.

She had cleaned up nicely since our confrontation this morning, now wearing a red sweater with a long skirt, and stylish boots. And she didn't look particularly concerned about her safety, despite my Chicken Little routine this morning.

"Aren't you listening, Dad?" Taylor said, annoyed by my distraction.

"Sure I am, honey. I'm happy that you've found the Christmas spirit. I told you a trip to see Santa would do you good."

"You're totally not listening to me. Mom's right—she says you never listen."

Alex picked the least opportune time to finally say something. He pointed at Nicole and said, "He's totally checking out that chick."

"I'm not checking anything out," I countered.

"I'll bet she's totally into guys with reindeer antlers," Taylor said, and Alex laughed so hard I thought he was going to pass out. On any other day it would have been great to see, but today it was drawing unwanted attention to us.

The line inched closer to the entrance of the 13,000 square-foot fantasy Christmas village, which ends with a meeting and photos with Santa. I kept "checking out" Nicole, who spent most of her time doting on her children and making a couple of calls on her cell. I continued to watch as she disappeared into Santaland.

I grew impatient as the line seemed to stall. I wouldn't feel comfortable until I entered, and was able to regain visual contact with her. My eyes bounced around, looking for signs of trouble. Boersch still had me in his sights, but he was the least of my worries at this point.

I suddenly felt a tap on my back. When I looked, it was Nicole. I was confused, but before I could even grasp what was going on, she picked up where we left off, "Don't think I didn't see you. I guess I wasn't clear this morning—leave us alone!"

The only thing that was clear to me, was that she shouldn't have let her children out of her sight. They were standing about fifteen feet from us, waiting patiently for their mother to kick my ass. And the woman moving toward them.

CHAPTER 34

Justin Duma had been following Nicole Closs, just as Kris had requested. He watched as she made it look like she was entering Santaland, but circled around to ambush Collins. Well played ... except that she should have paid more attention to her children.

When Duma saw the predator making a move for them, he made a mad dash. But he was too late. So he did the next best thing—trying to cut off her path to the escalator.

"Get out of my way," she warned.

"Sorry, Jacqueline ... looks like you've brought a knife to a gunfight. Let them go and I'll let you walk out of here in one piece."

"No need for a gun when a scarf will do." She slid her scarf off and wrapped it around the neck of the scared-looking, redheaded boy named Peter. "If you're still standing there when I count to three, I'm going to snap his neck."

Duma didn't move. During his career as an NFL defensive lineman he used to obsessively study his opponents, to the point that he could predict their next move before they even made it. And the common trait embodied by all the great running backs he went up against was patience. They would take that extra second or two to wait for their blockers.

In this case, the extra seconds gave Wintry the time she needed to get to the woman, and she hit her with a perfect form tackle. They fell to the ground, with Wintry's granny wig falling off in the process.

Wasting no time, Duma moved in. He grabbed the children and slung them over his shoulders. He rarely got to carry the ball during his playing days, but now he was on offense and heading for the goal line. He gripped on tight—he wasn't going to fumble.

He glanced back to see Agent Falcone of the FBI arrive on the scene. But he got too close to Wintry, and she hit him with the classic stripping move—whipping her leg around him and pulling him into a straddle with her impressive lower-body strength. She pretended that they'd accidentally got their legs entangled as she struggled with Jacqueline. Like most of the dancers she oversaw at the club, she wasn't a very good actor.

But it gave Duma enough time to make it to the escalator. He pushed his way through the crowd. Most people looked frightened by the oncoming train in a Santa suit, but the kids in his arms had gotten over their initial shock, and their smiles said they were now enjoying the ride. The boy, especially.

With the end zone in sight, he took one last look back to make sure he was in the clear. He then ran for the goal line.

CHAPTER 35

Nicole was stunned, so much so that she briefly stopped yelling at me. But the moment that Duma grabbed her children, I could tell she was about to scream. So I whispered in her ear, "If you make any noise, you'll never see your kids again."

She nodded that she understood. I then instructed, "Push my children in their strollers like they're yours. Act naturally. That's the only way you'll get to see Peter and Janie again."

When she didn't move, I opened my jacket enough for her to get a good look at Alyson's gun, which I was carrying in violation of numerous New York state gun laws, and my parole agreement.

Nicole didn't respond, but Taylor did, "Dad! What are you doing with a gun!?"

I tried to shrug it off. "It's America—haven't they taught you about the Second Amendment in school?"

"We're still on the First, which gives me the freedom of speech to say—have you lost your freaking mind?"

I had no time for this. "Everyone move—now!"

"What are you going to do if I don't—shoot me?" Taylor was starting to remind me of her father, and it was annoying me. I grabbed her arm and pulled her ahead. Nicole begrudgingly pushed one of the strollers, while Alex manned the other.

We were able to slip out of the Santaland area with little interference. With the usual Christmas chaos and commotion going on, along with a runaway Santa careening down the escalator, we were hardly noticed. And since Nicole wasn't screaming at the top of her lungs that someone had taken her children, nobody outside of Falcone knew that they'd been abducted. Hopefully we could keep it that way for the next few minutes.

I noticed that Jacqueline had removed herself from Wintry's grasp and had begun retreating to safety. Part of me wanted to stop her, but right now was about self-preservation.

Just when I thought we might be home free, I realized that we were back on Boersch's radar. We picked up the pace, but not fast enough. It was time to ditch the strollers. The twins protested. "Grandmother says Wainwrights were meant to be chauffeured," Franny stated.

"Well, when the FBI is chasing you, it's best to channel the Collins side of the family," I provided some fatherly advice, and as a compromise I took Zooey in my arms. Alex followed my lead and picked up Franny. We began a fast jog toward the elevators. The Christmas shopping zombies barely took notice of us.

We hit the elevator at just the right time. I hurried everyone inside, looking back over my shoulder to see Boersch the Elf running toward us. The elevator was empty—I had visualized melding into a crowd, but this might be better.

"I thought we were going to see Santa," Franny whined as I jammed the 'close doors' button.

"You promised," said her echo.

"I promised you Santa, and you'll get Santa," I said, hitting the button harder as if that would help. Boersch was about ten feet away when the doors finally shut, and he was banging on them by the time we began to descend.

We didn't get very far before the elevator stopped on the seventh floor. I had no idea what waited on the other side. So I moved to the side, out of view of the incoming, and trained my gun on the door.

It wasn't the FBI, mall security, or Jacqueline Helada. It was a couple, probably in their early sixties, holding numerous shopping bags. They smiled at Nicole and "her children."

"Well, aren't you adorable," the woman addressed the twins. "What are your names?"

"Franny and Zooey," the girls answered in unison.

The woman looked to Nicole. "Sounds like their mother was a big JD Salinger fan."

Nicole turned to me. "Actually their father was the one who chose the names."

With the gun safely tucked back under my jacket, I reached out to shake their hands. "Holden Caulfield—nice to meet you."

The couple got a chuckle out of that one. But Nicole wasn't smiling. She shot me a look to kill, and said, "If I recall, Holden Caulfield turned out to be a certifiable nut job who ended up institutionalized."

"I think he was just a confused teenager. You know how teenagers can be," I defended.

"We get it from our parents … they can be really bad influences," Taylor said, staring directly at me.

We could have continued with a full critical analysis of *Catcher in the Rye*, but the couple got off on the fifth floor. I held my breath, and gripped the gun, but no new passengers entered.

It seemed like it was taking days for the elevator to go, and then a noise rang out, almost sending me through the roof. It was a phone—Taylor's phone.

"Don't answer it!" I demanded.

"I have to—it's Mom."

Taylor looked to Nicole, who was staring at me in horror. "He's actually been much better since prison," she said, then answered cheerily. She went on to tell her mother that we were having the time of our lives—she didn't get the lead in the Nativity play for nothing—before handing the phone to me.

"I tried to reach you on your phone, but I had no luck. It seems to be a trend," Libby said.

"Sorry—I left it in the car. Good thing that Taylor brought hers."

"She has become quite dependent on it. She tells me you've been enjoying your day, and it seems that everyone is in one piece."

"It's been great. Except for all the crowds—we still haven't got to see Santa yet. The twins are getting a little impatient."

"Well, you better hurry it along. My reason for calling is not to check up on you, but to remind you to have the children to their grandparents by six tonight for Christmas Eve dinner. I forgot to inform you in my haste this morning."

"I'll have them there. Is there anything else?" I said, needing to end the call ASAP, but trying not to raise suspicion.

"Yes, Kris, I just wanted to apologize for last night … and my tone this morning. I know that you're a very responsible father, and I should display more trust in you. I know you would never purposely put our children in danger."

I looked around the group. "You know me, father of the year," I said, as the elevator started to go down once again.

CHAPTER 36

The elevator opened on the bottom floor, and Taylor and Alex strolled out.

As they got about fifteen feet away, Taylor glanced back over her shoulder. And just like Dad had predicted, the stocky guy in the elf suit approached the elevator. He stepped inside, and when he reappeared, he looked pissed.

His response was to head toward her and Alex. But they had already reached the Macy's security guard. And following Dad's orders, they told the guard that a "crazed" man in an elf suit was chasing them, and they believed he had a gun.

When security apprehended the man he looked doubly angry. He claimed he was an Agent Boersch from the FBI, but they weren't buying it.

They didn't have time to revel in their victory. Their instructions were to get out of Macy's immediately, and take Dad's car directly to their grandparents' house.

They left the department store through the 34th Street exit without any hassle, and walked to the vehicle was parked at the nearby Herald Square Hotel. But when they pulled the Volvo SUV out onto 34th Street, Taylor had another idea.

"Dad's acting weird," she said.

"Ya think?"

"It's too bad you don't share your sarcasm with everyone. It's so insightful."

"I mean he pulled a gun on some lady, and then made us run from an FBI agent in an elf suit … weird might be an understatement."

"We need to figure out what's going on."

Alex perked up. "If that involves us not going to Wainwright Manor, I'm in."

"I'll bet if we go to his apartment we can pick up some clues. I know where Alyson keeps the spare key."

She figured they could get to Brooklyn, check out his apartment, and still make it back to Greenwich for the six o'clock borefest. But the gridlocked traffic on 34th Street wasn't cooperating. It seemed like it would take them an hour to get from Sixth Avenue to Fifth.

"What's with all these military trucks?" Alex commented on the vehicles in front of them that were holding up traffic. "Is there a war going on in Manhattan that nobody told us about?"

"I think Dad might have started one," Taylor replied.

"Yeah, with that Nicole woman."

Taylor laughed. "Did I mention you should talk more often, little brother."

CHAPTER 37

My paranoid eyes bounced from side to side as we made our way across the third floor. Just because the cavalry wasn't waiting for us when we got off the elevator didn't mean they weren't hiding in the weeds … or the men's clothing section.

We had made our way through the sportswear section when Franny whined, "Daddy—my legs are tired."

"Mine too!" Zooey exclaimed.

"We're almost to Santa, girls. Just hold on a little bit more."

Unlike the twins, Nicole and I weren't a tight team. She said nothing, her face distressed, and mind focused on one thing—getting back her children.

We entered the "A Pea in the Pod" maternity section, and I led us toward the fitting room where we were to meet up. When Nicole heard her daughter's giggle she ran ahead and pulled back the curtain.

What she saw was a three hundred pound Santa happily trying on maternity wear with her children … sorta.

It was a "magic fitting room" that featured an eighty-inch mirror display, which was able to superimpose clothing on their reflection. To the kids … and perhaps Duma, it was as much fun as any video game they'd ever played.

Nicole shoved Duma away from her son, shouting at the oversized Santa, "Don't you ever go near him again!" She hugged young Peter so hard that he looked like he was in pain. She inspected every inch of him, searching for any sign that he was harmed. "Are you okay?"

"I'm fine, Mom," he said, seemingly confused about the fuss.

She pulled him into another intense hug. "I was so scared that I wouldn't see you again."

"Why wouldn't you see me? Santa was just getting me away from that crazy lady. He said Mr. Collins would bring you to me."

Nicole ignored that inconvenient truth and ran her hands over his neck. "Does it hurt, Peter?"

"I'm fine, Mom," he squealed, uncomfortable with the babying.

"You're really brave, you know that, right?"

He just nodded.

She turned her attention to her daughter, who was busy trying on virtual maternity wear.

"I think I want this dress for Christmas, Mom."

"You're a little young for that type of clothes, honey," she said, and then gave her daughter the same hugging treatment. She appeared more receptive to it.

I observed the twins, who had been rendered speechless by the sight of Santa. "You did bring us to Santa!" Zooey finally spoke.

"You always come through in the end, Daddy," Franny added.

"And because you two have been so good today, I'm going to let you spend some time with Santa, while I take care of a few things. Would you like that?"

They began jumping up and down on the legs that were too sore to walk just minutes ago. I took that as a yes.

"Can we spend more time with Santa, too?" asked Nicole's daughter.

Nicole grabbed Janie by the arm and pulled her away. I took that as a no.

Before she could leave the fitting room, Duma reached out and grabbed Nicole by her shoulder, stopping her in her tracks. "You're not going anywhere."

"Get your hands off me!"

"You need to start listening before you end up hurt."

"Leave me alone."

"It's not me you should be worried about. That woman who tried to take your son is on the loose. And because you didn't listen to Kris the first time, she almost got him back there."

"The FBI wouldn't be after you if you weren't some sort of criminals."

"Kris will explain when you're on your way."

"I'm not going anywhere with him!"

"I'm sorry I got you involved in this, but right now this is your best chance to keep them safe," I pleaded.

Then Franny spoke on my behalf, "Daddy always comes through in the end ... you'll see."

Nicole didn't appear convinced, but she had trusted the "system" to protect her family once before, and it failed miserably. She peered right into Franny, just like she'd done to me that day in the courtroom. "You better be right."

Duma looked to me. "You know where to go, correct?"

I nodded.

"And remember to wait for your blockers," he instructed, before picking up Franny and Zooey like a couple of feathers. He then led us out of the fitting room and into plain sight.

I spotted Falcone interrogating a Macy's employee in the distance. He was closing in. Duma pointed for us to go the other direction, while he walked right toward trouble. When Falcone spotted him, he shouted, "Freeze! FBI."

Duma set my children down, and put his hands up in surrender—giving us the opportunity to slip out undetected.

CHAPTER 38

"I told you—I'm babysitting."

Falcone feigned laughter as he paced the small detention center room below Macy's. "Babysitting … good one. You shoulda been a comedian."

"Ask them," Duma said, pointing at the two girls sitting in adjacent chairs, wearing reindeer sweaters and plastic antlers.

"Our daddy said we'd get to spend time with Santa while he took care of some things," Franny said. Or maybe it was Zooey. Duma always got them mixed up.

"I'm sure he was *taking care* of things," Falcone said, returning his attention to Duma. "So why did you abduct Nicole Closs' children? Was that also babysitting?"

"I didn't abduct nobody. I saved them from being taken by one of Stone Scroggie's thugs. Maybe you should check out the security video."

"So your story is that you're some sort of superhero who swooped in to save the day?"

Duma smiled. "I guess my suit didn't give it away—I'm Santa Claus."

Falcone's face flushed with anger. "Where are the Closs children?"

"For the millionth time—they're with their mother. Safe and sound … thanks to yours truly."

"Then where is she?"

"What do I look like, her keeper? If I knew, you'd probably accuse me of stalking her."

"I think she's with Kris Collins," Falcone said. "And for your information, we did check the security video."

He picked up a remote and clicked a button. The video feed played on a monitor. It showed Nicole walking off with Kris outside of Santaland, right after Duma took the kids.

"Is that a crime?"

"If she didn't go of her own freewill it's a very serious one. And we both know she didn't."

"All that shows is her attacking him. The only gesture he made toward her is whispering in her ear—probably to comfort her, since that lunatic Jacqueline Helada was trying to steal her kids."

"Since you had her children, I think he was using that as leverage."

"Leverage to do what? Get the children back to her safe and sound?"

"When we find Ms. Closs, and she can confirm your story, then you'll be free to go. Until then, you're not leaving."

"What happened to innocent until proven guilty? I'll bet if I was a white Santa, you'd be giving me a medal for helping those kids."

"Don't even go there, Duma. The only thing color-related in this is that black and white security video that shows you running off with somebody's kids … and then assaulting multiple people on the escalator to get away."

"You're just mad because I did your job for you. The FBI was lying down on the job while an average citizen had to step in to save the day."

"I wasn't lying down—your girlfriend dragged me down. She's lucky that I didn't bring her in for conspiring to assist in a kidnapping."

"What's wrong, Falcone—a girl was too tough for you? Maybe she was trying to alert the authorities that she'd tackled the real culprit. But it seems you decided to let Helada go. Are you working for Scroggie?"

The door of the detention room opened, and two Macy's security personnel walked in with an elf.

"Where the hell have you been, Boersch?" Falcone asked.

"I was trailing Collins and Nicole Closs, and this clown apprehended me."

"I'm not the one in an elf suit," the head of security shot back. "He claims he's one of yours—that you can vouch for him."

"And thanks to you, a kidnapper might have gotten away with two children," Falcone angrily spat.

"He had no ID on him, and was carrying a weapon. What were we supposed to think? We were not informed of any FBI investigation taking place in our store."

"That's because it was a highly confidential investigation—for your sake, we better get those children back."

Falcone looked to Boersch. "What happened?"

"I followed Collins and the Closs woman to the elevator on the eighth floor. Then I backtracked to the main floor—even if they got off on another floor, they eventually had to get to the main floor to exit the store."

"If security had been informed, we could have had a man on every floor, and locked down all exits," the security guy stated, further pissing off Falcone.

"We didn't have time. Children had been abducted—every second was crucial."

Boersch pointed to Franny and Zooey. "They were on the elevator, along with their older siblings—what did they say happened?"

"They're not talking—they lawyered up."

"Lawyered up? They're six."

"Their mother is on the way—Libby Wainwright, the attorney. She instructed them not to say anything to us."

"Just our luck, the only kids left on the planet who listen to their parents," Boersch said with a shake of the head. "Anyway, when the elevator reached the bottom floor, it was empty ... except for Collins' two older kids. When I approached them to discuss the situation, I was taken into custody."

Falcone rubbed his chin. "I apprehended Duma and Collins' younger children on the third floor. Obviously, they met up and did the old switcheroo."

"Does that mean this Closs woman is in on it?"

"She's involved, but I don't think she wants to be. Collins has her hostage."

"We can lock down all exits, and set up checkpoints in the store," Security said.

Falcone glared at him. "No, you've done quite enough already. You stay with Duma and the kids—I think the babysitter needs a babysitter."

"They're long gone from the building. I'll put out an alert on Collins to all law enforcement in a ten-block radius," Boersch said.

As Falcone headed for the door, Duma smiled at him.

"What's so funny?" he snapped back.

"Santa Claus knows everything, so he knows you're wasting your time."

"We'll see about that."

CHAPTER 39

We made it out of Macy's and sped down Sixth Avenue.

Duma was able to hold off Falcone and the FBI long enough for us to get out of the store before it was locked down. But my bigger concerns were Scroggie and Jacqueline Helada, and the latter was still on the loose with her deadly scarf.

"Where are you taking me?" Nicole asked with frustration as we hit 33rd Street.

"Gimbels," I replied.

"You do know that Gimbels closed in the 1980s, right?"

"Not all of it."

I made a sharp right turn, falling in behind the heavy crowd that was entering the Manhattan Mall, which occupied the building that once housed the Gimbels department store.

"You're safety plan involves bringing us to the mall?" Nicole asked with skepticism.

But her kids didn't seem too upset. In fact, they were all smiles. I still hadn't figured out the attraction the mall had for the modern child. When I was a kid, all shopping was evil, and time away from playing wiffle ball.

"Macy's might have had a Thanksgiving Day parade, but Gimbels was one of the first department stores to have a bargain basement," I said.

"Thanks, that really clears things up. Sorry to question your wisdom in bringing us to a populated area filled with security and cameras. There's only a killer after my kids—I feel really safe."

I felt like Columbus trying to convince folks that the world wasn't flat. But before I got my own holiday, we had a lot of work to do.

We kept pace with the thick crowds, passing all the standard mall stores—Aeropostale, GNC, Radio Shack. From a Christmas point of view, going from Macy's to the Manhattan Mall was like going from the North Pole to North Jersey, but the place was packed, which was good for our purposes. But it was also full of security, and I had no idea if there had been any type of alert put out on missing children, and their mother.

"I have one last Christmas gift I need to get," I said as we entered the JCPenney anchor store.

"You really think this is the time for that?"

"It's Christmas Eve, so it's not like I have much of a choice."

I found a section called "Home Environment" and picked out flashlights for each of us. A security guard eyed us a little too closely as I purchased them, and I felt my stomach tighten.

We made our way back through the store, and took the stairs down to the lower level. "This used to be the Gimbels basement. There is a direct entrance to the Herald Square subway stop," I said.

"So we'll be taking the subway out of here then?"

"Not exactly."

As I pretended to browse through a rack of clothing, a man stepped next to me. He spoke in a low, guttural voice. "I'm looking to buy my kid a Jets jersey for Christmas. I've been searching for a Justin Duma one—he was my favorite player back in the day."

He had my attention. I wasn't fluent in code, but I didn't need a translator either.

"And what the hell is a mall doing in the city? It's like sacrilege," he continued.

"Tell me about it—sometimes I miss the gritty New York of the past. Now it's like a big theme park."

"What if I told you I could take you back in time?"

"I think that would be the best Christmas gift I ever received."

"It's open, just make sure to lock up once you're inside." He handed me a badge. "And if anyone hassles you, just give 'em this, and they won't be giving you any more problems."

It was good to have friends like Duma who had friends in high places … or perhaps low ones.

I was already headed toward the entrance to the subway station when I saw the security guard from earlier—he was heading in our direction … and fast. Word had gotten out about us—it was just a matter of time.

The man remained calm. "And one last thing, Kris—remember to wait for your blockers," he said as he moved toward the oncoming security guard.

Armed with only flashlights, we entered the subway station, and I could see that a checkpoint had been set up. But we weren't going to be riding on any trains. We took a detour to a door marked *Off Limits*. I creaked it open, and slid inside. Nicole and the kids followed.

CHAPTER 40

The Gimbels Passageway was an underground tunnel that ran from the east side of Broadway at Herald Square to the west side of 8th Avenue at Penn Station. It connected the basement of Gimbels, the Hotel Pennsylvania, and Penn Station. It was closed in the 1970s after it became a haven for drug dealers and rapists. There had been talk for years about revitalizing it, but nothing has ever come of it.

When we flipped on the flashlights, Nicole looked like she was going to scream. We'd awoken a rat the size of a small motorcycle, and it scampered across the narrow corridor. The smell wasn't much better—the tunnel reeked of spoiled garbage.

But this was no time for the meek—we needed to move before they could trace us. We only had to go one city block, but it would seem like an eternity in this hellhole. I heard a noise, and couldn't tell if it was a human or some sewer monster, and wasn't sure which I feared more. The only thing we could do was move forward—one hand on the flashlight and the other over the nose—so that's what we did.

Grimy signs still hung on the cinder-block walls like out of some apocalyptic movie. Including one for the *Gimbels Brothers* store, surrounded by graffiti. We almost tripped on rubble and the debris of construction past, and passed rattraps that I doubted would be any match for the vermin that called the tunnel home.

Finally, we saw the ancient sign for *Pennsylvania Station*, and after a few more spooky moments, we slipped into its basement through another door that was meant to be sealed shut. Back in civilization, we made our way up a staircase to the terminal, acting like tourists who'd gotten lost.

I braced, expecting to be jumped by someone as we stepped into the crowded Penn Station—I just wasn't sure who it would be, or what they looked like. But since we were just spotted in the mall, and all exits and the subway were being guarded, they most likely thought we were still there, or at least in the vicinity. The tunnel, which had been locked off from the public for decades, would have been the last thing on their minds.

I checked the digital schedule to locate the train-line we were to catch—the Vermonter. We had five minutes. I purchased tickets, and we ran as fast as we could toward the tracks, Nicole gripping tightly to her children's hands.

I could tell that she was questioning her sanity. But no matter what she thought of me, after witnessing Duma rescue her kids, and then deliver them back to her, she must have concluded that we were the best option to get her children to safety, and alerting the nearest security guard would be the same thing as alerting Scroggie.

As we boarded the train, I smiled at the engineer—Zee Thomas—before leading Nicole and her children down the aisle. They sat on one side of the train car, while I took a seat across from them, next to a military man dressed in his fatigues. He made room for me by removing his large army duffel bag from the seat.

I extended a hand. "My name is Kris, and I just want to thank you for your service."

We shook, and he said, "Nice to meet you, Kris. My name is Herm, and I appreciate your support."

Not as much as I appreciated his.

CHAPTER 41

When Hope closed her eyes, she could see her father singing it to her. "The candyman can … the candyman can."

The song was from her favorite childhood movie, *Willy Wonka and the Chocolate Factory*, which she would watch over and over. She refused to fall asleep until her father sang the song to her. And now she was singing it to keep from waking up from her dream.

When she first laid eyes on Candi Kane and the judges, she thought she would faint. But she'd promised herself that she wasn't going to leave with any regrets. So she entered the competition thinking she had nothing to lose, which allowed her to perform without the burden of pressure.

She'd made it through the interview process and the rigorous acting scenes. The contestants had been whittled down to a final four. And suddenly the nerves were back—being so close, she now felt like she had *everything* to lose, and would regret a poor performance for the rest of her life. The room began to spin.

But when the music started, she could hear her father singing backup in her head, and she grabbed the moment. *"Who can take a sunrise, sprinkle it in dew. Cover it in chocolate, and a miracle or two? The candyman can … the candyman can."*

With each note, her confidence grew, and when she hit the final lines—*The candyman can cause he mixes it with love. And makes the world taste good. And the world tastes good cause the candyman thinks it should!*—she felt as tall as the Empire State Building.

All that was left was to wait for the judges' reaction—it seemed like it took an hour! But it was worth the wait when they responded with a standing ovation, and Candi Kane was smiling right at her.

The other contestants were kept back in the dressing room during the performances, so for all Hope knew, the ovation might not have been unique to her. But she figured it couldn't be a bad thing.

When all the contestants completed their final performances, they were brought back to the dressing room for what turned out to be the longest twenty minutes of Hope's life. And when they were brought back before the judges, her legs were jelly once more.

The auditions were being taped to be used in the show, so they eliminated one girl at a time for dramatic effect. Hope braced when they called the name of the first girl. But it wasn't her name. And when they got down to three, she was still standing. But since she couldn't feel her legs, she wasn't sure for how long.

As Candi prepared to send the last contestant home, Hope rationalized that no matter what happened, she'd made it far beyond her expectations. The perspective allowed her to smile as she braced to be eliminated.

At first it didn't register when Candi called out a name that wasn't hers, but then the other girl to make it—a blonde with giraffe legs who looked like she'd just leaped off the cover of *Maxim*—crushed her with a hug.

"Congratulations on becoming the final members of *Candi Kane & the Candy Stripers*," Candi announced with a smile. She then walked out from behind the judges' table and greeted Hope and Maxim.

When the filming was completed, and the cameras were turned off, Candi said, "I've never been accused of breaking up a party before, but we have no time to waste. We have an escort waiting for us outside to take us directly to the airport for the trip to Afghanistan, so gather your things from the dressing room, and meet me back here in five minutes."

Hope suddenly felt sick. "I don't think I can."

Candi looked confused. "You don't think you can do what?"

"My mom ... she doesn't know I'm here. I can't just leave the country."

"But you signed the consent form. It made it clear that we'd be leaving directly from the audition if you were selected."

A lawyer-type in an expensive suit spoke up, "And it gave the US military the right to do any necessary background check, using any information at their disposal including your Social Security number, and can terminate your participation at any point."

"I um ... I didn't think I'd win. It was kinda a last minute decision to come," Hope replied, leaving out the part that some random woman she'd met in the mall had filed her information for her.

Candi looked disappointed, but the show must go on. She looked to the lawyer. "It's not too late to get the runner-up, right?"

He nodded, but Candi gave Hope one last chance. "What's it gonna be?"

She felt like an entire ocean was perspiring through her *Candy Stripers* uniform. "Um ... I don't know."

"We don't have all day," the lawyer said, his tone unyielding.

"I'm going to be grounded forever."

"The only thing that grounds us in life is not following our dreams," Candi said.

Hope thought for a second, and felt the stares of everyone in the room. She still wasn't sure ... until Mrs. Claus' voice popped into her head, and made it clear in no uncertain terms that she was to get on that plane to Afghanistan.

"You're right. It's a once-in-a-lifetime chance. I'm going!" Hope blurted out and rush of excitement shot through her body.

"You're not going anywhere," a voice came from behind her.

Hope turned to see her mom. Her arms were crossed across her chest, and she was looking more pissed than Hope had ever seen her.

"Mom—what are you doing here?"

She held up a brown paper bag. "You forgot your lunch this morning, so I thought it would be a nice gesture to drop it off at the Christmas tree lot before I went to work. Turns out you weren't there."

Hope found some fight. "I'm going, I don't care what you say. This is my chance to catch my dreams and I'm not letting go."

"Since you're fourteen, and someone forged my name on the consent form, you don't have a say in the matter. When you're eighteen, you can do anything you want, but right now I'm taking you home."

The slamming of a door stopped the sparring match, and the sound of clapping echoed throughout the room.

"Bravo, bravo … what great drama. I suspect you will have a ratings winner, Candi—too bad you won't be around to enjoy it."

Candi turned white as a ghost and took a step back. "Gooch," was all she said.

Before anyone could respond, he pulled out a gun and fired at the lawyer, who fell to the ground. Then the two other judges. Hope screamed.

As did the *Maxim* girl. Gooch pointed the gun at her chest. "Please, no," she begged.

"You're very pretty—what pleasure would you provide me not to shoot?"

"Anything you want. Please …"

"I'm afraid that's not enough," he said and fired right at her.

The moment she hit the floor, he returned his attention to Candi. "Stone Scroggie sent me to teach you a lesson in loyalty. Depending on your cooperation, it will either be short and painful, or long and excruciating."

Hope suddenly felt she was playing the lead role in a horror movie, and the jelly legs were back. This Gooch character was staring right at her and her mother. There was something scary in his eyes. Or maybe it was what wasn't in them—any sign of compassion.

Candi stepped in front of them. "Leave them alone—they have nothing to do with this."

He laughed. "Candi Kane is concerned about someone besides herself—now I'm sure that the apocalypse is near. Somebody call the Mayans."

The laughter then came to an abrupt end as Gooch crashed to the floor.

CHAPTER 42

Alyson dropped the nutcracker that she'd just purchased on the second floor. It was for her Christmas collection, so she was annoyed that she was forced to break it over Gooch's head.

She rolled him over so that she could drive her boot into his nose. "Doesn't feel too good, does it?" she shouted at the unconscious hitman.

She picked up his gun and moved to the victims—three men in suits, and a pretty blonde who was going to miss out on her big break. She checked their pulses, and reported to the others, "They're fine—it was a taser. It's going to feel like they got hit by a truck when they wake up, but it just knocked them out."

She dragged them into the dressing room and locked the door. It should keep them safe until security could arrive. She then tied up Gooch. But there was no time to waste, so she guided Candi and the stunned group back into the busy department store. She held up Gooch's taser and yelled, "Security— out of the way. Move it!"

The heavy Christmas crowds parted at the sight of the gun, clearing the way for them to run down the moving escalators. When the shoppers spotted Candi Kane, a buzz began to ripple through the store.

"Will you slow down—it's not exactly easy to run in these Christian Louboutin heels," Candi whined. "Some of us have a fashion image to uphold—we can't be running around in combat boots."

Alyson stopped in her tracks and whipped around. "If you haven't noticed, I'm trying to save your sorry ass."

"If *you* haven't noticed, my ass is far from sorry."

"You would know—your head is usually so far up it that you can't see reality."

They started moving again, but the sniping didn't stop. "You barely know me," Candi said as they hit the fourth floor.

"I know the damage you've caused to people's lives."

"And by people, you mean Kris. He's a grown man, he doesn't need you to protect him."

"You're right—he needed a full suit of armor and a shot of penicillin to protect himself from you."

Upon reaching the main floor, they made a mad dash out onto 34th Street.

Despite the cold temperatures, Alyson remained hot under the collar. She couldn't believe she was risking her life to save this narcissistic home-wrecker. Kris really owed her. But when she caught a glimpse of a scared and shivering Hope Roberts, huddled next to her dazed mother, she found motivation.

"Stay here—I'm going to flag down a cab," she instructed the group, as they stood curbside.

"No cab—we need to stay right here," Candi argued.

"Sorry—there's no limo service today, princess. You're going to have to rough it."

"Are you deaf? I said no cabs."

Alyson ignored her as she viewed the surrounding scene. Anyone in the bustling shopping crowds could be one of the bad guys—the socialite-looking woman draped in shopping bags, the bell ringer from the Salvation Army. The possibilities were endless. And none of them were good.

Her attention returned to Candi. "This isn't Hollywood fantasy world— you don't know who you're dealing with in Scroggie!"

"I know exactly who I'm dealing with."

"I forgot—of course you do. Your usual way of moving up the ladder."

"What's that supposed to mean?"

"I just think it's interesting how you've suddenly made a career comeback after you started sleeping with Stone Scroggie."

"You have no idea what went on, but I don't respond to the haters."

"If that means you'll finally shut up, then I'm all for it. Now I'm going to get that cab before Gooch wakes up and decides to give you that loyalty test—I'm betting that wasn't your best subject in school."

"Do what you want—I'm staying here."

Alyson successfully flagged a cab, helped by the taser gun she brandished as if it were a Glock. She ushered Hope Roberts and her mother into the back, but Candi wasn't budging from the curb. So Alyson forcefully grabbed her by the hair extensions and shoved her inside the cab.

As they began to drive away, the driver asked, "Where to?"

But when he turned back to face them, they knew they had no choice in the matter. They all edged back in their seats.

It was Gooch.

CHAPTER 43

He handed the nutcracker back to Alyson, "I think you dropped this."

"I guess we're even now for my nose."

"After I kill you we will be."

Alyson attempted to shoot him with the taser, but he swiped it from her hand before she even knew what happened.

He had a good laugh at that one, and turned to Hope Roberts. "I'm sorry you won't be going to Afghanistan. But if it's any consolation, where you're going is much more dangerous."

"Please let my daughter go," Marilyn Roberts said through sobs. "She's just an innocent girl."

"It seems your tune has changed. It never fails to amaze me how the specter of death can bring people together. Unfortunately, most don't realize this until it's too late."

Candi shot Alyson a dirty look. "I told you to stay on the curb, but your ego wouldn't allow you to listen to me."

"My ego? You have some nerve."

Gooch interrupted, "Nerve she has, but its attention that she craves. Don't worry, Candi—you'll have my undivided attention very soon."

"Maybe if you let us off right now, I'll try to forget this ever happened. You can't just abduct an international superstar in broad daylight and expect to get away with it!"

He laughed condescendingly. "But if I recall, your ascent has always been star-crossed. So no one will be surprised when you turn up in the next couple days, dead of a drug overdose … especially after your erratic behavior at that charity event last night."

"You're going to have to go through me to get to her," Alyson challenged.

He appeared amused. "How fascinating—two mortal enemies teaming up in the name of survival. But why do I think it has more to do with your mutual loyalty toward Kris Collins?"

When nobody answered, Gooch continued, "I was sent to provide a test, and now is the time. Here are the rules—the first one to prove their loyalty to me, by telling where the treasure is, will get to live. Simple, no?"

Nobody moved a muscle. Alyson was surprised that Candi didn't blare out the location and offer to drive Gooch to it.

He stared out the front window of the cab, seemingly unaffected by the lack of action. "Take your time—it looks like we'll be sitting here for a while. They call me the magician, but even I can't find a way to make Manhattan traffic disappear during the holidays."

The cab continued to stop and start in the bumper-to-bumper traffic, and Gooch became distracted. Alyson noticed that he had zeroed in on an SUV that was turning on Fifth Avenue. Maybe too much so.

"Look out!" Alyson shouted out, and the normally in-control Gooch slammed on the brakes. They stopped just short of the military vehicle that had come to a stop in front of them. When Alyson looked closer, it wasn't just one military vehicle in front of them—they were surrounded by them.

Without a word, Gooch stepped out of the vehicle and casually walked away, leaving them parked in the middle of the busy street. He melded into the crowds of Herald Square, before disappearing. Alyson's first thought was that he was spooked by the military presence surrounding the cab, but something told her that it had more to do with that SUV he'd been focusing on. She wished she'd gotten a better look at it, wondering what the connection was.

When they stepped out of the cab, a friendly face greeted Alyson.

"Rudi?" said Sergeant Cherry, whom she had served with.

Alyson was equally surprised to see her. "What are you doing here, Sergeant? Is Manhattan under siege?"

They shook hands. "We have orders to escort a Ms. Candi Kane and her guests to the military transport plane that will take them to Afghanistan. We were supposed to pick them up curbside, but when we saw you leave the area, we followed. We assumed there had been a breakdown in communication."

Candi flashed another "I told you so" look as she strutted toward the military vehicle. As she neared the Jeep, Candi pirouetted on her expensive heels. She looked back to Hope, who was still shaking from the experience. "Are you coming, or what?"

Hope looked to her mother, who nodded that she should follow Candi. "Go follow your dreams, baby."

Tears began streaming down Hope's face. She wrapped her arms around her mother and they held on to each other for what seemed like minutes. It reminded Alyson of how much she missed Robbie.

They broke the embrace and Hope practically skipped toward the Jeep. But Candi never took her eyes off of Marilyn Roberts. "What about you?"

She pointed at herself, as if confused. "Me?"

"What do you say we go visit that husband of yours on the other side of the world? You'll be my guest."

She looked overwhelmed, and froze. So Candi took her hand and led her to the vehicle.

Alyson figured she must be in some sort of dream sequence, because she couldn't believe what she'd just seen. What was next—Ebeneezer Scrooge helping an old lady across the street?

"So you got any plans for Christmas Eve, Rudi?" Sergeant Cherry interrupted her thought.

"Robbie is spending the holiday with Herm, so I'm going to be heading up to Vermont."

"Sounds like a good time."

"It's more like a business trip."

"How you getting there? Train?"

"No—helicopter. I do some private flying work on the side. Got it parked over at the East 34th Street Heliport."

Sergeant Cherry laughed. "Sounds like you can take the girl out of the army, but you can't take the army out of the girl. You want a lift to the heliport, soldier?"

"Thanks, but I think I'll walk. I can use the fresh air," she replied, thinking that the army was less dangerous.

She made it safely to the heliport, but still did a double check for Gooch when she climbed into the pilot's seat. He wasn't waiting for her, but an envelope was. When she opened it her heart filled with joy. It was a hand drawn picture of Alyson flying a helicopter with Santa's reindeer pulling it through the air. *Merry Christmas, Mom. I miss you. Love you, Robbie.*

But how did he …

Her thoughts immediately went from jubilation to horror. Had one of Scroggie's people gotten hold of him? But then she found another note, and this one put her at ease.

Rudi,

Robbie wanted you to have this picture he drew for you, and since I can't say no to our son, I made a trip to the city to deliver it before Christmas. We will miss you this year—it's not the same without you.

Herm

PS. I left your gift in the luggage compartment. Be careful, it's fragile.

CHAPTER 44

Agent Falcone stood in the cramped security room inside Penn Station. He was flanked by NYPD officers Parillo and Mendoza, and a DOT official named Lipper.

They were viewing the security video of Kris Collins boarding the "Vermonter" with Nicole Closs and her two children.

"We stopped the train in Stamford. Searched the thing three times—no sign of them," Parillo said.

"There was no place to get off between Penn Station and Stamford," Mendoza added.

"That's because they weren't on the train," Falcone responded angrily, and froze the video. "There!"

It showed Collins and the others getting off the train before it ever left the station. They didn't pick it up at first because the escape was partially hidden by a military man with a large knapsack that was shielding them from the camera.

Mendoza shrugged. "I guess we missed it."

"You guess you missed it?" Falcone was about to blow his top, but regained his composure—now was not the time to set off any alarms.

"So what do you want us to do with the train?" Parillo asked.

"If our suspects aren't on it, there is no reason to keep those people from their ski trip any longer. Let them proceed."

"But what about Zee Thomas? It can't be a coincidence that he was driving the train that Collins used for his escape—those two are tied at the hip."

Falcone was well aware of this—of course it was connected. But he needed for Zee to get to Vermont and get him the information by using the wire, so he needed to divert the subject matter.

"Now you're gonna tell me how to run my operation, Officer Parillo? Where were you two when we put out the APB? We had all the subway entrances guarded, and they were trapped in a mall for God-sake … how the hell did they escape!?"

"There is evidence that they used the old Gimbels Passageway," Mendoza stated.

Falcone stared at the DOT official, Lipper. "And how would they get in there? That rat-trap has been closed down since the 1980s."

"There are a few people who have access to it. It's a small list, so it should be a quick investigation."

"I got a kidnapper on the loose and you're talking about investigations? Are you for real!?"

"We have a video from the JCPenney store in the Manhattan Mall, which has access to the subway line … and the passageway. It shows Collins talking to a man. I bet we learn that he was the one assisting them."

Falcone didn't doubt it, or even that the military man shielding him off the train might not have been a coincidence. He sighed deeply. "Let's face facts—Collins is long gone."

"We will put out an alert. His face, and the woman's, will be splashed over every TV station in the city. And we'll block all entrances to bridges and tunnels. We should have them in custody by Christmas Eve dinner," Parillo said confidently.

A little too confidently for Falcone. The last thing he needed was to disrupt what Collins and his crew had planned for tonight. He had to come up with some way to stop an alert from going out.

Falcone's phone vibrated—an incoming text. It was from Macy's security, letting him know that Duma's lawyer had arrived.

"I guess I was wrong," Falcone said, as he read the text.

"What do you mean?" Mendoza asked.

"I said Collins was long gone, but I was just informed that he was apprehended on Fifth Avenue. The woman and her children are safely in police custody. I need to get over there right away to question them."

"That's a nice Christmas present," the DOT official said, and Falcone agreed. They shook hands out of professional courtesy, and he was off.

It looked like he'd be spending his Christmas Eve in Vermont—everything in this case went back to the ranch in Vermont, and he was sure that was where Collins was right now. As was the money, which Zee Thomas was going to help deliver to him.

The bad news was that he now had to call his wife and inform her that he wouldn't be home tonight. When her yelling stopped, he promised that he would make it up to her by taking her out to the finest restaurant in the city on New Year's Eve. When the call ended, he was standing right in front of the 34th Street entrance to Macy's, with the large *Believe* sign staring back at him. He got the feeling that she didn't.

CHAPTER 45

The first person Libby saw when she walked into the room was Agent Boersch, dressed as an elf. She thought it was fitting.

Her eyes moved to the holding cell where Justin Duma was sitting on a bench with Franny and Zooey. She looked back at Boersch, as mad as she remembered ever being. "You put my children in jail!?"

Boersch shrugged. "It's not jail—it's a detention center where Macy's holds its shoplifters until they turn them over to the authorities."

"And my children stole merchandise?"

"No, but your client took something that didn't belong to him, and since he claimed to be babysitting your children, we thought it was best to keep them here until their mother arrived."

"Where is Agent Falcone?"

"He is making his way back from Penn Station. He's trying to track down a kidnapper—your ex-husband."

"I need to talk to my clients alone."

When Boersch opened the barred door of the cell, Libby ran to the twins and inspected them. "Did they hurt you?"

They looked confused. "Jail is boring," Franny said.

"Yes it is—all more reason not to end up here." *Like your father.* "Now please tell Mommy what happened?"

Zooey answered, "Daddy took us to see Santa, but then that mean man started chasing us." She pointed at Boersch, which he took as a sign to leave the room.

Franny took over, "But then we found Santa, and got to try on video clothes. Daddy let us stay with him so he could do errands with the nice lady."

"And this nice lady wanted to go with your daddy?"

"Daddy said he would keep her kids safe, and she wasn't sure, but then Franny told them that Daddy always comes through. She said 'you better be right' and they left."

"Just so we're clear, your daddy didn't *make* her go with him?"

They both shook their heads.

Next up was getting the version of events from Justin. They conferred for fifteen minutes before Falcone arrived and they moved the party to a table in the next room. Libby started right in on her offensive, "On what grounds are you holding my client?"

He played a video that showed Justin, dressed as Santa, tossing the Closs children over his shoulder and making off with them.

But it also showed another person that Libby knew all too well. Although, in hindsight, she didn't really know her as well as she thought.

"My client claims he was keeping the children from Jacqueline Helada, who you mentioned in our earlier conversation as one of Stone Scroggie's thugs. The video backs him up—she appears to be threatening the boy, wrapping something around his neck."

"That's what we are trying to get to the bottom of."

"And of course, Ms. Helada was also taken into custody and questioned like my client?"

"I had to make a choice to go after one or the other—and I chose to save the children."

"So where are these children you so *courageously saved?*"

"They are with your ex-husband."

"And also their mother, I'm told. It seems rather odd that my client would kidnap these children, only to give them back to their mother. Unless he was protecting them, as claimed."

"He handed them off to Kris Collins, not the mother. We believe that he is currently holding her hostage."

"And you have proof of this? Because your security video paints a picture of her going with him on her own volition. And she was the one who came up behind him, while he was waiting in line for Santaland."

"We both know that once her children were abducted, Collins held all the cards, and she had no choice but to go with him. And how do we know that he didn't have a weapon under that coat he flashed open for her to see?"

"I only deal with what we do know. And what I know is that the mother walked right out of the store with Kris *and her children,* which would mitigate these cards from your previous scenario. She didn't appear to be harmed or threatened in the slightest, and she chose not to alert any of the numerous security or other patrons within close proximity."

"We would have liked to talk to them to find out, but unfortunately Collins fled, using an abandoned tunnel to avoid us, and made a run to the train station. Does that sound like an innocent man to you?"

"If they tried to leave by train, then it shouldn't be that hard to apprehend them. If these children are in such peril, as you describe, then I'm sure you've stopped and searched every train that left Penn Station."

"We know what train they entered, but they got off before we were able to get to them. He is a very cunning criminal."

"So you have no idea where they are?"

"No, but I get the idea that your client does," he said, sending an accusatory look right at Justin. Falcone was a brave man, she'd give him that.

"My client is an innocent victim in this. He protected those children from the clutches of a dangerous woman, and returned them to their mother. For all we know, she could be forcing Kris to go with her, and not the other way around."

"You do know who Nicole Closs is, right?"

"All I was told by my clients is that she's a nice lady, and Kris didn't force her to go with him."

"You didn't follow the Kerstman trial?"

"I didn't, although I'm very aware of how it ended."

"Nicole Closs became front page news when she verbally assaulted Kerstman's lawyer in front of the entire courtroom."

"So now you're saying that Kris took this woman as some sort of revenge? Even by your standards, that's a reach, Agent Falcone."

"What I'm *saying,* is that the Kerstman trial is the common thread in this, and that the only act of *revenge* will come from Stone Scroggie, unless he gets his money back."

"While an interesting theory, it certainly isn't grounds to hold my client any further." She zipped her brief case and stood. "So if there isn't anything further, we'll be on our way."

"Your client is complicit in this, as is another client of yours, Zee Thomas, who just happened to be the driver of the getaway train. You're right, I can't prove it … yet. But in the meantime, you should spend less time concerned with enabling Mr. Duma and your ex-husband, and more about the well-being of others in this room." He looked at Franny and Zooey as he said it.

"Are you threatening my children?"

"No—I'm trying to warn you of the threat your facing. Just like I tried to do in your office yesterday. Stone Scroggie has no problem going after anyone to get what he wants. Including your children."

"The only person threatening my children's safety is you, Agent Falcone. You're the one who took it upon yourself to put two six-year-olds in jail, while letting Jacqueline Helada roam free."

"Where are your older children? They were with their father in the store, and now they seemed to have disappeared."

"Why, so you can follow them and then throw them in jail?"

"We're not following them, but it wouldn't surprise me if Stone Scroggie and his people are."

Libby felt the hairs on the back of her neck stand up. But her exterior remained cool. "If you're done with your threats, we'll be on our way. I wish you and yours a happy Christmas, Agent Falcone."

"Thank you, but the only way any of us will enjoy it this year is if Collins hands over the money. Stone Scroggie won't be taking the holiday off."

Libby grabbed Franny and Zooey's hands and led them out of the detention area, as Justin followed.

"Thanks for watching the children," Libby made small talk as they marched out of the department store. "If you need me tonight, I'll be having dinner at my parents, and then will be meeting up with Ned in the city. How about you—do you have any plans tonight?"

"I'll be working," Justin said.

"How sad for people that have nothing better to do on Christmas Eve than go to a strip club ... no offense."

"None taken—the club is closed tonight. I'm doing an appearance. Shake some hands, sign some autographs, get paid, it's all good."

Libby was no longer listening—her mind focused on Falcone's words. She pulled Justin away from reach of the twins' ears. "Is what he said truthful—are my children in danger?"

"Santa would never let anything happen to your kids."

She looked at him, bursting out of his red suit. "How can you protect them if you're working tonight?"

He chuckled. "I'm just a middle-aged ex-jock in a costume. I'm talking about the real Santa."

Libby didn't believe in leaving her children's safety in the hands of a mythical figure. So after parting ways with Justin, she dialed Taylor and Alex on their cell phones. There was no answer.

CHAPTER 46

We walked the blindfolded prisoners into the tunnels below the main house. This wasn't exactly the way I wanted this to go down, but the circumstances didn't leave me much of a choice.

Alyson took the lead, as my legs struggled to work after spending over two hours crammed in the luggage compartment of a helicopter. Nicole wasn't going easy. She was kicking and screaming. Alyson pushed her up against the wall and removed her blindfold, but was smart enough to leave the rope that was restricting her hands.

I removed the blindfolds from her kids. The girl seemed scared, hooked into her mother's emotions, and understanding the gravity of the situation. But the boy was oblivious. Sort of typical of men and women in the grownup world.

"That was cool," the boy gushed. "Is this the Bat Cave?"

I was about to tell him the truth—that indeed this was the Bat Cave—but before I could blow his mind, Alyson removed the gag from his mother's mouth and I was stabbed with a sharp tongue.

"Get away from them!" she screeched. "I trusted you!"

As someone who had experience in letting down the women in my life, I knew those three little words actually meant: *I was wrong to put my trust in you, which became abundantly clear when after leaving the train station, my children and I were thrown into the back of a truck, bound, gagged, and shoved into oversized bags—then loaded onto a helicopter like luggage. And now I'm a hostage in some subterranean prison in God knows where.*

Her kids ran to her and they did a group hug, as best she could with Nicole's hands tied behind her back. "That helicopter ride was cool, Mom— this is the best Christmas ever ... and it isn't even Christmas yet!" Peter exclaimed, still on an adventure high.

If I thought such a declaration would bring me goodwill, I was sadly mistaken. And things were about to get worse.

"And now the real fun starts," Alyson said to the boy, and led him and his sister away. "It's time for pancakes."

"Nooo!" Nicole shrieked, but there was nothing she could do, as she watched the kids disappear through the door.

"Where is she taking them?" she called out.

Since I was the only other one in the room, I assumed she was talking to me. "She's taking them to get some food. It has been a long day ... and it's kind of a tradition."

"Like it's becoming tradition for you to rip apart our lives!"

"You agreed to come."

"If I did, I've changed my mind—it was a huge mistake. I wanna go home right now."

"It's too late for that, I'm sorry."

She shook her head with exasperation. "So for the record, I am no longer here by choice. You are holding me hostage!"

"It's noted."

She sighed heavily. "I can't believe I had the choice of the good guys or the crooks, and I chose to go with you. I must be the worst mother ever."

This time I think she was talking to herself. But just to be sure, I answered, "You're a great mom."

"Real comforting coming from the guy who's holding us hostage in some musty basement in ... where are we, anyway?"

"The North Pole."

"Why didn't you say so? Can I meet Santa? Oh wait, he's in New York abducting children in department stores."

"Since he gave them back, I think the proper term is 'borrowing' them. And it doesn't matter if the FBI are the good guys or not—if they couldn't keep us from taking your kids, there was no way they would be able to protect them from Scroggie's people."

"But you'll be able to?" she asked with a shake of the head.

"This is the safest place I know. It's the only place I can guarantee everyone is on my side."

"I can't imagine that anyone would be out to get such a nice guy like yourself."

"They think I stole their money, and that I know its location."

"You mean *our* money … and *do you* know where it is?"

I chose not to incriminate myself. Besides, I think she already knew the answer, and her mind had already moved to the next piece of the puzzle.

"I get that they want to get you, and I don't blame them, but I don't understand how they can hurt you by getting to me … as you claim."

"Because they think I have a … it's not important."

"It's the reason I'm here, so it's damn important to me. I think you owe me that much."

She had a point, I did. So after a few starts and stops, some nervous chuckling, and stutters, I came clean, "They think I have a thing for you."

She looked confused. "And why would they think that? We've met once before today, and if I remember correctly, it wasn't exactly a friendly meeting."

"I didn't say I did, I just said they think I do," I dusted off some of my lawyerly avoidance skills.

She spared me some dignity by not pushing it. But that didn't mean we were on the same team. I handed back her phone that I'd confiscated during our escape. "Call your mother and let her know that you and the kids went on a trip and won't be home for your dinner plans. Tell her you'll be back first thing in the morning."

"How do you know what our plans are tonight?"

I chose not to mention that thanks to Marcus Hacker, we knew tonight's plans for all former Kerstman employees. "Everybody has a family dinner on Christmas Eve, it's what people do."

"How do you know I won't tell her that you have us held hostage?"

"Because you don't want to worry her. And since nobody knows where you are, including yourself … where would they even start to look for you?"

She knew I was right, which appeared to annoy her. And with Scroggie out to get her children, she was beginning to figure out that she was better off with nobody knowing where she was.

She called home and made up a story about winning a Christmas themed train-trip upstate while at Macy's, a real life Polar Express, and she couldn't turn it down for the kids. The sponsor of the trip would put them up for the night in a bed-and-breakfast and return them in the morning. She wasn't that far off.

The good news was that her mother didn't mention anything about seeing Nicole or the kids on the news. That meant Falcone wanted to keep the missing kids low profile. Because he knew any search for them might lead others to me, and possibly the treasure. And he was determined to get to it first.

Nicole's mood improved slightly when her children were returned, along with a big plate of pancakes for her. She refused to eat them at first, believing we were plotting to drug her, but eventually the Harry Crawford syrup wore her down, and she dug in.

I spent the next few hours guarding the prisoners. Mother and daughter wouldn't talk to me, but I'd dealt with the silent treatment before from Libby and Taylor, so I was accustomed to the tactic. On the other hand, the boy, Peter, wouldn't stop talking. Since my only son was Alex Collins, this I wasn't prepared for.

Another hour passed by before Alyson returned. This time she had someone with her—the sight of Zee brought a smile to my face.

He explained that they'd searched the train at the first stop in Stamford. But when they didn't find anyone or anything, they allowed him to proceed, eventually making it to Vermont about three hours after our helicopter arrived.

This surprised me. By now, Falcone had seen the security video that showed me getting on the train with Nicole and her children, which would give him enough cause to take Zee into custody. No different than he did with Zee yesterday or Duma in Macy's. His strategy had been consistent. If he kept the pressure on, one of us would eventually break. And here he had a chance, and passed. I noted it as interesting.

Alyson read my mind. "I did a full search when I picked him up at the station, and it was all clear. And I made sure we weren't followed to the ranch."

The ringing of a phone interrupted our conversation. It was Alyson's. Her face fell when she answered, and I immediately knew something was wrong. She handed to me with an eerie warning, "It's for you."

THE NIGHT BEFORE CHRISTMAS

Chapter 47

Libby drove her Mercedes up the long driveway and parked in front of the manor house. Wainwrights were always on time, and she had five minutes to spare until the six o'clock dinner.

She arrived with her mind more at ease. Alex had finally texted her back—she wasn't sure why they called it a phone, when all he ever did was text. He wrote that their father had asked them to feed Alyson's dogs in the Brooklyn apartment, since he was going on a trip … one that he had failed to mention to Libby. And that his sister's phone battery had died, which explained why she didn't answer Libby's numerous calls. It sounded like an elaborate story to excuse their tardiness, so she warned them of the unprecedented consequences that would occur if they were a second late.

Alex responded that they'd kept proper clothing at the apartment from the last time they'd visited their father, so they could go straight to Greenwich without stopping home, which would allow them to arrive on time. Libby and her children usually had a different definition of "proper attire," but it was too late now.

Libby was relieved they were safe and on their way, but concerned that they'd acquired their father's off-the-cuff style, which often led to trouble. She thought they could learn something about structure from their younger sisters, as she unhooked them from their car seats. They wore matching red and green plaid

Christmas dresses with bows in their hair. The outfits would probably spark another lecture from Taylor about how dressing them the same would limit their creativity. But since the creative side of their genetics was working on his second trip to prison, she thought that it might be a good thing.

Before they left their home in Pound Ridge the twins had to have everything organized for Santa, down to the placement of the cookies and milk. They were worried that spending the night at Ned's place in the city might cause St. Nick to pass by their house, so every light in the house had to be turned on. They were leaving nothing to chance.

Libby adjusted her dress—a classic sheath that was refined enough for dinner with her parents, but would be able to put Ned in the Christmas spirit later on tonight—and headed for the front door. She was surprised that no security or house staff met her. She hoped that they'd been given Christmas Eve off, but that didn't really sound like her parents.

The door was open, which was not normal, and caused a hesitance in her step. The lights were on, but the house seemed empty. "Hello?" Libby called out.

"Hello ... hello," her little parrots echoed.

"We're in here," Libby's mother called out.

This sparked the twins to make an excited dash to the dining room, their Mary Janes slipping on the slick floor. But they wouldn't be deterred until they got to their beloved grandparents ... even if Grandma constantly threatened to lock them in the coal cellar.

The grand dining room looked like it did every Christmas Eve. Her parents sat at the long table, underneath the twinkling chandelier that was decorated for the season—her father in a sharp suit, and her mother in a sequined gown, looking like a politician's wife with her blonde hair even more helmet-y than usual. But there was one major difference. While her father was present, he wasn't sitting at his usual position at the head of the table. Stone Scroggie sat in that seat.

Libby stopped in her tracks, pulling Franny and Zooey back toward her. "What's going on?"

"We have a guest for dinner this year, Elizabeth," her mother said with a forced smile. "Please take a seat."

"That's what I love about you Wainwrights," Scroggie rose to greet her. "Always on time ... and so predictable."

"Either tell me what's going on, or I'm going to call the police," Libby pushed.

"Your father is right—you *are* the rebel of the family ... although, nothing can compare to your ex-husband in that regard."

She pulled the girls even closer to her side. They were on the verge of tears—they thrived on organization, and to use one of Taylor's terms, they didn't "go with the flow" very well. She pulled out her phone and began to punch in the number for the Greenwich police.

"Before you make that call I'd like to give you your Christmas gift," Scroggie said. Right on cue, a handsome man in a suit entered the room. It was the man that Falcone had showed her the picture of—Gooch. And he had Taylor and Alex with him.

Alex looked placid, as usual, refusing to show his emotions. But his sister looked ready to introduce her captors to one of her lacrosse sticks.

"Seems he found them sneaking around their father's apartment. Looks like they trust him as much as their mother does. Not that I can argue with the sentiment," Scroggie said.

"I'm sorry that they didn't have time to change into the proper clothing like I mentioned in the text," Gooch said. They were still in the sweaters and jeans they'd worn on what Libby thought was a simple trip to the mall with their father. But nothing was simple when it came to Kris Collins.

Libby had no choice but to put the phone away and take a seat. Scroggie remained at the head of the table, with her parents closest to him, facing each other. Libby made sure that she sat between Gooch and her children—just the thought of him near them made her shudder.

A satisfied smile came over Scroggie's face as he took a seat. "Now that we're all here, it's time for Christmas Eve dinner to be served."

CHAPTER 48

Scroggie tapped his glass with a spoon and a waitress entered, carrying a tray of soup bowls. She wasn't wearing the same disguise she wore when they'd met in her office last month, but Libby still recognized her. But just in case, Scroggie reintroduced them.

"Libby—you might recall Jacqueline Helada from the work she's been doing for you, tracking your ex-husband. With all of Kris Collins' deception, one would think that would monopolize her time, so I consider us lucky that she was able to squeeze us in tonight."

Jacqueline just grinned as she placed a bowl of minestrone in front of her.

Taylor turned her anger to Libby. "I can't believe that you hired someone to follow Dad!"

Alexander spoke up in his daughter's defense … sort of. "Your mother should have hired her the day she met that cheating louse."

Scroggie shook his head. "I can't believe you're pointing fingers at others, Alexander. How many clients did you bilk out of money over the years with those fictional IPOs? I should know—half of them were mine. And then you'd trade favors and inside information with me in exchange for helping you artificially jack the prices up."

"Question my ways all you want, Scroggie, but at the end of the day I'm a businessman, and you're an extortionist."

"You were so offended by my tactics that you've willingly invested my money all these years. And even took an extra fee for laundering services."

"I made you what you are, and how did you repay me? By leveraging our relationship so you could steal from me … that's how!"

"It was business, Alexander, and it's not like I twisted your arm. You couldn't wait to get in on the Kerstman deal once I gave you that *insider information* about Harry Crawford's imminent return."

When her father didn't deny it, Libby felt hurt. She didn't think he was a saint, but she never thought he was a cold-blooded thief. And she had always defended his practices to Kris. She hated when he was right.

Her mother looked stunned by the accusations, but it didn't strike Libby as sincere. "Alexander—I can't believe you'd stoop to such a level."

"I might have been in business with Stone Scroggie, but at least I didn't sleep with him!"

"Mother!" Libby blurted out.

Beatrice rolled her eyes. "Spare me the indignation, Elizabeth. Compared to that unmitigated disaster you called a marriage, my relationship with your father is practically pristine."

"I think I'm going to throw up … gross," Taylor said.

Alexander re-joined forces with Beatrice. "This is all your fault, Elizabeth. If you hadn't brought Kris Collins into our lives, we wouldn't be in this predicament."

"This is not my mom's fault—own your mistakes, Grandpa," Alex surprisingly spoke up.

"The boy speaks—who says there aren't Christmas miracles!" Alexander sneered.

Libby appreciated the support, but she could fight her own battles. "Kris is far from perfect, but at least he didn't purposely go into business," she shot a disapproving look at her mother, "and do *other things,* with a known gangster."

"I told you he was a bad seed and you failed to listen to me. And now we're all paying for your mistakes," her father shot back.

"Kris has more integrity in his little finger than you have in your entire being, Father."

"You're as delusional today as you were then."

Scroggie nodded at Gooch, who stood and walked to Alexander ... with a knife in hand. He swung the weapon toward the table in one swift motion.

Libby thought she was going to be sick, but scrambled to cover Franny and Zooey's eyes. Gooch had chopped off her father's pinky finger.

"We have no time to be debating little fingers," Scroggie stated coldly. "Too much is at stake tonight."

Libby's mother didn't move as the blood poured out over the tablecloth. When it inched close enough to threaten her dress, she called for the servants. But they had long been sent away.

Taylor ran to the kitchen and got a wet rag and ice. She returned and wrapped it around her grandfather's hand. His skin had lost all color and he appeared to be in a daze.

And just when Libby thought it was safe to look, an even worse sight was before her—Stone Scroggie was staring directly at the twins.

He talked in a calm voice, "Do you know why we are celebrating tonight?"

Nobody answered at first, and then Franny hesitantly said, "Because Santa is coming?"

"Yes, I'm sure Santa will be coming this year and bring you everything you want. But the real reason we celebrate Christmas is because of the birth of the baby Jesus. Do you know who that is?"

"It's his birthday tomorrow," Franny said.

"I played him in the Nativity play this year," Zooey stated proudly.

"I played one of the Wise Men. We followed a star to Bethlehem to bring gifts to the baby," Franny added.

Scroggie looked to Libby. "Your children are very smart. And if I'm to assume they inherited their intelligence from their mother, you'll call Kris Collins and invite him to dinner. And if he's a *wise man*, he will also bring gifts ... specifically the money he stole from me."

CHAPTER 49

Libby stared up at the cathedral roof. She focused on the twin Juliet balconies and kept hoping that someone would swoop down and whisk them away. Or that Santa would enter through the chimney, place Scroggie on his naughty list, and turn him into a blubbering child. Ironic, since she'd never believed in Santa Claus throughout her life.

They sat in the Great Room, waiting for Kris—it had been over two hours since Libby was forced to make the call. It was clear that nobody was leaving, at least alive, until Scroggie got his money. He did allow her to call Ned and let him know that they were running late—citing a medical emergency concerning her father, which wasn't completely untrue. Ned was understanding, mainly because Ned was always understanding.

Scroggie sat patiently on the couch between Libby's parents. Part of her felt sympathy for her father, who was pale as a ghost, with his pinky-less hand wrapped in ice. But the bigger part of her was angry with him for his cheating business tactics. And speaking of cheating, she agreed with Taylor—the thought of her mother and Scroggie together made her nauseous. She couldn't forget how sanctimonious her mother was when the subject was Kris' infidelity. She couldn't look at either of them right now.

Jacqueline was pacing the room with gun in hand, while Gooch remained disturbingly still. He stood like a statue, barely moving a muscle, and rarely blinking. Libby marveled at how anyone could stand in one place for so long, but also found it a little scary. It was like he wasn't human.

The monotony was broken by a *flop-flop-flop* sound coming from outside. It drew closer ... and louder.

Jacqueline slid the drapes enough to peek out, and announced, "It's a helicopter."

It was hovering directly over the manor house, the whirring of the blades sounding like they would slice right through the roof.

Gooch finally moved, pulling what looked like a high-tech, sawed-off shotgun from underneath his suit-coat. Libby really hoped that Kris knew what he was doing.

The next sound was a loud thud on the roof, followed by footsteps. Everyone looked upward, as if they could see through the roof. Libby wasn't ruling out the possibility that Gooch could do so.

The helicopter moved away from the house. It hovered not far away, its sound still present, but fainter.

The phone rang, startling everyone. Libby's father walked to the glass table in the center of the room and picked up the receiver. "It's about time," he barked at the caller, sounding like his old self. He then put it on speakerphone for all to hear.

"Hello everyone, I just wanted to drop in and wish you a merry Christmas," Kris' voice filled the room.

A couple of loud, quick footsteps coming from the roof broke the moment. "Whoa—there's a lot of ice. I don't know how Santa does it—you could lose your ass up here!"

"Daddy!" the twins shouted in unison.

"How are my girls doing?"

"We got to wear our Christmas dresses," Franny exclaimed.

"And Grandpa got his finger cut off, but Mom says it was a magic trick," Zooey added.

"From what I'm told, your grandfather hired the renowned Dutch magician, Goochelaar, for the night. What a great Christmas surprise."

"It seems that he is full of surprises," Libby spoke up, looking at her father for the first time since dinner. "He turned out just as you said. I guess I just wouldn't listen."

"Cut him some slack, he must have done something right if his daughter turned out so well."

A slight smile slipped through her misery. "Thank you."

"I'm just glad you didn't force me to take your parents in the divorce."

"From what I hear, I should have asked for half of this lost treasure that you seem to know the location of."

"Sounds like you've been talking to my old friend Stone Scroggie."

"He was here when I arrived—and they already had Taylor and Alex. I had no choice but to call you."

"You did the right thing, Libby—is everyone okay?"

"We're fine."

"That didn't sound very convincing."

Taylor could sense that Libby was at the end of her emotional rope, and took over, "Hi, Dad!"

"Hey, sweetheart. I hear that you and your brother didn't follow my directions. I guess the more things change, the more they stay the same."

"I'm sorry, we went to your apartment to see if we could find out what was going on. We shouldn't have been snooping—that Gooch dude was there."

"Now that you've re-acquainted yourself with your family, I think you have something for me, Collins," Scroggie interrupted.

"I got what you want—perhaps you should come up here and get it."

"I don't think you're in any position to be dictating terms."

"I'd like to come to you, but I don't know how I'm going to fit down this chimney. I've put on a few this year—I can never turn down those damn cookies."

"Stop stalling!"

"Okay, okay … I'll just drop it down."

An object crashed down into the fieldstone fireplace. Jacqueline pulled it out to reveal a bag. But it didn't contain a billion dollars. "It's full of candy," she said, holding up a box of Milk Duds.

"I've been to these Wainwright dinners, so I know that minestrone soup and white fish isn't cutting it. I figured my kids could use some real food."

"You would know all about candy," Alexander spoke up.

"I'm sorry, *Dad,* would you have preferred some finger food?"

The color in his face went from nonexistent to angry red. "Get your ass off my roof, and give the man his money!"

"Nobody gets their gift until the Christmas Eve traditions are complete," Kris' voice shot back through the phone. "What's tonight, Taylor?"

She smiled wide, understanding. "It's the night before Christmas."

Libby remembered when Taylor and Alex were younger, and they couldn't go to bed on Christmas Eve until they recited "The Night Before Christmas" with their father.

Scroggie grew more impatient, but Kris went on undeterred. "Twas the night before Christmas."

"And all through Grandpa's house," Taylor followed.

"Not a creature was stirring."

Taylor looked at her brother, pressuring him to join. As usual, she won out. "Not even a mouse," Alex said. The scampering of feet across the roof accentuated the point.

"Are the stockings hung?" Kris asked.

"By the chimney with care," Taylor answered.

"In hopes that St. Nicholas would soon be there," Alex said.

"Are the children nestled all snug in their beds?"

"No, they are on the couch, surrounded by Mr. Scroggie's goons, but I can tell that sugar plums are dancing in their heads," Taylor said.

"And mama?"

"In her kerchief."

"And for the record, nobody ever looked hotter in a kerchief than your mother."

"Dad!" Taylor squealed. "Ick."

"And I in my cap," Alex picked up where his sister left off.

"You're about to get your kids sent to a permanent dirt nap," Scroggie chimed in.

"I didn't know you were a poet, Stone. Anybody else want to join in— Jacqueline? Gooch?"

When nobody answered, Kris continued, "When out on the lawn arose such a clatter."

As if scripted, the helicopter flew near the house again. It buzzed the tower, and the draft from the whipping rotors shook the windows. "I sprang from my bed to see what was the matter."

"Away to the window I flew like a flash," Taylor said.

"Tore open the shutters and threw up the sash," Alex followed.

As if the poem was a clue, Jacqueline moved to the window and slid the drapes open. It was too dark to see anything.

So she pulled out her gun and headed out of the room. Libby wanted to scream out to Kris, but she looked up to see that Gooch had Franny in his clutches. He peered at Libby. "One peep and it won't be a very merry Christmas for you."

CHAPTER 50

Jacqueline stepped out into the dark night, her gun drawn. The helicopter was gone, and the night was quiet and still. The only thing visible was her breath.

She could still hear Collins' voice on the speakerphone in the Great Room. "The moon on the breast of the new fallen snow, gave the luster of midday to objects below. When, what to my wondering eyes should appear …"

As she tried to find the best vantage point to locate Collins on the roof, something jarred her mind. Why could she hear his voice coming from inside the house, but not out here … where he actually was?

"But a miniature sleigh and eight tiny reindeer!"

Just as she looked up to confirm her theory, a heavy object landed on her face and she crashed to the ground. Pain tore through her body and her gun slid away. But she didn't get this far by being weak. She fought off her attacker to regain control of the gun.

She held it at him, and instructed him to slowly get to his feet and show his hands. The first thing she noticed was that he was shorter than expected. And when she examined his face, he was pudgy and looked to be Hispanic. This definitely wasn't Kris Collins. What was going on?

"Who are you?" she demanded.

He smiled smugly. "My friends call me Berto."

"Since I'm going to shoot you, I'm hardly your friend."

"Then you can call me Woby."

She laughed through the pain. "Like the whale? It does fit—try mixing in a salad in the afterlife, Woby Dick." She raised the gun to his head.

"No … it stands for Watch Out Behind You."

Before his words could register, a shoulder drove into her lower back and sent her to the ground once more. The man pounced on her and put his hand over her mouth. The last thing he said to her was, "Merry Christmas to all, and to all a good night." And then Tomás knocked her out cold.

After Berto helped him up, they both glanced up to the rooftop. When they did, Gustavo winked back at them.

But this was no time for celebration—there was much work to do.

CHAPTER 51

"Now Dasher, now Dancer, now …" I recited, and then suddenly my phone disappeared out of my hand.

I instinctively turned. Even in the dark coal cellar I was able to make out Gooch—his pearly whites glowed as he mocked me with his smile.

He clicked off my phone, which he held in one hand. But I was more concerned with the large gun he had in the other.

"I think Dancer is how we met—a feisty blonde that I'd mistaken for one of my students, if I recall correctly."

"No cookies this time?"

"Sorry, I left them out for Santa tonight. You were very lucky that your friend showed up that night—have you ever suffocated a man to death?"

"Haven't had the pleasure."

"I've killed many men, but it's the one method that I've never felt good about. Although, I imagine cookies would be more preferable than coal for a last meal."

"So is that how you plan to get rid of me?"

"It's up to you. You're a very lucky man—most of us won't be able to dictate the way we leave this planet. But you'll get to choose."

"Sounds like I won the lottery. I'm assuming that big gun is one of my choices."

"That's the easy way out. If you deliver me our money, then I will put one bullet in your head, and it will be quick and painless."

"And if I don't?"

"First, I will make you watch when I put each one of your children in there," he pointed to the large coal furnace, powerful enough to heat the entire manor house.

Those were fighting words. I rushed Gooch, but before I could get near him a roundhouse kick landed right in my throat. I fell backwards into the cinder-block wall and collapsed to the cold floor. It was starting to become eerily reminiscent of our last meeting. I could still hear the helicopter in the distance, but unless it was able to fly itself, Alyson wouldn't be able to save me this time.

He tossed away the gun, mentioning something about wanting a fair fight, but my head was spinning too fast to fully comprehend his words. He walked to my slumped body and ordered me to get up. I wasn't sure that I could even if I wanted to, and I definitely didn't want to.

So he grabbed a handful of my hair and pulled me to my feet. A lightning quick right-hook pummeled my face.

He let go of my hair and I dropped to the floor again.

"This is your last chance to make a decision. And just so you know, if I am forced to make it for you I'm going to start with Taylor. But before I cook her, I'm going to enjoy her as an appetizer."

"You win, you win," I called out the best I could with my kicked-in throat. "Just give me a minute to catch my breath." I was struggling to breathe and the air quality in the musty cellar wasn't helping. "Then I'll bring you and Scroggie to the money."

Gooch laughed. "You really think I plan to share the money with Scroggie?"

I said nothing, surprised.

"It doesn't seem fair that I'd only take ten percent when I'm doing all the work, now does it? And since the others think I'm out looking for you on the roof, they'll never see you ever again … at least until your body washes ashore. But I'll be long gone by then."

Before I could respond, Gooch was heading back toward me. This time I was more prepared and tried to put up my hands to protect myself. But the weight of his body was too much and he crashed down on me.

Despite the darkness, my eyes had adjusted enough to see the blood on his back. I was also able to see the dark silhouette holding a gun with an attached silencer.

"Good help is just so hard to find these days," Stone Scroggie said.

CHAPTER 52

"See what happens to those who steal from me?" Scroggie said.

"It happened really fast, could you shoot him again so I can get a better idea?"

He pointed the gun directly at my throbbing cheek. "You always have the smart answer, don't you? Which is a good thing, because the only smart answer left for you is to tell me where my money is."

It seemed that my captor had changed but my luck remained the same. As did the terms of the deal—I would hand over the money in exchange for the lives of my family and friends (without any real guarantees, other than the word of a sociopath), and I would get to die.

He shrugged. "I never wanted to kill you, Kris—I've actually found you to be a worthy opponent, and I've gained respect for you."

"From what I hear, Stone Scroggie always gets what he wants, and I wouldn't want to make an exception this time."

He shook his head, as if sad for me. "Even this last maneuver was fearlessly creative. But when you used the helicopter to create a distraction with that flyby, I knew it was so you could move inside the house to plan your sneak attack. If you were up against a lesser opponent, you'd have probably pulled it off."

He still hadn't figured that I was never on the roof, but it didn't seem to matter at this point.

"But letting you live would be a bad precedent—people need to know that when someone steals from Stone Scroggie, there is only one outcome."

"I have your word on my family?"

"They will be safe."

"And Candi?"

"She's as guilty in this theft as yourself, and should be held accountable. But because I'm in the Christmas spirit, I will put out the order that she isn't to be touched. Along with Zee Thomas and Justin Duma. I hope they understand the sacrifice you're making for them."

It sounded like it would be the ultimate one. I nodded acceptance. "Then it's a deal. I'll take you to the money tonight."

"That would mean it's close by. Statia was nothing but a diversion."

"No different than the claim during the sale process that Kerstman would only accept an all cash, no financing deal, because he urgently needed to pay off his many debts and liabilities. Even if it meant accepting a lesser bid."

"I can assure you that Diedrich Kerstman's financial problems were very real."

"But of course, his real liability was that he went into business with you. And the real reason he sought a cash deal was that way he could easily turn the money over to you. But the structure of the deal also allowed him to screw over the man who was extorting him."

"It made it possible for him to hide the cash, and then run to the authorities seeking protection. I see that now. I underestimated him."

I nodded. "He was going to use it as leverage during his trial. You were the one the FBI really wanted, and he would offer to testify against you, and in return he'd get a reduced sentence, along with getting to keep a good chunk of the money. And while you spent your remaining days in jail, he would be living happily ever after in the Caribbean."

"But hiding the money turned out to be harder than he anticipated. He needed help."

"And for the right price, I was willing to help him do that. I covered for him, so that he was able to sail to Statia to throw you off the scent. The official report was that when the authorities closed in on him, he decided to go out on his own terms ... but I have a feeling his end had more to do with an unexpected meeting with a friend of yours," I said, looking down at Gooch, who remained on the floor in a lifeless hump.

"So that left his greedy lawyer with an unexpected windfall. But he'd also assumed his client's liabilities—people wanting their money back, and willing to kill him to get it—so he needed to find a hiding spot for the money. The trick was for you to be able to keep the money, but remaining alive so that you could spend it."

"Just like Kerstman, I found that I needed a partner to be able to pull it off. And I found one who was motivated to get revenge on Stone Scroggie."

He smiled like he had it all the way. "Alexander Wainwright."

"We had to keep up appearances—make it look like he believed I'd stolen the money—which was made easier by the fact that his vile attitude toward me is genuine. But that couldn't eclipse Wainwright's joy of winning a deal. And it looked like he was going to win this one, even if he had to throw a few bucks to his disgraced former son-in-law.

"And while he didn't make the best father-in-law, he sure did make a great money laundromat. He could slowly move the money into his investments without drawing attention. All this investment in 'clean coal' is one example, and he could filter my share to me through funds set up for my children, making me the executor."

Scroggie looked perplexed. "I understand everyone's involvement ... except yours. You had a great thing going—married into the Wainwright family, a thriving law practice, banging pop stars. It makes no sense to risk your life for this. You had to know this would be the likely ending."

I shrugged. "I guess I always resented the Wainwright money. It was like they owned me. So when my practice started losing money, and I barely got to keep the clothes on my back in the divorce, I grew desperate. I felt like the Wainwrights were trying to steal the life I'd earned—I had worked my way up from Tarrytown to Greenwich, and I wasn't going back—this money was how I was going to get to keep a seat at the table."

Scroggie glanced at his watch. "Where's the money, Kris?"

"It's on the property—hidden by the Lake House. We laundered some like I said, but it's a slow process, so the majority of it is still there. That's why Alexander had the Amigos evicted."

"Then let's get this over with."

"First you let my family go."

"That's not how this works, and you know it."

I nodded with resignation—it was worth a shot—and began walking toward the external door of the coal cellar. When I reached the spot, I stopped. I looked back at Scroggie and said, "You really weren't very nice this year."

"You know what they say—nice guys finish last."

"In fact, you've been very naughty. I'll bet you're going to get coal in your stocking."

I jumped out of the way.

Scroggie looked stunned as the coal rumbled down the chute like a waterfall and knocked him to the ground. It kept coming and coming, until he was buried underneath.

I looked up at the "coal hole" window and Gustavo winked at me.

CHAPTER 53

"Dad—your cheek," Taylor exclaimed.

After my date with death, I'd almost forgotten about the shot Gooch delivered to my face. I touched the red, swollen flesh and pain shot through my entire body. Nurse Taylor ran and got me a bag of ice.

"Daddy—you got dirt all over your reindeer," Zooey pointed out, and didn't seem happy about it.

I looked down to see my reindeer sweater coated in soot from the cellar, mixed with some blood that gave it an edgier look.

"We can wash it, honey," I told her, still unable to shake the vision of Gooch tossing my children into the coal furnace. "The important thing is that you're safe."

I wanted to take the twins into my arms and not let them go. But I didn't have that kind of time. And knowing them, they would want no part of me dirtying up their Christmas dresses.

"Somebody needs to call the police. Scroggie and Gooch are in the cellar," I said.

"And Jacqueline was found tied up on the porch," Libby added, staring suspiciously at me.

I looked away. "Seems as if they turned on each other. But the important thing is that they'll be going away for a long time for taking you hostage."

"And they're not the only ones," Libby said, glaring at her father. "Someone else admitted crimes here tonight, and needs to pay the consequences."

Alexander was indignant. "I told him what he wanted to hear, Elizabeth. Those men were crazy—they cut off my finger, for goodness sake!"

I couldn't believe that I was about to defend Alexander Wainwright, but, "Anything your father said was under duress. Having worked in the legal department at Wainwright & Lennox, I would be willing to testify that their business practices were always on the up-and-up."

I think the only thing keeping Libby from strangling me was her confusion. But Taylor also risked a lengthy grounding to take my side, "Yeah, I didn't hear Grandpa say anything."

I'd taught her well, at least when it came to maintaining that trust fund.

With an annoyed look, Taylor signaled Alex to join forces. "I didn't hear anything, either," he added.

Before Libby could question our turncoat status, a visitor surprised her. "I figured if you couldn't come to me tonight, I'd come to you," Ned said in his usual enthusiastic style as he bounced into the room, carrying a large bouquet of flowers.

They embraced, and then Ned asked, "How's your father? I was worried."

Libby peered across the room at her father. "He's going to be fine. Just a carving accident with his finger. I thought it was much worse, but I guess I was mistaken."

I smiled at Alexander. He didn't return it, but at least didn't look like he'd bitten into a lemon like he normally did when he saw me. I did save him from a potential prison sentence, or at least an embarrassing arrest and the possibility of being prosecuted by his own daughter, and my smile told him that it wouldn't come for free. He would owe me a favor, a big one. And I would be collecting tonight.

This was about as close as we'd ever get to joining forces. Scroggie must have thought pretty low of me to think that I'd ever work with Alexander, or that I'd trust him to hide the money on his property. Perhaps I was the one who should have gotten the lead in the Christmas play.

"It's still not too late to come to the city," Ned said. "I was hoping the girls would help me trim my tree."

"I'd like that," Libby responded. The twins looked excited by this news—the events of tonight already washed from their mind.

"And for Taylor and Alex, I have movies. I wasn't sure what you like, so I think I got every Christmas movie ever made."

Taylor gave me a "do we have to?" look. And I nodded that they did. It was important to their mother, and who knows, maybe Ned would become a permanent part of their Christmases from here on out. And worst-case scenario, now that their trust funds were secure, he might be able to get them a great deal on a penthouse apartment one day.

Then Ned surprised me, asking, "You're welcome to come, Kris, if you're interested."

Libby's face told me that I better not be interested. And I wasn't. "Thanks for the offer, but I have to work tonight."

He looked surprised. "You have to work on Christmas Eve?"

I smiled. "My boss doesn't pay me enough, so I had to pick up a second job."

***

The Greenwich police arrived at Wainwright Manor approximately twenty minutes later. Stone Scroggie—once he was dug out from the rubble—was arrested and charged with hostage taking, among a litany of other crimes. As was Jacqueline Helada.

But after an extensive search of the coal cellar, Gooch was never found.

CHAPTER 54

The Roaring Twenties-style yacht cruised slowly around New York Harbor.

Justin Duma stood on deck taking in the Manhattan skyline, the row of skyscrapers decked out in green and red lights. It was quite a sight. And night and day from the welfare Christmases he used to spend back in Oakland.

He had worked to set this night up with the head of the Kerstman Survivor Community. The group was the main way in which the former employees and colleagues kept in touch after the downfall. They did most of their connecting via Facebook and Twitter, and would often organize events like happy hours and family picnics. Some were even able to help others get new jobs.

By using the KSC, Duma was able to get a high turnout for the Christmas Eve harbor cruise without much effort. Especially since he was willing to pay for the boat, and volunteered himself to MC the event. He played the role of the famous football player for the adults, and jolly old St. Nick for the kids, which made him almost as popular tonight as the champagne. But little did the guests know that they'd be spending a lot more time together tonight than they expected.

A beautiful woman brushed up against him. "Brrr, Santa, it's cold out here."

"For someone who calls themselves Wintry Mix, you sure don't do well with the cold." It had been a constant negotiation for years—the heavy-sweating Duma preferring the room at meat-locker chill levels, while Wintry was always trying to jack up the heat. Of course, the kids usually sided with Mom and he lost out.

She gazed out at the dark water. "Look at those chunks of ice. Hopefully we won't go all Titanic tonight."

"Well, if we do," he grabbed his belly. "I got me a floatation device. If you're nice to me, maybe I'll let you grab on."

Wintry rolled her eyes and turned away from the harbor. She viewed the festive party inside through the porthole windows. "These people are amazing—they were basically screwed over to high-heaven, had everything taken from them, yet look at them ... they're happy."

"They wouldn't be so happy if they knew someone was breaking into their houses right now while they're chowing down on shrimp cocktail."

"If the smiles haven't been knocked off their faces yet, then there's nothing they can't handle."

"We've both been through worse than anything these people have faced."

"No we didn't—it's all we knew. It's much tougher to have something ripped away. Just shows that Christmas isn't all about material objects."

Duma boomed a laugh, which annoyed Wintry. "What's so funny?"

"You're cute when you're naïve. Christmas is a religious holiday, and the main religion in this world is money."

"That's really cynical."

He shrugged. "I just report the news. The truth don't lie."

"Well, if that's all Christmas is about, the one thing I know about finance is that if you wanna make money you gotta invest. These folks invested in each other, and you know what their ROI was? Friendship, family, belief, hope. You can't buy that. And I also know that if you don't invest, and just stick your money under your mattress, then all you get is to wake up on Christmas morning in a cold, lumpy bed."

"Investing can be risky if you don't know what you're doing. You can lose everything. I'd rather wake up in that cold bed with my twenty million dollars."

She shook her head with disgust. "I can't believe you took that money from Kris. He saved your business, the least you could do is help him save his ass without getting paid for it."

"I put all our futures on the line to help him, so I took my fair share. It's business. You wanna keep believing in your fairy tales, knock yourself out."

"You mean like marriage?"

Duma sighed. "It always gets back to that with you."

CHAPTER 55

We drove the half hour from Greenwich to the sleepy town of Bethel, Connecticut, which was even sleepier than usual on Christmas Eve. This made it the perfect spot to launch our operation.

Bethel also happened to be the birthplace of PT Barnum, which I thought was fitting for the three-ring circus I was running tonight.

We pulled off Route-53 onto a winding rural road, which took us to the gates of a deserted industrial park. As we did, it began to snow. Another bad omen in a day of them. We weren't the first to arrive. In fact, we were in the middle of a convoy of 18-wheelers that were pulling in as if this were a rest-stop along the interstate.

Alyson had left the helicopter at Wainwright Manor, and we took my vehicle, which Gooch was nice enough to bring to Greenwich tonight for me, while also driving my children to their grandparents' house. He must have really been in the Christmas spirit.

Thoughts of Gooch made me nervous. His disappearance was disconcerting, to say the least. But based on our brief history together, if he *was* here, we probably wouldn't know it until it was too late.

I squinted through the darkness to view what was left of the building that used to be a warehouse for Kerstman Publishing. The place where they'd store the books prior to being shipped off to bookstores around the world, back when there were still bookstores around the world. The government had confiscated and sold off all of Kerstman's assets, but this warehouse, along with its many broken-down delivery trucks, was considered a liability. Especially after someone, presumably making a statement about Kerstman greed, attempted to burn it to the ground. It had remained abandoned ever since.

I gripped tightly to the coffee-filled Styrofoam cup as I stepped out of the vehicle. It seemed that it was ten degrees cooler up here, and the strong wind made it feel like I was going to be blown away. But there was no time to whine—the trucks kept rolling in, each driven by one of Harry's elves. And my fears about their sobriety level was put to rest—as far as I could tell the only things the Puff Daddies had brought along for the ride were veggie burritos and tie-dye parkas.

The moment each truck came to a stop, the back doors were swung open, and the loot was transferred into the many abandoned Kerstman delivery vans. Toys, clothing, bikes, you name it—one truck was completely filled with Christmas trees. More trucks kept arriving, rinse and repeat. Alyson and I joined in—all hands were on deck, there wasn't a second to lose. We needed to get out of here before our presence attracted any attention.

The Amigos were present, prepping as they always did—carefree laughter from Berto and Gustavo, while Tomás was his usual tense self. When they spotted me, specifically my reindeer sweater, Gustavo couldn't resist busting my chops. When I told him that my daughter made me wear it, Berto broke into laughter. But Tomás was quietly focused on the bloodstains, a reminder of the danger we faced tonight.

"I think reindeer sweaters are hot," a female voice came from underneath the hood of one of the vans.

The mechanic smiled at me. She was dressed head to toe in black, except for the strand of blonde hair hanging out of her visor beanie hat. She had engine-grease smudged on her pretty face, adding to the camouflage. But

I doubted she'd ever go unnoticed, and was fairly certain that her plentiful curves would show up on Google Earth.

But when Sophie looked closer at me, she grew concerned. "Kris—oh my God! What happened to your face?"

I made the obligatory joke about 'you should see the other guy', but if she did, I hoped she'd let me know so we could try to make a run for it.

She ran her gloved hand over my cheek and planted a soft kiss on it. It actually made it feel better. I was no doctor, but I was convinced that Sophie was capable of curing diseases with just her touch.

She pointed a wrench-filled hand at one of the vans that she'd been working on—they hadn't been driven in years. "I got three more to check, but the rest are good to go. For the most part, they were in better shape than I would have expected. Mostly needed new batteries and air in the tires."

"You are a woman of many talents," I commented. I would have never guessed in a million years that she had this skill-set, until she came to me seeking advice in regards to her plans to open a garage when her dancing days are over. When she offered to do some work on my vehicle in return, I found out that she was the real deal.

"Maybe too many," she said, shamefully looking down at the ground.

"What do you mean?"

"You need to know something."

I was in a major hurry, and anybody else I would have been short with, but it was impossible to be mad at Sophie. "Can this wait until later?"

"I'm worried that you guys are going to end up in a trap tonight. And it will be all my fault."

"What's this about, Sophie?"

"My past."

"We all have a past—welcome to the club." I smiled at her, but she didn't return it.

"After I left home and moved to California, I ended up working as an escort. And I think you know what kind I mean."

I did—every time a Hollywood madam got busted running an "escort" agency, my phone would ring off the hook with my freaked out clients worried that names were going to be named. Specifically theirs. "Does Zee know?"

"I've been totally honest with him. He was the only person I've trusted with my secret … until now."

"Then I don't see the problem."

"A lot of the girls who worked for the agency were underage, and when I got busted by the feds, I was given immunity to testify. The guys who ran it went to jail. They threatened to get revenge on whoever was responsible for taking them down. So I moved across the country, changed my name, and altered my appearance."

"If you need some sort of protection from these people, we can get it for you. I'm just not sure what this has to do with us ending up in a trap tonight?"

"The FBI ran my picture in their system, after the fight in the club the other night. My real identity came up, and Falcone tried to use it against me. He cornered me at Zee's apartment and tried to get me to convince him to wear a wire, so that he could get the dirt on what you guys were doing up in Vermont. He made it be known that if I didn't, he would let it slip about my new life to the people I helped put away. And they're some bad dudes."

She began to cry, and the black grease ran down her face. "So you agreed to work with Falcone?"

"I refused—so he went directly to Zee. You know how loyal Zee is, if it came down to protecting me he might agree to help them."

"I've known Zee since we were kids—there's no way he'd ever put us in jeopardy."

"He's in a no-win situation. If he chooses you, then he'll feel horrible that he put me in danger. And if he chooses me, and hurts you, he would never be able to live with himself."

"That's when Zee's at his best."

"What do you mean?"

"Did you ever see him pitch?"

"No, I never watch sports."

"The thing about him was that the more trouble he'd get in—like when he loaded the bases with nobody out—the better he'd get. When most pitchers would be stressed by the situation, Zee would find calm. And you know what, more times than not he'd get out of the jam without any damage."

"But this isn't baseball."

"You're right, it's not—it's high-stakes gambling. And I'm willing to bet my life that he'll find a way to get out of this one."

CHAPTER 56

The semi-truck crossed over the Massachusetts border, and Zee pulled it into the rest area. He found driving a train much more natural.

He parked, leaving the truck idling, and entered "the sleeper" behind the driver-cab. He untied the rope that held Nicole Close' hands together, and removed the blindfold. Her children were sleeping and he tried not to disturb them.

"Where are you taking us?" she demanded. She'd given up being scared long ago, and was now just pissed off.

"I'm going to leave the truck in Boston. I will help you get a ride home at that point, and will cover the costs."

"Wow—he actually speaks," she said. It was the first time he'd uttered more than a sentence since Kris put him in charge of her.

"I hope that will be agreeable to you."

"Suddenly you care what I think? I don't remember having a say in any of this."

Without any better options, she joined him in the driver cab. "I don't get it," she continued, as the truck rolled out of the rest area and back onto the dark highway. "You people hijacked us because you claimed we were in danger. But now you're just going to drop us off and pay for a ride home like nothing happened?"

"You are no longer Scroggie's target—he's going after Kris' children."

She momentarily stared out the front windshield at the endless highway—every parent could relate, no matter what she thought of Kris.

"He told me the reason they came after me was that they thought Kris had, to use his words, a thing for me. What's that all about?"

"I think it's pretty self-explanatory."

"How is that even possible?"

"Your attractive, intelligent, and very passionate. I would think it would be very possible."

"You guys are the strangest hostage-takers ever. I met him once, and I made it very clear what I think of him."

Zee shrugged. "Once Kris connects with someone he will go to the end of the earth for them. That's why so many people are loyal to him."

"We never connected—we never even had a conversation."

"You might not have connected with him, but he did with you."

"Sounds like you're describing some psycho, or a stalker."

"No, I'm talking about a loyal friend."

"From what I've heard, he was more loyal to the crook who stole my life than to his own wife."

"Everyone loses their way sometimes. All I know, is that when things got foggy for me he was my guide."

She blew out a frustrated breath. "And now you're returning the favor? I hope it's worth it, since you're probably going to end up in prison."

"He saved my life, but it's more than that. He has a way of making people believe in something, and he made me believe in the most important thing there is."

"Based on what I know about Kris Collins, he thinks the most important thing is Kris Collins."

"No—he made me believe in myself. And when you believe in yourself, and only then, can you give yourself to others. And life can get pretty lonely if you don't figure that out."

"I'm happy that he helped you turn your life around, I really am. But I didn't ask for any of this. He put my children at risk, and that's unacceptable."

"That wasn't his intention. And I know this, he'd take a bullet for you before he'd let anyone hurt them. How many people do you know that would give up their life for yours?"

After a long silence, she said, "The man who vowed to do that decided to give up his life to solve his own pain."

Zee completely understood. The pain would never go away, but hopefully the guilt would. "It's not your fault, you know."

"For a guy who supposedly doesn't talk, you sure have a lot to say."

"I blamed myself for the longest time. I know it's crazy, but I thought I could have stopped it if I just did things different that morning. But I eventually realized that you can't control people—in the end they're going to do what they're going to do."

Nicole began to get emotional, but then she glanced into the rear-view mirror and her expression changed. "You were starting to get me to believe that you and your friend Kris Collins were trustworthy guys. But these police lights coming up behind us reminds me that you two are involved in transporting stolen goods in this truck … just like the money that was stolen from us and the other Kerstman families who won't be having Christmas this year … again!"

Zee pulled off to the side of the road, and watched as Agent Falcone walked slowly toward the truck.

CHAPTER 57

"I thought we had a deal, ZT?"

Zee remained quiet as Falcone patted him down.

"It seems you removed the wire. And here, I thought your word was good. Luckily, I made sure I'd be able to find you." He pointed to Zee's necklace to let him know it contained a tracking device.

"And it's a good thing I did, before you were able to escape with these hostages." He turned to Nicole. "Are you okay?"

She nodded her head, and then surprised him, "But I'm not a hostage. Mr. Thomas offered us a ride home and I accepted it."

"I have security video of Justin Duma taking your children, and then handing them over to Kris Collins," Falcone responded.

"They were worried for my children's safety. That woman in Macy's threatened to choke my son. She worked for a gangster named Stone Scroggie, isn't that correct?"

Falcone's face contorted, as if he was fighting back an angry response. "I don't understand why you'd protect Kris Collins, the man who helped Diedrich Kerstman … and who you publicly accused of being responsible for your husband's death."

Nicole held it together. "I am not pressing any type of charges, so I hope we're free to go."

"Once I search the back of the truck and find the stolen items that I'm sure are there, then we're all going to be spending the night together down at the police station."

"Nicole had nothing to do with any of this. So if you assure her a safe trip home, we can do this the easy way," Zee said. "If not, you're going to have to impound the truck and get a court order to search it. And I know you don't have that kind of time tonight."

"Our intent all day has been to assist Ms. Closs and her children. But you and Collins were able to convince her of your lies."

"And Sophie's identity will be protected?"

"I hope you don't really think we would have released that information. Getting inside was the only way we could get the money back to the Kerstman families, and we needed to convince you to help."

Zee was skeptical of his motives, but flipped him the keys. He then watched as Falcone made his way to the back of the truck.

Since the tunnels under Harry Crawford's ranch were part of the Underground Railroad, there was also a back entrance to the property, which had been sealed up by a past owner. On the outside, the entranceway was hidden within a rock formation near the main roadway. During the reconstruction of the tunnels, Harry unsealed the entrance, and made sure it was large enough to fit a truck. So while the FBI was scouting the main entrance to his property, the trucks that contained what Falcone was looking for were headed out the back.

Zee had figured that he was being traced, even if he was unaware of the tracker being in his necklace. So he'd purposely led Falcone away from the ranch, pulling an empty trailer.

Falcone stormed back, red-faced. Instead of addressing Zee, he turned to Nicole. "You don't know the people you're dealing with here. And by choosing to associate with them, you could be putting yourself and your children in danger!"

"You're right, I don't know. But I'm starting to get a clearer picture," she said.

CHAPTER 58

In less than an hour the loot had been transferred from the trucks to the vans. The Puff Daddies drove the vans to specific locations to provide support to the Amigos, as they systematically hit the targeted homes.

Alyson and I drove just over the Connecticut border into New York, landing in the small, upscale town of Pound Ridge, where we were to set up the Command Center. A thick fog had settled over the rural, winding roads, but it didn't slow Alyson down.

We entered the secluded driveway of my former house, even though I was rarely here during the final years of the marriage, back when Libby was busy turning it into a home. The large white colonial on three acres was a relative bargain at two million, which was the Wainwright equivalent of living in a tent.

Just as we arrived, I received a text from Zee. It simply said *Merry Christmas*. It calmed my nerves; it was code for Nicole was safe and headed home with her children.

We turned the headlights off, as to not announce our presence, and used the well-lit house to guide us. It seemed as if every light was on, along with the floodlights in the backyard. I was suspicious at first, but then I remembered Franny mentioning something about leaving the lights on so

Santa wouldn't miss them. I thought to tell her that Santa never misses the Wainwrights, but I liked that she hadn't figured that out yet.

The driveway turned into a bridle path that led to a red barn. Back when we bought the place I had made it into a garage for my car collection, most notably my fire engine red, mid-life-crisis Ferrari. But based on the smell, it seemed as if it had been returned to its original roots.

The horse stalls that were once ripped out to make room for the cars were back. And sticking out their heads, looking curiously at their visitors, were Franny and Zooey's new ponies. At least they would be tomorrow morning. One was reddish brown with a black mane, while the other was completely black.

Alyson went right to them and began petting, seemingly very comfortable. "They're Welsh Mountain Ponies," she informed me.

"You think I don't know that?" I said with a grin. "They're my Christmas gift to my daughters. I thought the best way for them to learn responsibility would be to care for another living creature."

"I think I'll get Robbie a goldfish. And I must say that *Libby* has great taste—the Welsh breed are known for their trustworthiness, stamina, and intelligence."

All things we needed tonight. "I didn't know you were a pony connoisseur?"

"I spent a lot of time at Herm's family farm when we were first married. I picked up a few things."

I detected a melancholy in her voice—the family farm was a reminder of Robbie being away from her for Christmas.

I stopped to say hello to an old friend—the Ferrari. I lovingly ran my hand over the hood, as if to tell her that one day our relationship could be out in the open once again, and not consist of secret meetings like this in the dark of night. But I forced myself to move on.

We entered the small living quarters that were built into the garage/barn. It had a small kitchen and a shower. And for tonight's purposes, it contained the two essentials—plug-ins for the laptop and a coffeemaker.

Alyson scrambled to set up the laptop, hooking into the secure feed that would allow us to visually follow the movements of the Amigos throughout the night. She also fitted me with a headset, so I could hear the audio of the conversations between the Amigos and Hacker—and could communicate with them when necessary. I was Mission Control and they were the astronauts.

The Amigos had already hit homes from North Salem to Lewisboro, and were now in Bedford. I watched as a van driven by one of the Puff Daddies arrived. Seconds later, Tomás dropped off Gustavo and Berto, and made his way around the block.

"Give me the details," Gustavo said.

"Occupants left forty-five minutes ago for church. Only thing you need to worry about is a German Shepherd," Hacker replied.

"Dogs love me," Berto said, flashing the reason why they love him to the camera—a handful of treats.

Hacker provided the security code, which Gustavo was already punching in. "Like taking candy from a baby," he said, as Berto unloaded the items from the van, which then backed out of the driveway and left the scene.

The camera took us into the house—it was like I was in there with them. I almost jumped out of my skin with each creak of the hardwood floors, but they showed no signs of nerves. Gustavo moved from the kitchen to living room, and then to the fireplace, methodically taking care of business, while Berto moved the heavy items.

Three minutes in and out, no resistance from the dog, and even time left for Berto to take a couple of bites out of the cookies that were left for Santa, along with a sip of the milk. It was his calling card.

"Done," Gustavo said, re-setting the alarm.

"I'm closing out of their bank account. Transaction has been made," Hacker added. Seconds later, the van driven by Tomás slowed by the curb, and the black-clad burglars made their way across the lawn and jumped in. They were already off to the next house in North Castle before anyone spoke.

We planned on three to five minutes at each home, depending on the amount of loot involved. But nobody was naïve or arrogant enough not to expect complications at some point tonight.

The order of the houses was determined by geography and difficulty. The plan was to hit the less populated areas early in the evening, and move to the more congested areas as the night grew long, and people set in for a long winter's nap … or at least tried to get a few hours of shuteye before the chaos of Christmas morning.

It was impossible to hit every home. First of all, many of the former Kerstman employees didn't live in the area any longer. And for the few that still could afford to live in New York City, we couldn't risk going over bridges, and make Falcone's job easier.

But 78% of the former employees still lived in Westchester County or Fairfield County, Connecticut, and we targeted the ones who were left most vulnerable by the Kerstman demise. And those we couldn't get to, we would still be able to get into their bank accounts.

I continued to watch in awe as the Amigos marched through Westchester County like Sherman through Georgia—Rye Brook, Harrison, White Plains, Scarsdale, New Rochelle. While I was a nervous wreck, the Amigos seemed to become invigorated each time the challenge heightened— getting into apartment complexes, or homes where the occupants were sleeping upstairs. Since Hacker could read the emails and texts of the residents, we knew which ones had plans tonight, and the others we attempted to get out of the house, and keep out—for example: Duma stalling the yacht on the harbor. But it didn't seem to matter to the Amigos.

At three in the morning, they arrived at a dark home in Sleepy Hollow, the home of Jeffrey Yu and his family. Berto slipped and fell in the living room. And being no small man, it caused a loud bang. A rustling could be heard upstairs.

My screen immediately changed to boxes like in the television show *24*, and I was watching action in different parts of the house in real time. In one box, I saw Mr. Yu reach into the drawer of a bedside table and pulled out a .44. He threw on a robe, and headed toward the living room, gun in hand.

But Hacker had already relayed the information, and Gustavo was waiting for him as he stepped out of his bedroom, and chopped the gun out of his hand. Before he could get a good look at the man in the ski mask, Mr. Yu was tied and gagged, and tossed into a hallway closet. Gustavo then moved into the bedroom.

Before Sharon Yu could scream, Berto had his hand over her mouth from behind. She received the same treatment as her husband, and was placed in the closet.

I picked my heart off the floor, but my hands didn't stop shaking until they arrived at their next stop in Tarrytown. I recognized the street—it was the one I grew up on—and suddenly I flooded with childhood memories of Christmas. As they slowly drove down the street it looked exactly the same as when I used to stare out the window, waiting for Santa in the wee morning hours, even though my parents warned me that if I didn't go to sleep the big guy wouldn't come.

Hacker informed them that Stu and Mary Reed planned to be spending Christmas at the home of Stu's brother in Rhode Island.

"I have a note that Zee was able to get a copy of the spare key on a reconnaissance mission, so you should have it, and everything should be set up for you inside," Hacker said.

I suddenly remembered who the Reeds were—the ones who accused Zee of stealing the wife's jewelry. And that Zee did get the key, but he gave it to the absentminded professor who forgot to pass it along.

I adjusted my headset and said, "I got this one."

CHAPTER 59

The Ferrari probably wasn't the best choice for our drive to Tarrytown in the wintry conditions—the fog had lifted as the temperatures dropped, but a light snow had continued to fall, and hidden ice was always lurking.

I'd convinced Alyson that people would be suspicious of a dark SUV driving around a suburban neighborhood in the predawn hours, but not a Ferrari. If criminals drove cars like this they wouldn't need to be criminals, I told her. She countered that I was just looking for an excuse to drive my car one more time. She was right, but let me have my way. It was like the good old days at Kris Collins Esq.

Main Street was empty, but the marquee of the Tarrytown Music Hall was lit up like the show was about to start. I spotted the café where my parents used to bring my sister and me for lunch on summer days, and we'd eat outside on the patio. And Shea Polo's Pizza, where Zee's father used to bring our Little League team after wins … and losses … or any excuse he could come up with.

From Main Street was a view of the beautiful, majestic bridge that crossed the eastern bank of the Hudson River—the Tappan Zee Bridge. Okay, there was nothing even relatively attractive about the Tappan Zee. It looked like a child built it with an erector set and painted with rust. But it was our bridge, and if not for it's horrendous daily traffic crossing to and from New Jersey, Zee would have been named Mike or Steve, and we'd have missed out on those witty *Baked ZT* tabloid headlines.

Tarrytown was a village within the town of Greenburg. We shared a school with neighboring Sleepy Hollow, which became famous for the Washington Irving classic *The Legend of Sleepy Hollow,* even though the story actually took place in Tarrytown. Irving was also responsible for the modern American version of Santa Claus. Before his 1809 book *The History of New York*, Santa never had a "flying sleigh" or filled stockings that were hung by the fireplace with care. He also added the girth to his belly.

As I turned up Overland Drive, I felt like I'd traveled back in time. I could visualize the bike races, the kick-the-can games … and of course, baseball. The Reed residence was similar to the other houses on the street, four lots down from my childhood home, and on the same side of the street.

We were met there by an aging hippie named Barry, who smelled like he hadn't showered in a week. He helped me unload what I needed out of the van, and was off. "Rock on, dude," he told me before he left. It had been a long time since I rocked anything at this time of the morning, but I would do my best.

Alyson drove around the block, just as the Amigos would have, and I pulled on my ski mask. Before we left Pound Ridge, I'd changed into the all-black, form-fitting running gear that I had purchased with plans to continue the healthy fitness habits I'd picked up in prison. Kind of ironic that I would be wearing it when I performed the act that might get me sent back.

I took out the key and headed for the front door.

CHAPTER 60

Even though nobody was home it still felt odd, and wrong, being in somebody's house. So I unnecessarily tiptoed, and made as little noise as possible as I took care of business.

It would take me much longer than the allotted three to five minutes, and require multiple trips in and out—the Amigos had probably hit ten houses since we'd left Pound Ridge. But that was all right. I had started to feel useless in my CEO role back in Mission Control. I'd been the one plotting this for years, and had been involved in every part of the planning and execution up to this point, and when the big night came I felt like I wasn't pulling my weight.

My work in the Reed house was just about completed, and I was about to make a move for the door, when I heard the footsteps. At first I thought I was hearing things, but they were very real. I wasn't alone.

It sounded like the footsteps were heading for the living room, so I slipped into the kitchen. Big mistake—since the Reed house had the same circular floor-plan as my childhood home, I should have known the person could have been just as easily heading for the kitchen.

The lights came on and there stood Mary Reed. She hadn't gone to her brother-in-law's house. And she was holding a shotgun!

We'd thought this would be an easy in and out, with the key and nobody home, so all the assistance was with the Amigos. I was all on my own.

She looked disheveled, wearing a bathrobe with no makeup. Understandable, at this hour, but her eyes also looked wild, and I could smell the booze across the room. She was drunk.

"I knew it was you, you gutless son of a bitch!" she yelled at me. "Did you come to steal more of your own wife's jewelry!?"

I wasn't sure if it was a good thing or not that she thought I was her husband. But the way she was aiming that gun at me, I was leaning toward no.

I thought about taking off my mask and revealing my true identity, but in her irrational state, it might spark her to pump a round into my chest. So I remained silent, and still.

"I called your brother to wish you a merry Christmas, but he told me you left without telling anyone. Just like around here when you wander off. You know I followed you one day."

I continued my strategy of silence, letting her continue, "Yeah, that day when you went down to the Hudson and just looked down at it for an hour, like you were thinking about jumping. Is that what you were doing, Stu?"

This time Mary wanted an answer. She shot over my head, the shells lodging into the wall. I instinctively jumped to the floor.

"Answer me, Stu—is that what you're going to do … kill yourself!?"

I was about to rip the mask off and take my chances, when she shouted, "If you're too big of a coward to do it, I'll do it for you!" She shot again, this time the bullets pinged off pots and pans.

"Were you going to tell Bailey that you're going to let him grow up without a father!? The poor kid bought you that baseball glove because he wants his father back. He doesn't care about the money or our credit rating or any of that. He just wants his goddam dad!

"So go ahead, steal everything in the house, and sell it, if that's what you need to do to live for our son. God, Stu, do you remember when we lived in that tiny apartment and ate ramen noodles for dinner every night? We didn't need a will to live, we just lived. And that was enough."

She waited for an answer, but none came. "Talk to me, Stu! Please talk to me," she pleaded.

When I didn't reply, she pointed the gun at me again. I tried to inch away across the floor. "I guess I have my answer then, Stu, don't I? Well, here's my solution—I'd rather have it look like you died in an accident, sneaking into the house and surprising your wife ... than have your son live with the guilt of knowing his father didn't care enough to stick around. So that will be my final Christmas present to you—I'll set you free."

She cocked the gun and her finger went to the trigger. But before she could shoot, an angel grabbed me by the stretchy material of my running top, and dragged me into the living room.

Alyson flashed me her typical "what would you do without me?" look. But there was no time for relief. Mary Reed bolted into the living room, ready to fire. "Get back here you coward," she screeched.

But when she saw it, she stopped in her tracks, and dropped the gun. A look of shock came over her face, before she fell to the floor and passed out.

I moved her into a Barcalounger and found a stool to put her feet on. I covered her with an afghan.

Alyson picked up the gun and shook her head. "How does it go from children waiting up for Santa, to mom shooting dad?"

I looked at Mary Reed, who was now soundly sleeping it off, and then at pictures on the mantle of her and Stu in happier times. I thought of the Washington Irving story that re-defined Santa Claus, and Christmas as we know it. But one element that remained in the transition was belief, and as long as it's present, we always had the power to change the story. "Maybe they'll have a chance to write a different ending," I said.

Alyson looked skeptical. "I don't know, Collins. Sometimes we get too far down the road and there's no going back."

CHAPTER 61

Edmund Woods' flashlight scanned the dark parking lot until he found the small bolt. "Got it," he called out to Dora.

She looked relieved. They had come so far in building this dollhouse, and there was no way one little bolt was going to stop them.

Edmund laughed as he handed it to her. "What's so funny?" she asked, her teeth chattering.

"I was just thinking about when it took us all night to put together that bike for Payne."

She joined his laughter. "We're not doing much better on this one. I guess there was a reason we worked in publishing, and not home building."

"What was he, like five?"

"Six, I believe. A lot has changed since then, but directions still suck."

Edmund thought it might be more related to pilot-error, but kept that to himself. Susie wanted a house for Christmas and she was going to get one. Even though it wasn't the type she meant.

He took another glance at Payne and Susie, sleeping in the backseat of the Range Rover. After the kids fell asleep they had found a pine tree in Tibbets Brook Park in Yonkers, where they'd stopped for the night, and decorated it with lights and tinsel. The plan was to put the few gifts they could afford around the tree before the kids woke up in the morning—a pair of skates for Payne, and this dollhouse for Susie … that is, if they ever finished putting it together. It wouldn't be their usual Christmas, but there would be Christmas nevertheless.

Suddenly a voice boomed through the parking lot, causing Edmund to jump.

"The park closes at dark. So I don't know what you think you're doing here."

It was him again. The only difference was that tonight he was wearing a "Santa hat" over his mask and red coat that he probably stole from jolly old St. Nick.

"What do you want?" Edmund said.

He smiled. "Just because you got lucky last time, doesn't mean that lightning will strike twice, Edmund."

"I'll do whatever it takes to protect my family."

The man didn't seem to take the threat seriously. He moved to the dollhouse. "Man, I've been here—I think directions are a conspiracy to make us all feel like idiots."

Edmund and Dora couldn't disagree.

"I think I see what the problem is—you're missing a bolt right here."

The second he touched the dollhouse, Edmund rushed after him. "My daughter wanted a house for Christmas, and don't you touch it."

He bounced off the man like he'd hit a brick wall, and fell to the slushy ground.

The man just shook his head at him, as if offering pity. "I warned you, Edmund. And if I remember correctly, she asked Santa for a house, not you. Now somebody hand me the bolt, so I can help you finish this thing before morning."

Dora grudgingly handed it to him, and after a couple twists and turns of the wrench, the house was finished. "Voilà," he exclaimed.

Edmund didn't know whether to thank him or make a run for it, but he didn't have time to do either. In an instant, the man had both him and Dora pushed up against their vehicle, and was securing their hands behind their back.

"What are you doing?" Dora asked angrily.

"I told you—you're breaking park rules. Rules are rules."

"I knew I shouldn't have taken that wallet back. You must have put something in it to track us."

He laughed. "If I had those type of skills I wouldn't be freezing my ass off in some park at the ass-crack of dawn. Now I need you to shut your trap."

Moments later, he tossed them into the backseat, waking up the kids.

"Whoa—Santa's here," Susie belted out enthusiastically. "I knew there'd be Christmas!"

"That depends—did you leave me any cookies and milk?"

"Will you settle for Doritos and Sprite?"

"That'll do—I'm starving. It's been a long night."

"I imagine you're really busy on Christmas, Santa."

As she handed him the food, he looked at Payne. "How you doing, fighter?"

"Good, thanks … except that I'm jammed in here next to my little sister."

"Hang on—it won't be long before we get where we're going. How's cancer doing today?"

"Still losing."

"That's what I like to hear."

Before leaving, he carried the dollhouse and loaded it into the back of the vehicle. He then drove out of the park and onto I-95. They traveled for forty minutes, and daylight began to appear in the east. It was officially Christmas morning.

He headed through the gates of the estate and up the hill, passing a large manor house. He wound around the property until they arrived at the Lake House. He then walked Edmund and Dora inside like prisoners, while the children followed, carrying the dollhouse.

"I knew Santa would come through," Susie shouted, as Payne untied his parents.

Susie was already at the sparkling Christmas tree, going through the pile of gifts. "Look Payne—now I got skates too!"

Dora moved to the kitchen table, where a new laptop computer and power cord rested. She felt disorientated as she read the note, so she took a seat. It informed them to check out their bank account—the one that had less than two hundred dollars in it the last time she thought to look. When she signed on the account, she almost fell off the chair.

Edmund was at the kitchen counter, where he found the deed to the house. It was in their name. It was on the property of Alexander and Beatrice Wainwright, and the contract included a clause that stated that the Woods family could not be removed from this house, even if the Wainwrights sold the property. It was signed by Alexander Wainwright.

Susie was running in and out of the bedrooms. "I knew Santa would bring us a house!"

Edmund and Dora just looked at each other with amazement.

"This one is gonna be my room!" Susie shouted out.

"This one's mine," Payne's voice echoed down the stairs, trying to keep up with his little sister. They both bolted down the stairs and headed toward the door. "Look, Suse—a skating pond!"

As the children ran outside, Dora felt panic. But then she caught herself, as did Edmund. It was the one thing they'd been wishing for since Payne got sick—that their teenage boy would be a teenage boy again, even if that meant they'd likely be heading back to the hospital for other reasons, like broken bones.

They moved to each other, and hugged. "Merry Christmas, Dora."

"Merry Christmas, Edmund," she said with a smile … and when they looked up they found themselves standing under the mistletoe.

CHAPTER 62

Susie was exploring the pond with Payne when something popped into her head. "Hey—where'd Santa go?"

Payne shrugged. "It's Christmas morning, so he's probably headed back to the North Pole."

"I need to find him before he goes. We need to talk," she said, and was already running after him before her brother could respond.

It seemed like the driveway would go on forever, with no sign of Santa, but then she spotted him. "Hey—wait up!" she yelled.

He turned around, looking surprised. He'd taken off his mask. It was the Santa from the mall—he was the real one, not one of his helpers like everybody said.

"I just wanted to say thanks for coming through on my wish," she said, between huffs and puffs.

"Just doing my job, Susie. Do you like the house?"

"It was my second choice, but it does have the yard and tall trees I asked you for."

He smiled. "You're a tough audience. Just remember that it's only a house, and it's up to you and your family to turn it into a home."

"What do ya mean?"

"Your parents will help you understand, I think they finally get it."

"You gotta go, huh?"

"Been a long night—it's time for Santa to take a vacation."

"To the North Pole?"

"I'm thinking somewhere warmer." He watched as the car pulled to a stop at the end of the driveway. "But first I gotta go see my children open their presents. It's my favorite part of the day."

"I'll bet Santa's kids get the most gifts ever!"

He chuckled. "They'd still want more."

"I guess I'll see you next year, Santa."

"If you're a good girl you will, Susie Woods. Enjoy your new house, but don't feed the Wainwrights—I hear they bite."

She ran to him and wrapped a hug around his thick midsection. "You've come through on big ones two years in a row Santa, so I'll understand if you give my wish to somebody else next year."

***

He waved at Susie Woods as they drove away. He figured she was probably wondering why he didn't take his sleigh. He looked back at Jarren and Terrance and their big Christmas smiles, looking confident that there'd be plenty under the tree when they got home. "So how are my guys doing this morning?"

"We'll be doing better when we get to open our presents," Jarren whined.

"Yeah, when are we going to get our gifts, Dad?" Terrance added.

"Who do I look like—Santa Claus? Ask your mother."

He traded a glance with Wintry, as she drove them through the empty streets of Greenwich. She just stared back, unnerving him "What?"

She smiled. "I knew it wasn't all about the money."

WEDNESDAY DECEMBER 25

CHRISTMAS MORNING

CHAPTER 63

The moment I stepped through the front door in Pound Ridge my emotions were on overload alert. My first instinct was to run away, but I was too tired to walk, much less run.

It had been five years since I'd spent Christmas morning with my family. I could smell the buffet that was heaped with sizzling breakfast foods, mixed with the heavy pine odor coming from the stout tree that was decorated in orderly, Wainwrightian fashion. I remembered that smell fondly. And it sure contrasted sharply with the aroma of Christmas morning in prison.

My entrance was greeted by a piano rendition of "Jailhouse Rock." I looked to see a smiling Alex, sitting proudly behind a Steinway baby grand piano, that was his present from his mother.

He traded grins with Taylor, who obviously was the mastermind behind the prank. It broke the tension, and once again made me proud that I'd passed the Collins family snarkiness to another generation.

Taylor gave me a more traditional greeting—wrapping my weary body with a hug. "You shaved your goatee," she observed, "but I see you didn't take my advice about icing your cheek."

The swelling in my face was the least of my worries last night. Once the Amigos finished the final house, and we made sure we removed any trace of our involvement, I returned to the barn. I showered and shaved, and then Alyson and I went out for breakfast at the greasiest diner we could find.

When we finished with our feast, which included enough coffee to flood a small city, she dropped me off here.

"But you cleaned up well," Taylor gave her seal of approval to my simple button-down shirt that was tucked into jeans. This was much more casual than the black tie affairs at Wainwright Manor, which were Taylor's first images of Christmas morning.

She was wearing an orange and purple Clemson sweatshirt that clashed with a pair of sky blue and gold UCLA sweatpants. I loved the outfit because it showed that she still hadn't made up her mind, making her a typical indecisive teenager, which I hoped she would remain … at least for a couple more minutes.

The twins followed their sister to me. They were still in their Christmas dresses from last night, keeping the formal tradition alive. They listed off the numerous Christmas gifts they'd received as if they were delivering an address to their stockholders. There was no doubt that Franny & Zooey Inc. had a good year.

As I viewed the room, it was as if nothing had changed. For a moment I thought that the last few years were just one of those *It's a Wonderful Life* glimpses into an alternate existence, and once I realized I was on the wrong road, I returned home and we all lived happily ever after. But when I heard Ned's voice, it reminded me that things would never be the same.

He greeted me like I was his long-lost relative. There was no real downside to Ned's sucking up, but if the goal was for me to give my approval to his relationship, it wasn't going to happen. First of all, as he'd soon find out, Libby makes her own decisions, and if I intervened, either positively or negatively, it would make our divorce seem like eating ice cream on a summer day. So as long as Ned didn't threaten to lock my children in a coal cellar or embezzle money from their trust funds, I would choose to remain neutral.

We made our usual small talk. What great kids I have—I agreed.

Alex is an amazing musician—I had no idea, but acted like I did.

Can't believe how bad the Jets are—I could, I don't think they'd made the playoffs since Duma retired.

Ned had rented a hotel room overlooking Times Square for New Year's Eve, did I think the kids would like to go if he asked them?—I would never attempt to enter the minds of teenagers, but if it didn't involve them hanging out with their friends, and being out of the watchful eyes of their parents, then probably not.

Once that was out of the way, we got down to the important business of the day. "How's Operation Farmer on the Roof going?" I asked.

His face lit up, enjoying the covertness. "The fields are prepared for harvest," he responded cryptically, not making eye contact, as if we were a couple of Cold War spies.

I couldn't believe I actually understood what he meant. Or that I would respond with, "And the crops will be picked this afternoon?"

"I expect it to be a harvest festival," he said with a wink, then walked away before the KGB discovered our true identities.

As I watched Ned head toward the buffet, I felt a tap on my shoulder. I turned to see Libby.

"I'm glad you decided to come," she said and kissed me on the cheek—the one without the large red lump.

"It never feels like Christmas unless I'm here."

"You look tired. Did you go clubbing last night?"

I was 75% sure that she was joking. "My club-hopping partner is in Afghanistan, so I spent a quiet evening at home."

"You deserved a night of relaxation after what you did for us last night."

"The whole running for my life, hostage rescue thing just takes more out of me since I turned forty. I need a nap," I deflected with a smile.

"Joke all you want—you risked your life to save us, and we all will be forever indebted to you."

"Any father would do it for his children."

"Not every father."

I hoped she meant Alexander, whose shadier side she was introduced to last night, but I was fairly certain that she was referring to the man she was once married to.

My attention was stolen away by my son playing an up tempo version of "Hark! The Herald Angels Sing" on the piano. "I had no idea he even played," I said.

"You've been away the past few years, and your communication with each other leaves much to be desired. So it's not surprising."

That's the literal Libby I know and love.

"He's able to communicate better through music, and I think his true personality comes out. His gift from my parents is a top-of-the-line music studio that will be installed in the basement."

"Soundproof?"

She smiled with a nod. "Absolutely soundproof."

I noticed Ned heading back in our direction. "Did you have a good time last night? You know, once the hostage thing was over."

"We did, thank you for asking. We went out to dinner at Norvell's and then midnight mass at St. Patrick's. By the time we got back to his place, we were all so tired that we practically passed out from exhaustion ... although, Franny and Zooey were rise and shine at five."

There were things I missed about Christmas, but the kids jumping on the bed at the crack of dawn wasn't one of them. And while I never experienced it with the younger ones, I'd bet that Franny and Zooey were even more relentless than their older siblings.

Ned arrived, handing us glasses of orange juice. When I sipped it and tasted the heavy dose of vodka, I decided that Ned and I might get along after all.

He informed us that he'd made a few calls, and confirmed that Operation Rooftop was in motion. He expected to close the deal this afternoon.

I turned to Libby. "Are you sure about this? It's your last chance to back out."

Her look was unflinching. It was the one that said once Libby Wainwright makes a decision, trying to change her mind is an exercise in futility. Ned would learn that look soon enough, if he hadn't already.

She raised her orange juice and the three of us clinked glasses. "To fresh starts," she toasted.

CHAPTER 64

My mother arrived. She presented Alex with a book on baseball that he'd wanted, and for Taylor, a case for her lacrosse equipment. They both hugged their grandmother like they didn't want to let go, which warmed my heart. It also made me wish that the older kids had gotten to spend more time with my father, and that the twins would have gotten to meet him.

Her gift to Franny and Zooey were a couple of store-bought outfits they seemed excited about, but not as much as the pony sweaters she had knitted for them. But their mood turned melancholy—mentioning that they'd listed ponies on their extensive gift list this year, and Santa had failed to come through with that one.

Some would call my girls spoiled, but since I'm their biased father, I would say they're two little love-letters to capitalism.

Thankfully, there was no pony sweater for Daddy. But she did bring something for me—her famous Christmas cookies. I'd lost my appetite for the oatmeal raisin ones, but still loved the snickerdoodles.

Not to be upstaged, Alexander and Beatrice's limo rolled in a few minutes later. They looked as if they'd dressed for a White House dinner, he in his best Armani, while Grandmommy Dearest wore a designer dress, along with a hat that would have been considered over-the-top at the Kentucky Derby.

I could tell it was burning up Alexander that I'd saved his ass last night—even if nobody was able to save his pinky. He now had to live with the indignity of being just another in a long line of celebrity clients that I got off the hook. And my fee was a few favors that I called in last night.

But he regained some swagger when he escorted everyone to the front of the house to view the new Escalade sitting in the driveway, a gift for Taylor. He said he wanted her to have a "safe vehicle" for when she drove to school next year. As if her three-year-old Lexus was some sort of safety hazard.

Taylor was thrilled, of course, but what I loved about this girl was that she didn't appear any more excited than when she got the lacrosse case from my mother.

When we finished examining every gadget on the ultra-expensive vehicle, we returned inside the house, and settled in for the remainder of the morning. I moved to the buffet table and grabbed a bagel, along with another very merry orange juice.

"You need to slow down—you've got to drive me to the soup kitchen this afternoon," I heard Taylor's voice behind me.

"Cut back on orange juice?"

"Can I have a sip," she said and reached for my glass. I pulled it away, proving her point.

She smiled, satisfied. "I wouldn't underestimate my observational skills."

"It's noted. Soup kitchen?"

"I'm working as a server this afternoon in Stamford. Mom said you were in charge of my carpooling until she lifts your suspension."

"Didn't you just get a new car?"

"Mom doesn't want me driving there alone."

I nodded that I would take her, and smiled proudly. "I'm impressed."

"I don't need compliments for helping people. Besides, it's in my blood."

She gauged my reaction like she knew something, waiting for me to walk into a trap. It reminded me of my courtroom days, which concerned me that she really might have her father in her blood. But maybe I was just being paranoid.

Our conversation was interrupted by a *Breaking News* report coming from the television, and the room went silent. A young female anchor, who probably thought she'd drawn the short straw by having to work on Christmas morning, was suddenly sitting on a big story.

"We reported earlier this morning about what is now being called the Santa Burglar, who broke into a Mount Kisco home last night. But instead of robbing the place, the burglar actually set up a Christmas tree and surrounded it with gifts. Stockings were hung by the fireplace, filled with goodies.

"What made this story even more amazing, was that the 'victims' of this break-in were former Kerstman Publishing employees, part of the group whose lives were ripped apart by the infamous scandal.

"As most are aware, Diedrich Kerstman became the poster child for corporate greed when he allegedly stole his employees' identities in part of a fraudulent sale of the company, which netted him in excess of a billion dollars, while the employees were left with nothing. Kerstman was never convicted—dying during an escape attempt in the Caribbean—but his lawyer, Kris Collins, served three years in jail for his role in the botched escape."

All eyes went to me—like they just realized that I'd gone to jail. Not real newsworthy. But I had a feeling what they were about to learn would be.

"But as the morning has progressed, we've learned that this wasn't just an isolated incident. Reports are coming in of a rash of break-ins across Westchester County and parts of Connecticut, which appear to be part of a systematic plot. As in the 'Miracle in Mount Kisco' these burglaries also brought Christmas to struggling former Kerstman employees. We are now going out to Teresa Rivera who is on the scene in White Plains."

A pretty reporter who looked like she'd just graduated college, stood in front of a house on a suburban street in White Plains. "Yes, Jennifer, it has been a morning of Christmas miracles. And the story of the Santa Burglar keeps growing," she belted out with enthusiasm, her breath visible on the cold morning.

I thought about pulling the plug from the television, while making it look like I tripped. But it was wireless. Damn technology.

"We have learned that not only did Santa Burglar provide traditional Christmas items like a tree and gifts for the children, but also dropped a much larger gift in their parents' bank accounts. A note was left behind to inform the families that all the money stolen from them by Kerstman had been returned, plus interest, and a million dollar bonus for hardships incurred since the heist."

"Sounds as if this would confirm our earlier reports that this is connected to the Kerstman victims," the anchor said, stating the obvious.

"We contacted as many former employees as possible this morning, and every one of them was touched in some way by the Santa Burglar. Even those who had no break-in, or had moved out of the area, still received the payment into their bank account. And one person we talked to said that the gifts left for their children were so specific, it was almost like the Santa Burglar was listening to their private conversations."

"Well, they say he sees you when your asleep, and knows when you're awake," the anchor said, laughing at her attempted witticism. "But it would also require a very sophisticated plan to be able to get into bank accounts, and to reach that many people in one night. It's mind-boggling."

"They say Santa has helpers, and this Santa appears to be no different," Teresa responded. "The internet is already buzzing with rumors of who might be behind this—one source said they saw two men run from their neighbor's house and enter a van, but that's unconfirmed at this time.

"We do have one confirmed report of a sighting inside a house in Sleepy Hollow, where a husband and wife, Jeffrey and Sharon Yu, stumbled upon the burglar, and were tied up and blindfolded, before being placed in a closet. They were unable to see a face or make an identification, but were convinced that there must have been more than one person involved. It seems there are more questions than answers when it comes to the Santa Burglar."

"Not exactly the traditional story of Santa and his reindeer, but I'm sure for those involved, they're just happy to get back what was stolen from them, and now can try to put this nightmare behind them."

"The ones we've spoken to certainly are, although they are stunned. And it's never a comfortable feeling to know someone could penetrate your home or bank accounts, especially for these people who've been victimized in the past."

"What is the reaction from the authorities?"

"The FBI, which handled the Kerstman investigation, and subsequent arrest, had no comment this morning. Although, a source told us that initial investigation showed little or no evidence left behind, confirming that this was a professional job. Strangely, one of the few pieces of evidence being tested were half-eaten cookies left for Santa, which are being tested for DNA.

"We also talked to the local police in many of the communities that were involved—all said they are investigating, but didn't consider it to be a high-priority at this time. But they did remind us that it is a crime to break in to a home or bank account, no matter the motive."

"I would imagine these 'victims' would not be so quick to press charges in this case, and it wouldn't be easy to get a conviction against the Santa Burglar."

"That is if they can ever find him or her."

"Maybe they should start at the North Pole," the anchor said with a chuckle. "We'll be looking forward to your reports the rest of the day, Teresa. Thank you for your work in getting this story out this morning."

A piece of paper then came across the anchor desk. "This just in—a statement was released by Alexander Wainwright, whose investment company, Wainwright & Lennox, was involved in the Kerstman sale. Mr.

Wainwright says that the money that was stolen from him, believed to be in the neighborhood of six-hundred-million dollars, had been returned in full, with interest.

"He went on to announce that he will be using a large portion of the returned money to set up a fund for victims of identity theft throughout the world. And his organization was looking into investing in technology that can protect future victims.

"In a related story, Stone Scroggie, who partnered with Wainwright on the Kerstman sale, is currently in jail for attacking Wainwright and his family on Christmas Eve, with other charges pending the outcome of an investigation. It's another strange twist in a case full of strange twists."

While the statement caused me to almost choke on my bagel, everyone else in the room seemed to buy the self-serving snake oil that Alexander was selling. "Way to go, Grandpa," Taylor exclaimed, and Libby gave him a hug, ending their brief cold war.

I returned my attention to the screen, where the anchor looked into the camera with the serious news-look usually reserved for major tragedies, and broke into editorial, "To repeat our breaking news this morning, we have confirmed that there really is a Santa Claus. In our increasingly cynical society, many question or doubt the existence of Santa. But today is no different than when Virginia O'Hanlon wrote to the editor over a hundred years ago, wanting to know if Santa really existed. And Francis Pharcellus Church's famed response has never been more relevant than this morning. I quote:

"Yes, Virginia, there is a Santa Claus. He exists as certainly as love and generosity exist, and you know that they abound and give to your life its highest beauty and joy. Alas! How dreary would be the world if there were no Santa Claus."

She looked directly into the camera, adding, "I'm glad it looks like we'll never have to find out. Thank you, Santa Claus, and your helpers, for once again reminding us of the importance of believing in you, and all you represent."

CHAPTER 65

"Why don't you just give the money back?" I asked Diedrich Kerstman. Just as I had numerous times before that day when he slipped out under my nose, only leaving behind instructions in case he didn't return. I had the feeling that he didn't think he would.

And the answer was simple. If the money was ever exposed to sunlight, Scroggie could have regained it, and they never would have seen it again. But if he handed it over to the FBI, the money would have been held up in the belly of bureaucracy. Good luck getting that back in full. The Kerstman employees probably would have had to sue to get back what was rightfully theirs, and the majority of the money would have landed in the pockets of bottom-feeder lawyers like myself, even if they won. The term 'class action lawsuit' is a legal term for 'lawyers get rich'. So we had to keep it hidden until the right moment.

But it was more than that. In Diedrich's final letter, he pleaded that I couldn't just write a check to his victims—it wouldn't make things right. He had stolen away something much more precious than money—he took their innocence, their trust, and most of all, their belief. He put it on me to restore it, and I accepted the challenge.

Maybe I saw the parallel to my own crumbling life, and my own loss of innocence and belief, or perhaps I'm just a lunatic thrill-seeker. Regardless,

I'm not sure what made me risk everything for a man I barely knew, and for a concept I no longer believed in. But as I stood in the rain at Diedrich Kerstman's funeral, which was attended by less than ten people, I vowed that I would restore belief. I said it was for those who had been victimized, but I knew it was just as much about restoring it to myself.

Following the funeral, I was offered a ride home by one of the mourners. But since I no longer had a home, Harry Crawford took me to his ranch. When we arrived, the FBI was awaiting at the front entrance to arrest me. Two days later I agreed to a plea deal that made sure I wouldn't see the light of day for three years.

"Any ideas on who might be behind these break-ins?" Libby quietly asked me, even though I was pretty sure she knew the answer.

"I think it might be Gooch," I whispered.

"Gooch? In our brief encounter I hadn't pegged him for virtuous."

"He wasn't—when he had me cornered in the cellar, he threatened everyone in the house if I didn't hand over the location of the treasure. So I didn't have a choice except to give it to him. But with Scroggie arrested, and likely to turn evidence against him, I think he tried to get rid of the money. And what better place, than to return it to the bank accounts of the original owners? Besides, who else would have access to the accounts, other than the people who were behind the original theft?"

Libby shook her head. "I find it incomprehensible that all those juries bought your delusional theatrics all those years. The answer is so obvious who is behind this."

"Then who do you think did it?" I asked hesitantly.

"Santa Claus."

I was puzzled. "I thought you didn't believe in Santa Claus?"

She held a firm stare on me. "I didn't, but I always base my opinions on evidence. And when new evidence comes to light, I am open to re-examining my position."

I was in need of a subject change, and it came in the form of ponies. We'd let the twins go almost an hour without a major gift, and I suggested we take them to the barn to meet their new friends. Mercifully, their mother agreed, and we made our way outside.

"It's the best gift ever, Daddy!" they exclaimed upon meeting their ponies. They also gave me a big hug, which was the true best gift ever.

"Did you take the Ferrari out, Dad?" Taylor suddenly asked me, interrupting the twins' jubilation.

"No, why do you ask?" I replied nervously.

"It seems like it was parked differently when I was in here the other day."

I shrugged. "The only time I've been at the house recently was to pick you up yesterday morning."

"I allowed the workers to move it, if need be, when the stalls were reconstructed. Perhaps that's what occurred," Libby backed me up.

"I guess," Taylor said, not exactly sounding convinced.

Capitalizing on his recent philanthropy, or more likely wanting to one-up me once more, Alexander led the twins out of the barn. Whatever the reason, I was happy to remove myself from the scene of the crime.

He took them into the backyard where a castle was awaiting them. It was technically a "play" castle, but a family of five could have lived comfortably inside.

"Don't worry, no gift can top what you gave them," Libby whispered softly to me, noticing my flailing self-esteem.

"They did seem to like the ponies."

"No, I meant that you gave them their father back. They'll never receive a gift with more value."

"But it will never make up for all the time I missed."

She put her arm around me, which surprised me. "Last night, at mass, the sermon was about the similarities between Jesus and Santa Claus. A lot of people in the church look at Santa Claus as a modern symbol of materialism that is a competitor of religion, and of what the day is truly supposed to represent. But in the end, at their core, Santa and Jesus both believe in the same thing—redemption. Forgiveness of sins through baptism and penance, on the one hand. While Santa wipes his slate clean each year. His naughty list starts over on December 26. It's what we do with that blank slate that counts. "

"I didn't get a blank slate with you."

"We will always be together, Kris," she looked out at the twins. I was pretty sure they were trying to sell the playhouse to Taylor and Alex. They were really going to get along well with Ned.

"A lot of people praised me as noble for trying to hold our marriage together. But I was being selfish. I knew that you had a much bigger destiny to fulfill, and no matter how much we loved each other, I was holding you back."

"You were holding *me* back? I think it was the other way around."

"No, things have never been more clear for me. When I walked down that aisle at our wedding, I firmly believed that we would stay married forever, for better or worse. But sometimes it takes a while for our destinies to be revealed, and once they are, we have no choice but to follow our calling."

"I'm not sure I understand what you're talking about."

"I think you do, Santa. And we both know that I was never cut out to be Mrs. Claus … so I think it's time for you to find her."

I followed Libby's gaze to the woman walking up the path.

CHAPTER 66

I met Nicole with a smile. She met me with a slap to the face. My cheeks once again matched.

"That's for putting my family in danger!"

Then she hugged me—I'd almost forgotten what it was like to be utterly confused by a woman. In other words, being in love.

"Thank you for what you did. We very much appreciate it," she said.

"I'm not sure I know what you're talking about," I played dumb. It worked about as well as it did on Libby.

"Zee told me everything on the way home, including why you did it. Don't worry, your secret is safe with me."

"That Zee—can't shut him up," I replied with a smile.

"He asked me to tell you that he had business to take care of in Boston, and he'll stop by tomorrow when he gets back."

It was the same business he had every year on Christmas, so it was understood. "I'm just glad that you and the children made it home safely."

"We made it home just in time to see that Santa had come."

"Was he good to you this year?"

"Too good … I don't think we can accept it."

"Sounds like he just returned what was stolen from you. With a little extra bonus courtesy of Stone Scroggie. But he won't be needing it where he's going."

"I guess I wouldn't know where to return it, anyway—the North Pole? And it would crush the kids. They got everything they asked Santa for, and then some. Although, Santa sure made my mother and me look bad with our measly gifts."

"Don't feel bad—look what I have to compete with," I said, pointing toward the backyard.

"Is that an actual castle?"

"They tell me it's just a playhouse."

"Wow—I think it's bigger than my first apartment."

We stood in awkward silence for a few minutes before she spoke again, "I said some terrible things to you. My mother taught me to never assume, and I guess she was right. So I apologize." She looked at her watch. "I have to get back to Peter and Janie. I just needed to stop by and tell you that."

Since we were on the subject of apologies. "I'm sorry I dragged you into this. It wasn't my intention. And that your kids missed meeting Santa this year."

"I'm not sure that they did," she said and began to walk away.

She stopped and turned hesitantly, as if she might regret what she was about to say next. "If you're not busy, I'd like to have you over for New Year's Eve, to cook you dinner as a thank you for what you did. It would make me feel better about accepting it."

"Like a date?"

Her face horrified. *"So* not like a date. My mother and kids will be there, and I was going to suggest you bring the twins. I think they'd get along good with Janie."

The old 'safety in numbers' trick. "The twins will be watching the New Year's festivities from a hotel room above Times Square. And I don't know if I feel safe in your home with this Santa Burglar on the loose. What do you say we go out to dinner, no parents or kids?"

"Now that sounds like a date."

"So not a date. And besides, the FBI is always following me, which means there's zero chance we will ever be alone."

"Will blindfolds be involved?"

"I thought you said it wasn't a date?"

She smiled. "Only on the condition that I get to pay."

"I hear that you came into some money recently, and I'm just a struggling paralegal, so I think it would only be fair."

"And that you have me home before midnight. The kids and I have a tradition of watching the ball drop together."

I glanced at my family and realized that getting them back was the best gift I could ever receive, not the other way around. "I would never think of standing in the way of a family tradition."

She nodded. "Then it's a non-date."

"A non-date it is," I said as I watched her walk off.

She came to a sudden stop and turned back to me. "I'm not sure this is a good idea. I've changed my mind. Sorry."

I stood confused, as usual, and watched her leave.

CHAPTER 67

Zee sat across the street from the house in the Boston suburb of Watertown, Massachusetts, just as he had the past fifteen Christmas mornings. Everything looked the same, including the old, leafless oak tree that he always climbed to get a better view.

Kris hadn't come up with his Christmas plan all on his own—he'd seen Zee do it for this family each year. It was a more scaled-down version, and Zee's gifts would arrive anonymously by courier, not break-in, but the spirit was the same—an attempt to return the stolen innocence.

They'd moved here not long after the trial ended. Their aunt and uncle took them in, and they still called it home, even though they were starting to leave the nest. The oldest boy, Joseph, was twenty-two now, having graduated from BU last spring, and recently got engaged. He planned to attend law school at Holy Cross next fall. His sister had just turned twenty last week, and also attended BU, where she earned a swimming scholarship, and won the American East championship in the 200-meter backstroke last year. The youngest brother was just a year old at the time of his parents' murder, and was currently a senior at Watertown High, where he starred on the baseball team. Ironically, a left-handed pitcher with the type of velocity that attracted the scouts.

A court of law declared that Zee Thomas was not responsible for their parents' murders. Witnesses had come forward, and by the time Kris finished with his summation, he made Zee look every bit a victim as the children.

But in the court of Zee Thomas's mind, he was guilty. If only he could have woken up in time—he still couldn't believe he was that close and wasn't able to stop it. Or maybe if he wasn't lying in a pile of his own puke on that club floor, and he couldn't be used as a scapegoat for the killers, maybe they wouldn't have been so brazen as to go forward with the home invasion. Logic told him that they'd go to any length to get money for their next drug fix, so it was doubtful anything would have stopped fate from playing out the way it did. And that's what haunted him the most. Because at that time he was no different from them—he would have done anything or hurt anyone to get that next fix.

And there was another law he broke. The law of the scoreboard. That's one of the things he loved about baseball—the scoreboard never lied. It wasn't complicated like a lot of things in life that get murkied up—you either won or you lost, there was no middle ground. And his father used to drill into him that there were no excuses in baseball. It didn't matter if Zee's arm was sore, or if the sun was in his eyes, as it was that day when he was ten and dropped that fly ball. The yelling lasted the entire car trip back to Tarrytown—it wasn't that he dropped it that angered his father, but that he'd made an excuse.

And on the scoreboard, these kids had their parents taken from them. It didn't matter if he was dragged to the crime scene without his consent, or any other excuse. He's the one who put himself in that position, nobody made him do those drugs.

After his father's suicide, Zee had vowed to protect other children from going through the same pain he did. But he ended up doing the complete opposite. Just like himself, these kids would never get to have a catch with their father ever again. And worse still, it happened on Christmas Eve, a day that symbolized childhood innocence. The least he could do was give them Christmas, even if he knew it would never change anything.

As the sun rose through the fog of Christmas morning, he watched from his perch. The curtain was always open just enough for him to see into the living room window. It was almost like they knew he was there and let him watch. He observed as they opened their gifts—the ones from him were marked *From Santa,* while others were exchanged between each other. Smiles abounded—it was a happy year. In the early years after the tragedy, the children had seemed to hold back their joy. As if they didn't completely trust happiness, or felt guilty for feeling that way.

Zee was always amazed at how much change occurred between each Christmas. The aunt and uncle were much grayer this year, and the children had crossed that threshold to adulthood. He imagined that in the coming years there would be weddings, followed by babies—he could only hope that the new additions would be passed down the unrestricted joy he'd witnessed this morning, and not the residue of that horrible day from years ago.

Zee gathered his emotions, and maneuvered his way back down the tree. He would always leave before the family headed out for Christmas brunch, as they did each year. But when his feet hit the ground the front door of the house opened, and the oldest boy, Joseph, began walking through the snow-filled front yard. By the time he reached the street, Zee knew he was heading in his direction. Part of him wanted to flee, but his legs felt paralyzed.

"Can I help you?" the boy asked him.

Zee took note of Joseph's beard. He was a child no more. "I was just passing through the neighborhood. I hope I didn't alarm you."

"My aunt thought she saw someone in the tree. Her brother was murdered in a home invasion when we were younger, so she can be a little paranoid."

"It's nice that you have someone to watch over you. I apologize for interrupting your Christmas morning. As soon as my ride arrives, I'll be on my way."

Zee noticed Joseph's baseball cap. A midnight blue Yankees cap with an interlocking NY. "It must not be easy being a Yankees fan up here in Boston Red Sox territory."

Joseph smiled. "My dad was a big Zee Thomas fan. So I guess when we moved up here rooting for the Yankees was a way of keeping his memory alive."

"My father taught me to play baseball. One year he gave me a new glove for Christmas, and we stayed out in a snowstorm the rest of the day working it in. I still have it—that's one of the ways I keep his memory alive."

"Do you want to have a catch?"

"Excuse me?"

"A baseball catch—would you be interested in having one while you wait for your ride?"

"I don't even have a glove with me."

He smiled. "I don't have a ball."

Zee followed Joseph across the street into the front yard. The one that the young man grew up in, even if it wasn't where he was supposed to grow up. He scooped up snow into his hand, the slushy kind that would make a perfect, tightly-packed snowball.

He tossed it to Zee, who caught it with his cold hands, and threw it back with his once famous left arm. Soon, the other children came out of the house, and joined in without a word. Zee threw the ball to Joseph, who sent it to his sister. She fired a fastball to her baby brother, who tossed it back to Zee.

They kept the circle going until their hands had practically turned purple. When it was time to get dressed for brunch, the children retreated back into the house, and Zee headed toward the street. As he did, Joseph called out to him, "It wasn't your fault."

Zee turned and nodded his appreciation. It didn't change the scoreboard, but it reminded him that the game wasn't over yet.

Fifteen minutes later a red pickup truck pulled to a stop at the curb, and Zee climbed in.

"Merry Christmas, baby," Sophie said to him with her brilliant smile.

And for the first time in as long as Zee could remember, it was.

CHAPTER 68

Bailey Reed ran into the house. The trip to Rhode Island was fun, but he couldn't wait to get home to see if Santa remembered to stop at their house.

He dashed right through the kitchen, and when he arrived in the living room, he froze—not only did Santa come, but standing before him was the biggest tree he'd ever seen. And it was surrounded by a pile of presents!

Stu Reed arrived moments later, unsuccessfully trying to keep up with the energetic youngster. "Good lord," he said, stunned by the sight before him.

"Did Mom do this?" Bailey asked.

"This looks like the work of Santa," Stu said.

"Where is Mom? I hope she's feeling better."

Good question, Stu thought. Maybe she was in bed, having not joined them on their trip due to a sudden stomach bug. But he knew she was faking, so she likely felt better the minute they left the driveway.

Stu started toward the stairway that would take him up to their bedroom, but then he saw her. She was laid out on a Barcalounger that was hidden by the branches of the large tree. She was in her bathrobe, and her face was as white as a ghost. As he drew closer, Stu could smell the alcohol.

His first thought was that she was dead, and pulled Bailey back as he tried to go to her. He then made his way to his wife. "Mary," he shook her, thankfully feeling warmth in her skin and noticing a breath. "Mary—it's Bailey and me. We came home for Christmas."

Her eyes slowly opened. "Stu?" she said groggily.

"Yes, it's me and Bailey. Are you okay?"

She sat up slowly and looked around the room with wonder. "I had a dream that you were here last night."

"Did you put up this tree, Mare? And all these gifts?"

"I thought it was you … last night … but I guess it really was Santa Claus."

She sounded confused, and was making little sense. "Did you see Santa Claus in this dream?"

"I thought it was a dream, but it felt so real." She began searching for something with her eyes.

"What are you looking for?" Stu asked, confused.

"The shotgun."

"Why would you have a shotgun? Did someone try to break in?"

When she couldn't find one, she said, "I guess I didn't. Maybe it was a dream after all."

Stu was confused. Dream. Not a dream. Maybe a dream. But there was nothing confusing about the hug she encased Bailey in. "Merry Christmas, Mom. I love you!"

"I love you too, Bailey," she replied, her senses returning. She looked at Stu. "I called last night. Your brother said you weren't there. I was worried that … something happened to you."

Stu handed her a wrapped package. "I was out looking for this."

She looked surprised by it, and unsure. "Go ahead, open it," Bailey urged.

When she did, her face lit up. "It's my necklace."

Stu smiled. "I tracked down the guy I sold it to. Cost me twice what I got for it, but I realized that there's a lot more important things in life than money." He took a long look at his wife and son, as if to remind himself.

Mary struggled to her feet and grabbed hold of him like she hadn't done in years. She kissed him. He'd almost forgotten how much he loved those lips.

"Don't ever do that again," she said firmly.

He knew she didn't just mean selling off her necklace without telling her. She was referring to the dark place he'd gone to. But there was something about the intensity in Zee Thomas' words at the police station. It was like he was an angel who'd come to warn him about the future. And it just wasn't any angel—it was Stu's baseball hero. He even bought a house on the same street Zee Thomas had grown up on. It couldn't have been a coincidence. Who says that heroes don't matter anymore?

"Who's up for Christmas breakfast at the Tarrytown Café?" Stu asked.

It was an easy sell for Bailey. But Mary wasn't so sure. "What about all these gifts? Shouldn't we open them first?"

"They'll be here when we get back, I'm starving," Stu said.

Mary smiled her approval, then headed upstairs to freshen up.

Stu strolled into the kitchen to get the car keys that he'd dropped during his pursuit of Bailey. He was drawn to a spot on the wall behind the stove, and examined it closely. It seemed that it had been filled in with Spackle. Strange. And there were similar touch-ups nearby. He guessed that Bailey had caused some damage while playing ball in the house, and attempted to cover it up. He had performed similar touch-up jobs at his parents' home when he was growing up.

When he walked to the counter to pick up his keys, he spotted the note. It was typed with instructions telling them to check their bank account immediately.

When Mary came into the kitchen, looking like a new woman, he showed her the note. She looked curiously at it, not remembering leaving it there, but she wasn't exactly the best witness of what happened here last night. She assumed it was junk mail from their bank that she'd dropped on the counter, but Stu thought it was connected to the large tree in the living room, and wondered if they might be part of another scam.

Mary shrugged. "There's barely any money in our account. It's not like anyone can steal anything if they got into it. We can check it out when we come back."

Stu agreed. There was no time to put the important things off any longer. He dropped the note back on the counter and headed for breakfast with his family.

CHAPTER 69

Hope Roberts couldn't stop shaking as she waited to take the stage. She wanted to blame it on the plunging temperatures at Bagram Air Field—it was in the forties during the day, but had dropped into the high twenties after nightfall—but she knew the real culprit was a bad case of nerves.

From her position offstage, she was able to view the huge crowd of army and air force members—it was like an endless sea of camouflage. And they had been hooting and hollering at the top of their lungs since the head of the First Infantry Division introduced Candi Kane.

The first portion of the show was all about Candi. She did singing numbers, dances, costume changes, and flirted with the servicemen. She even performed a Marilyn Monroe imitation, braving the temperatures in a body-hugging, spaghetti-strapped number, similar to the one that Marilyn showcased while entertaining the troops in Korea, and singing a sultry version of her classic hit "Diamonds are a Girl's Best Friend."

Some people were just made for the spotlight, Hope thought, as she watched Candi hold the crowd in the palm of her hand. But then she received a look from her mother, who gave her a smile and a thumbs-up. Her nerves immediately calmed.

It seemed like it was the first time she'd taken a deep breath since she made that life-altering decision to blow off work at the Christmas tree lot.

Within an hour of escaping that deadly cab ride, they were on a plane to Kuwait. During the trip, they had to provide information to the military security team, including blood samples and fingerprinting. Their phones were confiscated, so that no details of the trip could be sent out. There was no time to ponder the enormity of the moment. It was probably a good thing, Hope thought—otherwise, she might have passed out on the spot.

Candi made another wardrobe change. When she returned to the stage in her iconic *Candy Stripers* uniform, the crowd cheered wildly. Candi milked the ovation for all it was worth, and then sang the first line, "Who can take the sunrise."

It was the cue for the new *Candy Stripers* to take the stage, and they filed in behind the star. Hope could barely feel her feet, and she was sure that her voice cracked when she joined the group in harmonizing the next line, "Sprinkle it with dew."

By the time they got to the chorus it seemed like the entire crowd was singing along with them. And when the final note was hit, Hope could barely stand, and was struggling to catch her breath in the mile-high altitude of Bagram. But she would have a moment to recover, as Candi had an announcement to make.

"This past year I learned about the power of giving and sacrifice, which I know is nothing new for all of you … but it was for me.

"There are many unable to be here today because they made the *ultimate* sacrifice. And since there's no better day to celebrate this selflessness, as it's Christmas morning back home, I want to announce that on behalf of myself and the *Candy Stripers,* we have started a fund for wounded soldiers and their families … and I am going to make the first donation of twenty million dollars!"

The crowd went nuts—if a missile landed in this place, Hope wasn't sure anyone would even notice. Candi spoke over the noise, "It will be called Kane & Abled, because I met a number of wounded heroes at the medical center here on the base, and they are abled, not disabled!"

When the roars finally died down, Candi had the *Candy Stripers* introduce themselves to the crowd. And then each girl would call on a soldier to escort her to the Christmas feast in the dining hall.

First up was a girl from Seattle that Hope had sat next to on the plane ride over. "My name is Meredith Berkley, and I'd like to call up my hero, Lt. Major Jack Hood from Murfreesboro, Tennessee."

The fresh-faced soldier didn't look much older than Hope's high school classmates. His fellow soldiers cheered wildly, and practically pushed him up to the stage, where he hooked arms with Meredith and they walked off stage together.

Hope was to go last. Before she stepped before the microphone she traded looks with Candi Kane, who smiled encouragement back at her. Hope couldn't believe this was happening!

"My name is Hope Roberts from Elmsford, New York. And I'd like to call up my hero, Sergeant Maxwell Roberts ... my father."

She looked out into the audience and found her father in the cheering sea of green. It was like when he used to sit at the edge of her bed when she was a little girl, reading her to sleep. "Merry Christmas, Dad," she mouthed.

"You followed your dream, baby girl," he mouthed back.

CHAPTER 70

Alyson Rudingo pounded the pavement of her quiet Brooklyn Heights neighborhood, nearing the end of her afternoon run. If it weren't for the many festive decorations on the brownstones, she would have thought it was one of those weekends in the summer when everyone takes off for Jones Beach or the Hamptons, leaving the place a ghost town.

This year, Christmas was just the day between the 24th and 26th on the calendar for her. Without Robbie—and even though she didn't want to admit it, Herm—what was the point? Last night, while exhausting, had been a great way to keep her mind off things. But no such luck this morning. After she rolled in at around six, following her breakfast with Kris, she kept up her normal weekend routine, which included this five-mile run.

The run did provide time to think, and to put things in perspective. And she came to the conclusion that she better get used to this. Christmas was normally one of the few times of the year that Herm was in the States, and she knew it was important to use the time to build a relationship with his son. And even though he offered, she knew it wouldn't be healthy for her to spend Christmas in Pohio—it would send Robbie a mixed message—so she declined.

When she arrived at her apartment building, she climbed the fire escape, hoping not to disturb Olive and Oil. But just before she let herself in, she noticed that the window was cracked just a smidgen. Somebody was in there, and she knew Kris was spending the day with his family, so it wasn't him. As a rule, she believed it was always best to stand and fight, rather than to run away from your problems, so she slipped inside as quietly as she could. She heard a low voice coming from her bedroom, and footsteps.

"Damn," she muttered, remembering that her gun was in the drawer by her bed. But she had a backup plan. She removed the shotgun from under the couch. The one she took from the Reed residence, so that Mary Reed couldn't go on a psychotic shooting spree that would ruin everyone's Christmas. There wouldn't be enough Spackle in the world to fix that.

She eased toward the bedroom, hoping to get a good look inside, before she made her move. But just as she reached the door, two male figures leaped out in her sightline and shouted, "Surprise!"

Only, they were the ones staring down a surprise.

"Rudi—what the hell are you doing?" the adult voice shook her and she dropped the gun.

"You're scaring me, Mom," Robbie said, standing next to his father.

She lit up when she saw her boy.

"It just wasn't Christmas without you, Rudi," Herm said.

Then he caught a glimpse of her face. "What happened to your nose?"

"It's nothing. I got gooched."

"Gooched?"

"It's a long story."

"Does it have anything to do with why you're running around your apartment with a shotgun?"

"It was a long night, Herm. Can we talk about it later?"

Robbie ran to the kitchen, and returned with a mug, holding it steady with both hands. "We made your favorite, Mom."

She smiled lovingly at him as she took hold of the cup of hot chocolate. It hit the spot. She wasn't kidding with the "long night" stuff, and now that the run used up her last energy reserves, it was really starting to hit her.

Robbie pulled out the phone his father had got him for Christmas, and showed it to her. "It has video call, so Dad I can talk no matter where he is!"

She smiled, but it was bittersweet, thinking about Herm once again taking off to parts unknown.

The dogs began barking in the other room. "Why don't you go feed them, Robbie," his father instructed, and the boy headed off.

"Thank you for my Christmas gift," Alyson said.

"I don't know what you're talking about. I haven't given it to you yet."

"The one that was left in the helicopter? Feel like explaining how you just happened to make a trip to the city, and landed next to my roommate on a train?"

"It's been a long couple days, Rudi. Can we talk about it later?"

He flashed a sly smile—the one that had hooked her like a small-mouth bass the first time they'd met. The innocent farm-boy mixed with the hotshot fly-boy—for Alyson it was a lethal combination. His face was now lined with his travels and his buzz-cut had thinned, but he still had the same strong presence.

They were both thrill-seeking daredevils back in those days. But after Robbie was born, she'd lost her sense of adventure—last night notwithstanding—and became the protector, deciding to leave the nomadic military life behind. Herm never lost his, and continued on with his career, which took him to all parts of the globe. When the situation grew unworkable, they divorced. It was the best way to provide a healthy, stable environment for Robbie.

"Sure, we can talk about it later, but I'll accept my gift now," she said.

"I'm not gift enough?" he said with the same grin.

"You said you hadn't given it to me yet. Since you were already here when you made the statement, that must mean that it's something other than you."

"How about I show you?"

CHAPTER 71

They put on their winter hats and coats, and headed out with the dogs. Robbie tagged along in his own world, wearing his music-blasting headphones. Alyson's first thought was that they were headed to the Promenade, one of their favorite spots, but she soon found herself walking through Fort Greene and Williamsburg, before reaching Greenpoint, the most northern portion of Brooklyn. Between her run and now hour-long walk, Alyson figured she wouldn't have to work out for a month. But still no word on their destination.

"I have something to tell you," Herm finally said, sounding serious.

"What is it?"

"I decided that I'm not going to re-enlist when my commitment is up in the spring. I'm going to become a civilian."

She was caught off guard. But felt a twinge of excitement. "I thought you had decided to sign up again?"

"I guess I just started to think about what's really important to me. I've given most of my adult life to my country, and I don't regret a minute of it, but it's time for some stability. I'm not getting any younger."

"What are you planning to do?" she asked, feeling like everything had changed in a few precious seconds.

"I'm a farmer. That's what I was born and raised to be. And it's what I'm going to do."

She stiffened her upper lip. His family's farm was about a nine-hour drive from New York, but at least now there would be a consistent second home for Robbie. And Alyson knew that Herm's mother was getting to the point where she could no longer take care of the farm.

"That's great. I'm happy for you," she said, and she was, even if she secretly hoped the thing that made it worth leaving the military for would be moving back with her and Robbie.

"There's no chance you and Robbie will move out to the farm in Pohio?" he asked.

"I can't, Herm … we've been over this. My job, Robbie's school …" She sighed. "I guess a city girl and a farm boy were never meant to be together."

"Just checking to be sure," he said as they kept walking. To where, she had no idea. Every time she asked, he told her it was a surprise.

Alyson's feet were frozen, and she was getting ready to decline whatever gift/surprise he had in store, when Herm suddenly stopped. If she was expecting the prince to take her to the castle, she would have to settle for her ex-husband bringing her to what looked like an abandoned warehouse.

"What is this place?" Alyson asked.

"What do you say we go in and find out?"

Anything to defrost her feet. Robbie must have been thinking the same thing, because he was already running toward the front door. They followed him into a cavernous room that appeared to be under renovation.

All Alyson saw was dust. But beauty was in the eye of the beholder, and Robbie exclaimed, "This place is cool! I could ride my bike in here!"

They climbed a winding staircase up three stories to the top floor, which looked like it was once office space. If nothing else, with its large windows, it had a sweeping view of the East River and the Manhattan skyline.

Herm opened a door that led to the rooftop, and he helped them through. Waiting for them was Libby's boyfriend, Ned. Now she was thoroughly confused.

When she looked out over the expansive rooftop of the warehouse, her confusion changed to amazement. "What is this place?"

"It's going to be called Rudingo Farms—a 5,000 square foot green roof organic vegetable farm right in the heart of the city. I said I was going to become a farmer, I never said I was going back to Pohio." He grinned. "Well, unless you and Robbie agreed to go when I just asked. I wasn't signing the papers until I was sure."

"You're going to be a vegetable farmer in Brooklyn?" she asked.

"Merry Christmas."

Ned explained the details. He made them close their eyes and picture the greenery of summer, or the fall harvest with red tomatoes bursting to life with the sun rising over the East River. Radishes and lettuce flourishing on the rooftop. And while it looked barren and snow covered on Christmas day, there was a modern greenhouse, which would allow lettuce and other produce to be harvested through the winter, when many of the restaurants in the area struggled to get fresh local produce.

Alyson remained flabbergasted. "But how can you afford this?"

Ned spoke for him, "The farm received a hefty grant from the DEP's Green Infrastructure Grant Program, which will help. As will the fact that Morzetti's restaurant is waiting to sign an exclusive contract with Rudingo Farms to provide them fresh produce each day. An upscale restaurant like that only wants to use the freshest foods, which isn't easy to do in the city."

Herm added, "And the law firm of Wainwright-Collins & Rudingo purchased the bottom floor. They will be moving here after the construction is finished, and will be hanging out a shingle. That will cover a lot of the expenses for the farm."

Her mouth dropped open. "We're moving here?"

"Not until you sign off on it, since you're a partner in the firm," Ned added.

"Libby would do that for me? Her commute will be utter hell!" She looked at Herm and something hit her. "That's why you came—the helicopter."

More grinning. "I was supposed to meet with Ned and Kris to finalize the details. When Kris no-showed, we eventually tracked him down on his daughter's cell phone. Turns out he was in quite a predicament over at Macy's and needed some immediate help."

"So what do you say?" Ned asked.

She grabbed the pen and approval sheet, and signed it before anyone could change their mind.

When Robbie returned, Ned said, "Come on, let me show you the third floor. Herm will be turning it into an apartment, or I guess in this case it would be called a farmhouse."

"You're going to live here? Talk about taking your job home with you."

"Don't knock it until you try it," he said and looked intently at her. "But it's really expensive living in the city."

"Tell me about it."

"I was hoping to find a roommate to help cover the costs."

It took her a moment to realize he was talking about her. But when she did, she ran and jumped into his arms. With the sun going down behind the cityscape in the background, he swung her around as they kissed. The city girl was about to become a farmer.

CHAPTER 72

Just as I'd remembered it, the anticipation and excitement of Christmas morning slowly dissipated like a balloon losing its air, until it finally settled into an early afternoon malaise. But to be fair, the fun-factor of most parties plummets after Alexander and Beatrice Wainwright hightail it away in their limo.

My mother had received a special invitation to tour the twins' castle, so she ventured out in the cold like a trooper, while Taylor and Alex lay like lumps on the couch in the living room, fighting over control of the television. There were ten TVs in the house, give or take, but I guessed it wouldn't have been as much fun to find their own. Alex wanted to watch a basketball game, but Taylor preferred the ongoing coverage of the Santa Burglar. I was rooting for Alex to win out, but when it came to these battles of will with his sister, he tended to be the hopeless underdog.

The phone rang, annoying Taylor, as it interrupted her viewing of the news coverage. By the bounce in Libby's voice, I knew it was Ned. And suddenly I was very interested in this call.

When she hung up, Libby looked in my direction. "It's a done deal—I guess we're going to be moving."

This got the kids' attention, and they were finally unified. "What do you mean moving?" Taylor asked with an edge. "I'm not going anywhere for my senior year!"

"Not that you'd have any say in it, young lady, but I'm referring to our law office. We're transferring to Brooklyn."

Once they were convinced that this didn't affect their daily lives, Taylor and Alex returned to their struggle for television superiority.

I had run into Herm at a Labor Day picnic that Libby held for the employees of the law firm, and their families—all five of us—and he confided in me that he was thinking seriously about leaving the military next spring when his obligation was up. He'd asked that I not say anything to Alyson, since he hadn't yet made up his mind, and didn't want to get Robbie's hopes up.

So fast-forward to earlier this month, when I was searching for a special Christmas gift, as a thank you for her support the last few years. I didn't know where to start, so I asked Libby for advice. And as we discussed possibilities, Herm's words from the picnic came up. We both agreed that there would be no better gift than the opportunity for their family to be together again now that Herm was leaving the military, and we needed to find the bridge between New York and Pohio. Whether or not they chose to rekindle their love, which I'd long suspected was still there, would be up to them—I was the least qualified person on the planet to play matchmaker.

At that point, Libby got her boyfriend involved—still a strange concept for me. And in his words, he had "the perfect bridge to bring them together. And what place is more famous for a bridge than Brooklyn?"

Since all my assets had been turned over to Libby prior to my sentence, and she would be the one to sign on the dotted line in any purchase, she came along with Ned and me to view the warehouse farm. And that's when she fell in love with the possibilities of the future.

The building required a lot of work, and portions would need to be rebuilt from the bottom up. But it more symbolized Libby's vision of the law office than the glitzy building in Midtown. And it was more than just a fresh start—which remains the story she's sticking to—it was about the thing that was most important to Libby … keeping family together. Even if it was somebody else's family, as it was in this case. And once she decided she was all in, there was no way Ned or I could talk her out of it.

"So are you ready, Dad?" Taylor asked.

If she meant ready to go to sleep until next Christmas, then the answer was yes. But since she had a backpack slung over her shoulder and kept nervously checking the time, I realized she had something else in mind.

"The soup kitchen?" she said with a sigh, assuming correctly that I'd forgotten.

"Oh, yeah, of course," I said, pulling myself off the couch. It wasn't easy.

Taylor tossed me a set of car keys. "Mom said you can take the Ferrari."

I looked at Alex, who was engrossed in the Nets/Bulls game. "You wanna come? Maybe we can stop by an empty parking lot on the way home and let you practice driving."

He shook his head and returned his stare to the television. He wasn't giving up control of the remote. I shrugged and followed Taylor toward the door.

"Dad?" Alex's voice surprised me, and I turned.

"Yeah?"

"I'm glad your home."

I smiled. "Me too, Alex … me too."

We walked over the grounds and into the barn, passing the ponies. The twins had suggested that they name them Beatrice and Alexander. I thought to explain to them that they're ponies, not jackasses, so they'd have to come up with different names, but I didn't want to put a damper on their Christmas spirit.

I took the covering off of the Ferrari, and Taylor stared at it, deep in thought.

"Are you sure you haven't driven it recently?" she asked. "Something seems off."

"Maybe Alex took it out for a joyride," I offered what I thought was a plausible explanation.

"That would explain him turning down a chance to drive his dream car," she said.

"What do you say we take *your* dream car for a ride … at least until your grandparents get you another dream car in a couple years."

"Now that sounds like a plan."

We began the short drive from Pound Ridge to Stamford in the Escalade. This was the first time I'd been a passenger while one of my children was behind the wheel, and it was just as terrifying as I'd imagined. And the conversation wasn't helping matters.

Like her mother, Taylor had a knack for getting right to the point. "So you really like this Nicole woman, huh?"

But I was no pushover. "She seems like a very nice lady."

"She must have been to get on the Santa Burglar's nice list. Just like all those families. That was a pretty amazing story."

"Speaking of being nice, Ned is going to ask you and Alex to spend New Year's Eve with him. I think it would be a really good thing if you two went along without a fight—it would mean a lot to your mother."

"I'm there," she said with surprising enthusiasm. "Ned's starting to grow on me. Maybe one day him and mom can double-date with you and that Nicole lady. So are you two going to go on a date?"

"I doubt it."

She smiled. "You know, she'd really have to be Saint Nic-ole to put up with you."

I could tell she'd been saving that one for the right moment.

Having made her point, Taylor clicked on the radio, which was playing nonstop Christmas music. I was convinced, based on how much earlier they start each year, that within a few years they would be playing it all year round, maybe taking a break in July. Or perhaps have a winter and summer Christmas like the Olympics.

The Kinks' "Father Christmas" blared out of the speakers. My children loved the classics, which made their father proud. And by blared, I meant that blood was trickling out of my ears. The stereo system sure worked.

Taylor kept giving me strange looks as she sang along. *When I was small I believed in Santa Claus, tho I knew it was my dad. I'd open my stockings at Christmas and I'd be glad.*

When the song ended, she shut off the radio, with the comment, "I'm kinda sick of Christmas music. How about we watch a movie instead?"

She clicked on the DVD player, and I was looking at what looked like a department store security video. But when I looked closer it hit me what it was.

"When you got out of jail and you had all these guys after you, Mom was worried about us. So she had security cameras installed in the barn. Luckily, I was able to get the tapes away before anyone discovered what went on last night. It's really top of the line equipment—it was able to capture every word you and Alyson were saying."

I dipped into my lawyer bag of tricks, trying to come up with a defense, but I had nothing.

As I remained speechless, she turned to me. "I can't believe you guys pulled that off. You were in total beast-mode!"

"Taylor, it's not what you think … and can you please keep your eyes on the road."

"I want in!"

"What do you mean in?"

"Next year. I meant what I said about giving back—what you did for those people was amazing!

"There is no next time, Taylor."

"Whatever you say, Dad," she said with her teenage eye roll, not listening to a word I said. "And no matter where I end up going to college, I'll still be home for Christmas break. I already have some great ideas that I want to run by you for next year."

"It's important that nobody ever knows what happened last night, Taylor. Are we clear?"

She didn't respond, just staring out the windshield with a big grin on her face.

"Taylor?"

She turned to me, still smiling. "I can't believe my dad is Santa Claus. How cool is that!?"

TUESDAY DECEMBER 31

NEW YEAR'S EVE

CHAPTER 73

Justin Duma stepped out of the car and made his way to the passenger side. He assisted Wintry out and removed her blindfold.

Her excitement vanished. "A football stadium?"

"Not just a football stadium—the place where I left my heart and soul on the field for thirteen years."

There's gonna be some other parts of you on that field if you think I'm gonna be spending my New Year's Eve here!"

"Hey—I'm the one who wanted to leave the kids with my mother and head off to Statia this week for some fun in the sun."

"So let me get this straight, you had me doll up in this dress because you had some surprise that was so big I had to be blindfolded for it. And it turns out that you're taking me to a football game?"

"There's no game tonight. The game is Sunday. During which I'll be enshrined in the Ring of Honor, if you haven't forgotten."

"How could I forget, when you mention it like every ten minutes? Then why are we here now?"

"I thought you might want a sneak peek of your boyfriend's name up in lights."

"If that's what you're thinking, then you're not thinking."

He reached his hand out to her. She blew out an angry breath and grabbed on. He then led her toward the dark stadium. Huge mounds of snow from yesterday's snowstorm surrounded the parking lot. The lot had been plowed clear, but it was still a little slippery, and Duma's tux shoes weren't the best footing for the surface. He knew he'd look like a clumsy polar bear if he fell.

"Hey JD, what's shaking?" a security guard greeted him.

"Doing well Stevie, how's the family?"

"It was a good year, can't complain."

Duma slipped him a crisp hundred. "Now it's a better one."

He still knew most of the security staff from when he played here. Some of his teammates looked down on these guys or just plain ignored them, but Duma made it a point to get to know each and every one of them.

Stevie nodded a thank you, and then turned to Wintry. "I see you bought your wife something nice. That's a beautiful dress, Mrs. Duma."

"Thank you, but I'm not his wife," Wintry snapped. "And I bought my own dress."

Stevie was smart enough not to touch that one. He quietly took them inside and led them to the elevator.

They rode to the top level of the stadium. Then climbed the steps to the highest point. Wintry was growing even more frustrated. "Where are we going, Justin?"

"It's best to see it from the top."

"God forbid if we don't kill ourselves on account of your ego."

The lights suddenly came on, as if on cue, and lit up the 70,000-seat stadium.

They were momentarily blinded, but when Duma regained his sight, he pointed. "There it is."

Wintry focused on the ring around the stadium, known as the Ring of Honor, which displayed the names of the elite players and coaches who contributed most to the franchise over the years. It was an exclusive club, and the highest honor a team could give a player.

But he wasn't pointing there. He was trying to get her to look down to the field, where a snowplow was busily removing the snow cover for Sunday's game.

When she looked closer she saw that the plow had carved something into the snow.

Wintry Will U Marry Me?

When she turned back to Duma he was on bended knee. He held up a small box, and said, "This is the only ring of honor that matters."

Before he could even ask, she had tackled him with the same ferocity that he had attacked opposing quarterbacks in this very stadium.

"Yes, yes, yes!"

When they eventually returned to their feet, Duma gave a thumbs up to the grounds crew and security staff down on the field. They returned a standing ovation and serenaded them with the famed *Dooooma!* chant.

Wintry wiped the tears away and found her composure. "I already know what I'm going to do with my half of the twenty million," she said.

"Your half?"

"I'm going to start a performing arts schools in all major cities, for underprivileged kids. So the next Hope Roberts will get a chance. If we didn't step in, she'd be working at the Christmas tree lot today and not on the world stage."

"And the next Wintry Mix."

"There's millions of kids like us out there. So what do you think, husband?"

"I think it's a great idea, but you're too late, wife."

Her face fell in defeat. "You already spent the money?"

"I did," he said. "I spent it on starting a performing arts school for underprivileged kids."

Her face lit up, which made it worth every penny … well, almost. "I told you it's more about helping people than the money, Justin. It's about time I've started to rub off on you."

"I hope you remember that when we're at our divorce hearing."

She smiled. "Remember what?"

CHAPTER 74

We arrived at Morzetti's restaurant in Little Italy. It was one of the toughest tables to get in the city on a typical night, much less New Year's Eve.

I was met by the whirling dervish that is Sal Morzetti. Think Danny DeVito with ten Red Bulls in him. He hugged me, and then took Nicole's ankle-length leather coat, revealing a jaw-dropping, one-shoulder, black cocktail dress. Her gold earrings contrasted perfectly with her red hair.

Sal spoke for all his male patrons, "Madonna Mia!"

He sat us at a table in the corner of the dark, intimate eatery, and brought over his best wine. Wine always tasted the same to me, if it was five grand or five bucks, but I would take the world-famous television chef's word for it.

"I'm glad you decided to come," I re-started what had been awkward conversation on the drive into the city.

"My mother informed me that it was time for me to start dating. It made me feel like I was fifteen again."

"I thought this wasn't a date?"

"It's not, which is why I came. I can be a little bit of a rebel when it comes to my mother, so if she wanted me to go on a date, then I would show her by going on a non-date."

"You showed her. And I'm just glad you're here, no matter the motivation."

"Me too. I haven't been out on New Year's since ... I can't even remember the last time. I always thought it was forced fun—fun is supposed to be spontaneous."

I lifted my wine glass. "To spontaneity," I toasted, and we clinked glasses.

"This place is great," she beamed, looking around the small dining area, the tables draped with red and white checkered tablecloths, and the walls lined with photos of celebrities who'd eaten here. "Although, it does look a lot nicer on TV."

"I did some legal work for him back in the day," I mentioned.

He'd hired me after a restaurant reviewer filed a complaint, claiming that Sal had stalked and threatened him after receiving a bad review. I was able to get him off on that one—thankfully for Sal, just like real life, nobody likes critics, and the jury was no different. But the case Libby was currently handling for him would be much trickier. He allegedly assaulted his sou chef, and did so in front of the cameras of his reality TV show for the world to see. Since I was no longer a lawyer I would leave his guilt or innocence to the professionals, but I made a mental note to compliment him on the food tonight, regardless of how it tasted.

"It's also a safe choice," I continued.

"Safe from those people who were chasing us in Macy's last week, or safe in that you feared I'd poison your food if you came over to my home?" she asked with a smile. The conversation was starting to loosen up.

We had come a long way from that day in the courtroom, even if this was likely the last stop for the train. "Safe, as in I knew there would be no cameras. Sal is very protective of the celebrities who eat here."

"I almost forgot that I was dining with the famous Kris Collins."

"More like infamous, but I was referring to you. Can you imagine the field day the tabloids would have if they caught you on a date with the enemy."

"You mean a non-date."

"When your picture is plastered on the cover of the *New York Globe* tomorrow, I tend to think it won't mention that part. Pushing people off their pedestals is the favorite sport in this city."

She nodded, turning serious. "I still get recognized from that newspaper cover."

"Nothing under the tree," I said, repeating the headline.

"But there was this year … thanks to you."

"You mean the Santa Burglar."

"I stand corrected."

As an appetizer of fried calamari arrived, I went into the story about Alyson, Herm, the farm, fresh starts and building something new from the ground up. She seemed to relate to the concept.

"So you're going to stay in the apartment you're in now?" she asked.

"It will be nice to have a place to myself for the first time in a long time," I said. "And if I ever have a real date one day, I could have her over without my gun-toting roommate there."

I studied Nicole to see if she had any reaction to the "real date" comment, but there was none. So I moved on, "How about you? Do you plan on moving out of your mother's place now that you got your savings back?"

"No, I think we'll stay for a while. Obviously living on our own would be ideal, but the kids have had their lives uprooted so much the last couple of years, and I really think they're finally starting to settle into a routine."

"They seem like really great kids."

She lit up like a Christmas tree, and stroked her earrings. "They're my gift from Janie, and Peter gave me the coat I wore tonight. Although, I think their grandmother might have helped out with the shopping."

"So who helped out with the dress? That person deserves a medal."

She smiled at the compliment. "That was also my mother. She calls it my mating dress ... you know, for whenever I start dating again."

"I'm glad you decided to take it out for a test-run on our non-date."

She smiled again, but didn't seem comfortable with the subject. "How about you? I know how the *giving* thing went for you this Christmas, but how about the *getting*?"

"Taylor and Alex are taking me to the Jets game this weekend. We're going to make a day of it—tailgating, the whole thing. A family friend, Justin Duma, is being inducted into the Ring of Honor."

"I think I remember him, something about taking my kids."

"I believe he was saving them."

"I guess there's a fine line between scoundrel and saint."

I was living proof, but didn't want to labor the point, so I returned to the original question, "And the twins got me a gym membership—they said I was starting to get a 'Fat Albert tummy'."

"You're hardly fat. And isn't Fat Albert a little before their time?"

I smiled proudly. "Collins kids are all about the classics."

But just when the conversation seemed to hit a lighthearted rhythm, she suddenly turned deathly serious. "I need to tell you that it wasn't your fault."

"Excuse me?"

She began nervously playing with her hair. "My husband had suffered from depression for years. It would come and go—he would get on a new medication and it seemed like things were going to be fine, and then it would just stop working, and we were back to square one. He'd tried it before the Kerstman thing, a couple times, but I always believed his excuses ... because I wanted to believe them. The time I'd caught him in the garage with the car running, or when he drove off the road and told me that he'd fallen asleep at the wheel.

"It doesn't change the fact that my children lost their father and I lost my best friend. Or that your defense of Kerstman was insulting and nauseating. But that didn't make it right for me to blame his death on you. I had to blame someone or something, and you were in the wrong place at the wrong time. I'm truly sorry."

"No need. I probably would have done the same thing. I might have been an easy target, but I made myself an easy target."

She took a couple of deep breaths and blew them out slowly. "Okay, now that I've totally dropped a buzz-kill on New Year's Eve."

"Last time I came to the city for New Year's some drunk threw up on me on Metro North. Trust me, that was way worse."

Our food arrived—chicken francaise for me, pasta primavera for her. As we ate, and sipped another glass of wine, Nicole let out a big yawn. Not exactly how I envisioned the evening going.

"If you're tired, we can go," I offered in a neutral tone.

"No … no, I'm sorry. Christmas is just so exhausting that it takes me like a month to recover."

"Well, the good news is that you have 359 more days until the next one."

"I wish. Peter is already talking about next year. It's like a year-round thing now."

"I know what you mean. The twins mentioned that they are going to get me a sleigh next year, so that they can pull me behind their ponies."

"Sounds like Santa Claus and his reindeer. Speaking of which, do you think they'll ever find the identity of the Santa Burglar?"

Subtle she was not. There had been a feeding-frenzy over the last week in the media, and the internet was at fever pitch. The *New York Globe* listed its top ten potential suspects the other day. I made it, at number seven, one spot behind the ghost of Diedrich Kerstman, and just ahead of Donald Trump.

I thought about her question for a moment. "I don't think anyone will pursue it. There will be a bunch of unfounded theories on the internet and it will be eternal Mardi Gras for conspiracy nuts. But law enforcement, from the FBI down to the local level, all work for somebody. And those somebodies are usually politicians. The Santa Burglar is quite popular at the moment—you saw the outrage when the IRS even suggested that they might 'look into' going after the taxes from the gifts to the Kerstman families—and one thing you can count on in this world, is politicians associating themselves with what's popular."

She looked curiously at me. But on second glance, she was actually looking past me. "If that's the case, then how come the FBI is still following you?"

I followed her gaze to a table across the room. Sitting there was a smiling Agent Falcone, who raised his wine glass in my direction.

CHAPTER 75

Falcone stood to greet me. He introduced his wife, a pretty brunette with a wide smile. I figured that he must not bring his job home with him, because she greeted me kindly.

"So you're the one responsible for my husband not working tonight. It's the first time he's ever not worked on New Year's," she said.

"It was the least I could do—I apologize for keeping him away so much."

She waved her hand at me dismissively. "If it wasn't you, it would be somebody else. Paulie thinks if he takes a day off, the criminals will take over the world."

She politely excused herself and headed to the ladies room, leaving me alone with her husband—always a precarious place for me to be.

"I see that your incessant stalking finally got Ms. Closs to go out with you. It's good to see that crime still pays," he began.

"It's actually a non-date."

"That doesn't look like a non-date dress to me."

"From what I hear, this is your first date since the turn of the century. So I'm not sure you're an expert on the subject."

"That's because I was too busy chasing around guys like you."

"Well, I guess you caught me this year. Which must mean that you got back the money you were looking for."

"Not exactly."

"I'm sure it will turn up."

"Oh, it has. At least a portion of it. And on that subject, I noticed that your friends Candi Kane and Justin Duma both made large charitable contributions this past week. Was twenty million the going rate for helping you pull this off?"

"As you know, I no longer have a dollar to my name. But Candi and Duma are both very financially successful, and willing to give back to worthy causes. I think they should be commended for that."

"Perhaps, but how do you explain the Wainwright's landscapers being able to purchase what's left of Kerstman Publishing, including a burned-out warehouse, a sunken ship, and a house in Statia? Why hide the evidence when you can buy it, right?"

"No idea, but I know they've lived on the Wainwright property for many years, and probably know more than they should about what goes on over there. Keeping secrets can be a really high paying job in that world."

"As can hacking into people's bank accounts," he said and reached into the breast pocket of his suit. He pulled out a photograph that he handed to me.

It was of Marcus Hacker, leaving through the front entrance of Crawford's ranch. "Your old cellmate had disappeared since his release, but for some reason I wasn't surprised that he ended up here. I was pretty confident that you and Candi Kane weren't the ones who hacked into those accounts."

"I'm not sure why the FBI was looking for a free man," I said with a shrug and handed him the photo back.

"We weren't looking for him, we were monitoring Harry Crawford's ranch, which we both know was the epicenter of the crime. And like your other friends, Harry was very philanthropic this year, starting a charity that provided toys for underprivileged kids. We've learned a lot at the Bureau since 9/11 about how charities can be used to launder and funnel money. It's become a specialty of ours."

"Did you just compare Harry Crawford to a terrorist organization?"

He handed me another photo, this one was a scenic photo of what looked like a typical rock formation in Vermont. "It looks innocent, but with use of some high-tech equipment we were able to determine that it was a secret, back entrance onto Crawford's property, with access to the main thoroughfare. Just big enough to fit a semi-truck through. Well played."

I shrugged again, acting disinterested. "From what I heard, you got your man Scroggie, who's looking at spending the best years of his life in jail. And the money was returned to its rightful owners. So it sounds like you got everything you wanted, including that date with your wife … unless you also wanted the glory."

"Not all the victims had their money returned."

"I thought I read that all former Kerstman employees got their money back, plus a hefty bonus for their trouble."

"Stone Scroggie is still out over a half a billion dollars. Those hefty bonuses had to come from somewhere."

"Sorry if I can't find any tears for Scroggie."

"The law states that stealing is stealing, no matter how twisted and corrupt Scroggie is. Nobody gave you the right to play Robin Hood."

"I don't know what you're talking about, but I do know enough about the legal system to know that the money would have never been fully returned to those victimized. And as they drowned in their bills, Scroggie would be hunting down new prey."

Falcone shook his head, frustrated. "The system is flawed, but if you don't believe in it, then it's every man and woman for themselves. And without the system, the Scroggies of the world will always win in the end."

"If you believe in it so much, why don't you get a warrant and search those tunnels on Crawford's property? Bring us all in on suspicion of being the Santa Burglar."

"It seems those above me don't like bad publicity, which is exactly what they'd get if they went after you. So you're in the clear, Collins, along with the rest of your cronies. But before you celebrate, be aware that we no longer will be able to protect you from the likes of Gooch if he decides to take the law into his own hands—like I said, every man for himself."

He patted me on my dress shirt. "If I were you I might start wearing that bulletproof vest again."

He noticed his wife stepping out of the ladies room. "One last question, Collins, and then I'll be out of your life for good."

"And that is?"

"How did you get Alexander Wainwright to go along with it? Talk about a Christmas miracle—handing over the Lake House to the Woods family, and that fund for identity theft victims will cost him a small fortune."

I smiled. "I threatened to marry his daughter again."

Falcone laughed and headed across the dining area toward his wife. As he did, he looked back at me and said, "I can't believe you were willing to give up three years of your life to do what you did."

"I didn't give it up," I said. "I got it back."

CHAPTER 76

The afternoon storm had passed, and the Caribbean was now as calm as bathwater on the leeward side of the island. The sun was sinking into the sea in spectacular fashion.

Candi strolled through the sand toward the large house that was built at the foot of the dormant volcano. After a week that took her from New York to Afghanistan, and back, she had been looking forward to some R&R in Sint Eustatius over the New Year.

She could hear the festive sounds as she walked under the stately columns of the house, and into an open patio area.

She went directly to Tomás' wife, Mia, and handed her a panettone cake that she'd picked up in Oranjestad on her way over. Mia and the other women greeted her kindly, but going by their subtle looks, Candi wasn't sure how welcome she really was. It was a look she'd become familiar with. Their husbands had been the ones to invite her to the New Year's Eve party.

She made her way to where Tomás, Gustavo, and Berto, were sitting beside a small fire on the patio. It had been in the eighties when she arrived on the island this morning, but the storm had cooled the temperatures.

"Feliz Anos, Candi" Tomás greeted her. "Come sit down."

"Thank you for having me."

"Any friend of Kris Collins is welcome here," Tomás replied.

"And no woman as beautiful as you should ever spend New Year's alone," Gustavo said, eying her snug, neon-yellow mini-dress. That was another look she'd become accustomed to.

"Nice place you have here," she said, referring to the home that was last owned by Diedrich Kerstman. "And Statia is a beautiful island."

"It's been rough, but I think we'll eventually get used to it down here," Gustavo replied with a grin.

Speaking of beautiful, she took notice of the band that was playing salsa music in an adjoining courtyard. The bare-chested singer caught her attention. He appeared to be in his early twenties. His dark hair was wet, like he'd just returned from a swim, and his abs were a work of art.

"That's my son Angel," Gustavo informed, noticing her stare.

"Their good," she said.

"The band was becoming well known around New York before we moved. Maybe you can give him some pointers while you're here."

"He looks like he's doing just fine from here," she said.

Candi spent the last few hours of her year laughing, mingling, and dancing. It seemed as if every guy at the party had to dance with her at least once. Except for Angel, who continued to churn out song after song. She wondered if that type of stamina translated to other aspects of his life.

As the clock neared midnight she took a break from the dance floor, and walked out under the columns. She found a quiet spot with a view of the sea. The lights of the house reflected off it, coloring it a bright blue.

Suddenly she felt a cold sensation. She turned to find that it was Angel, pressing a bottle against her bare shoulder." Champagne for the pretty lady?"

She smiled. "Thank you, but I'll stick to my water."

"That doesn't sound like a fun way to bring in the New Year."

Maybe not, she thought, but it might save her from her New Year's tradition of waking up tomorrow with a guy she'd just met the night before, along with a couple of old friends named Headache and Regret.

"I had too much fun for a long time, and it wasn't all that fun," she said.

"Do you mind if I do?" he said as he removed the cork from the bottle.

"Don't let me be the skunk at the picnic … drink up."

He took a swig straight from the bottle and ate grapes, which he held in his other hand. "It's a beautiful night," he said.

"Yes it is," she replied, switching her view from his sculpted arms to the boundless water.

"Much more beautiful because you came."

Like father like son. "You're a great singer. I'm impressed."

"Gracias. Means a lot coming from a legend in the business."

"I'm not old enough to be a legend."

"I thought I watched you on the *Candy Stripers* when I was just a little boy, but perhaps I was mistaken," he said with a grin.

She smiled. "You were doing good up until that point."

"So what brings Candi Kane to little old Statia on New Year's Eve? I would think you'd be at the hottest parties in New York or Vegas … or maybe both in the same night."

"I came for some rest and relaxation. But I'm not sure this is the right place for that—your family really knows how to throw a party."

He handed her his stem of grapes, took her hand, and led her down to the beach. The water was completely still, the sand a dark gray. Not the prettiest beaches she'd ever been to, but the blue-glass beads that Angel picked out of the sand for her were something to behold.

He explained that they were considered collector's items, usually emerging after a heavy rainfall. "I will string them together into a necklace for you, and give it to you on our second date."

"Second date? I don't remember agreeing to a first one."

"I think you're on it right now." He moved his hand around to the small of her back. She didn't push him away.

"I usually only date older father-figure types."

"I would think it would take a young man to keep up with you."

He glanced at his watch. "Two minutes until midnight. There's a tradition in Peru of eating twelve grapes at the New Year—it provides luck for each month of the upcoming year."

She took a grape and fed it into his mouth, and he returned the favor. They slowly fed each other until they'd both eaten twelve. Just in time to ring in the New Year with a kiss.

When his lips touched hers, it felt like she was drinking champagne on one of her past New Year's benders. She heard fireworks going off overhead. Or maybe they were inside her head. She wasn't sure at this point, things were getting hazy.

She dug deep and found the strength to push him away. "I can't do this."

He looked stunned. "Are you sure that's what you want?"

"I'm not sure of anything. But a friend of mine taught me that to truly give yourself to another, you first have to believe in yourself."

"You wouldn't have gotten where you are if you didn't have belief in yourself."

"I don't know how I can believe in myself if I don't even know who I am. I was the stranger I woke up with."

He nodded as if he understood. He kissed her on the forehead and whispered softly, *"Feliz Anos,* Candi Kane."

She watched the beautiful creature walk back to the house, and rejoin the raucous party. A few minutes later she heard the band start up again.

She sat on the beach and watched the fireworks lighting up the small island. For the first time in her life, Candi welcomed the New Year by herself. And for the first time she didn't feel alone.

CHAPTER 77

The meal was unceremoniously slid under his cell door on a plastic tray.

Stone Scroggie looked at the soup and sandwich with contempt. He vowed that people would pay when he got out of this hellhole, starting with Kris Collins and Alexander Wainwright. Candi Kane would also feel his wrath.

And he would do it on his schedule. He always did things on his schedule, and to prove his point, he refused to eat the food until he was good and ready. This left him with more idle time to plot his revenge, which would be more delicious than any meal they could ever serve him, anyway.

His lawyer, Barney Cook, had promised that he'd make bail and be home to celebrate New Year's. A judge didn't agree, denying bail. When he attempted to call him tonight, Cook's voice message said he was out for the evening and would be in touch tomorrow. He envisioned him out at some swanky party in Manhattan—the one he should be at, spending the money that Kerstman and Collins stole from him. Cook was getting close to joining Collins and the others on his naughty list. He hoped he enjoyed his night, because it might be the last New Year's he got to celebrate.

Scroggie finally gave in and took a spoonful of soup. Not only was it nothing like the food in the finest restaurants in which he dined, but it left a terrible aftertaste. Like a film was forming over his throat.

He got up and banged on the bars. "Guard! Guard!" When nobody answered his call, he shouted, "If you can't even make a decent soup, let me do it myself!"

Still no answer.

He soon began to feel lightheaded. A sharp pain tore through his lower back.

He tried to yell, but nothing came out. His throat was frozen, and he felt the air being sucked out of him as he tried to breathe. He banged as hard as he could on the bars, and when that didn't work he threw the cup of soup against the wall. But the plastic made little noise. He started to panic.

He banged on the bars one more time, before collapsing to the cement floor. It felt like an animal was trapped inside his abdomen and was eating its way out.

Just before he passed out from the pain, the guard finally arrived. But he didn't do anything—he just stood there and grinned at him as he writhed on the floor.

When his eyes finally were able to focus on the guard's face, a horror came over Scroggie.

"I hope you enjoyed your soup," Gooch said.

CHAPTER 78

I delivered Nicole back to her doorstep at five minutes before midnight.

"You were good to your word," she said, glancing at her watch.

"I had a great time. Thank you for dinner."

"Thank you for fending off the FBI."

We had another awkward moment, before she said, "I'd invite you inside, but it's become kind of a tradition for it to be just us. And like I said, I'm trying to make things as stable and normal as possible for Peter and Janie."

"I wouldn't want to intrude, anyway. Tradition is really important to hold on to. There's not as much of it as there used to be."

She shook my hand like we just closed a business deal and turned to go inside. But just as quickly she turned back around. "On second thought, it's kind of sad that you would bring in the New Year alone in your car."

I pointed to my wrist. "My watch is five minutes fast. So it's midnight in my world, and I couldn't think of any place that I'd rather be spending it."

She smiled. "Happy New Year, Kris Collins."

"Happy New Year, Nicole Closs."

We stood there for what seemed like another minute, nobody moving an inch. And then we came to the end of our collision course.

"Tradition *is* a good thing," she finally said, "Like kissing on New Year's. And since your watch says …"

Before she could say another word, I'd taken her into my arms and our lips came together.

That day in court, I felt like a piece of her had been embedded in me. And as we kissed, I felt like she was reaching inside me once again and planting hope. That, and it had been a long time for me, since before prison, and she was looking seriously hot in that dress.

But she pushed me away again. "I'm not sure this is a good idea. I've changed my mind. Sorry."

And before I could say anything, she entered the house and shut the door, leaving me with a dumbfounded look and a case of … the blues.

I noticed her son, Peter, sneaking a peek through a window. He just shrugged and waved at me.

As I began to walk away I heard him call out to his sister, "Janie—I saw Mommy kissing …" his voice trailed off as I got further from the house.

I walked carefully down the icy path, rationalizing that if I had to usher in the New Year alone in my car, at least it was a Ferrari.

During the short walk I replayed the past year in my head. It started with my recurring nightmare of waking up in a jail cell on New Year's Day, and ended in the fairytale of Nicole Closs' lips … at least until the clock struck midnight and I turned back into a pumpkin.

In the end, I learned much about giving, but it seemed that I still had a long way to go when it came to getting some.

And most of all, I found out that it's not about how many gifts are under the tree on Christmas morning, but how many people are willing to guide your sleigh when things get foggy.

CHAPTER 79

Harry Crawford poked the fire back to life, as he waited for the New Year to commence. Or maybe it already had—he'd lost track of time. His mind had been racing all day. He couldn't remember that happening since Ginny died.

The house was quiet for the first time in a long time. He'd finally gotten rid of the "elves." He loved those guys and would do anything for them, but it seemed like they kept multiplying, bringing in their friends and friends of their friends' friends, and they never slept. It reminded him of when he and Ginny used to follow around The Dead. He must be getting old, he thought, because the silence was soothing.

It had been a week since Christmas, but he could still feel the magic in the air—at least that's what Ginny used to call it—so much so that he felt compelled to spend his afternoon cutting down a pine tree on his property and dragging it back here to the living room. He found the boxes of decorations stored in the cellar, and he spent his New Year's Eve trimming his Christmas tree. He just wasn't sure if it was for last year or next.

He hadn't put up a tree, or any decoration of note, since the day she left—it was the day that served as the benchmark for almost all of his "last times."

Ginny believed there was a universal theme about Christmas, whether it was seen through the prism of a religious holiday, or if it meant something else to others—that if you do the right thing, and strive to get on that "nice" list, mixed with a little belief and wishing, you would be rewarded in the end.

But the only thing it represented to Harry in recent years was loneliness. His belief had been swept away by the wind, and he had no desire to chase it down. He remembered back to Christmases past, in the days following the big day, he would feel a certain emptiness—post-holiday blues, they called it. But since Ginny left, he felt that way every day.

She was his hero, his muse, his inspiration. He knew she was the reason the Gin Rumy books sold like hot cakes—the world loved Ginny, just like he had. Without her, he was just that mediocre wannabe who shouldn't quit his day job, as one literary agent once told him. He hadn't picked up a pen to write since that day.

The last thing he wrote was the final chapter of the final Gin Rumy book, when the hero, who'd taken on everything from aliens to the CIA, and was able to miraculously survive the most dire of situations, succumbed to the most insidious enemy ever created—cancer.

Many of the fans were upset when he chose to "end" Gin Rumy. They wanted her to live on as a tribute to Ginny. To "keep her alive." He understood the sentiment, and appreciated it on some level, but what they didn't understand was that he didn't create her ... she was real. And now she was gone, and in many ways the author died with her.

He had been content to spend the rest of his life wallowing away on the ranch. But that was before Kris Collins returned. Just like he had once represented him in court, Harry felt that he was now representing Ginny. He was making her case from the Great Beyond that he shouldn't waste another minute, because life is never as long as you think it will be.

There was something about Kris. He saw the same fierce loyalty in his eyes as he'd seen in hers. And the storyteller in Harry was attracted to the delicious, layered character Kris was, filled with honor and fault, gallant yet fallible, as he set out on his noble quest for redemption.

And Ginny had seen it too. She used to joke with Harry during his trial that Kris was like the son they never had. And that the arrest was a blessing that brought him into his life at a time when he was about to lose his best friend. She was always so accepting of her fate, while he refused to admit she would ever lose the battle. But with some reflection, he knew she was right … just like always. So when Kris needed help, Harry didn't hesitate for a moment.

But Kris returned something else to him in the last few months—inspiration. Suddenly Harry was waking up in the middle of the night and jotting down a thought that came to him in his sleep, or losing track of time as his mind wandered to places he never thought it would ever go again.

He watched as the story unfolded in front of him, a classic story for the ages, centered around one of the most charismatic and mysterious characters ever created. And like Gin Rumy, it was a timeless character that the world had fallen in love with.

He walked to the Christmas tree and picked up the scrapbook he'd found in the cellar during his search for decorations. He'd brought it upstairs with him and left it under the tree. Ginny had made it for him during her final months, yet he had never looked at it. But tonight he took a seat in front of the fire and opened it.

He was in many of the photos, but he only noticed Ginny. Her look changed over the years, but the smile remained the same—from their hippie days with flowers in her long, straight hair, to the sophisticated woman in a sequined gown at some event where they were honoring Harry, to the bald woman sitting up proudly in her hospital bed, fearlessly living when everyone told her she was dying. He took a close look at their wedding photo, both of them clasping a knife as they cut the cake—it seemed like a million years ago and yesterday at the same time. It was a photo clipped from the local newspaper with the inscription: *The wedding of Virginia Johnson and Harold A. Crawford III.* She had crossed it out and written *Ginny and Harry.* That's who they were. That's who they would always be.

He shut the scrapbook and placed it back under the tree, a reminiscing smile on his face. As he did, he was drawn to the other objects he'd placed there. It was like they were taunting him, daring him to try avoiding them. Finally he gave in and took them into his hands.

He momentarily looked out the window at the falling snow that was welcoming the New Year, before returning to his seat by the fire. He had found his story, and the heroic but flawed protagonist to carry it out. He used to joke that he wasn't a writer, but a writer-downer—he would watch the wonderment that surrounded Ginny and just write it down. And now he would do the same with Kris Collins.

He took the cap off the new pen and touched it against the empty paper. It felt exhilarating as he wrote the first words. *"Yes, Virginia, there is a Santa Claus. He's just a lot different than we all thought ...*

ACKNOWLEDGMENTS

It's like Christmas every day for me because I get to work with the best group ever in making these books come to light. As always, thanks to the incomparable Charlotte Brown for her great editing. Carl Graves for the cover. Curt Ciccone on the formatting. And Sandra Simpson's proofreading.

EXCERPT OFFICER JONES

Midtown Manhattan

July 2

When you've risked your life in the world's most dangerous places, a long life expectancy isn't so expected. So it wasn't a surprise that I was having a midlife crisis in just my late thirties. The only question was why it took so long.

I sat at a small table on the patio of a trendy midtown restaurant called Norvell's, alone, but not by myself. The relentless machine of Manhattan traffic whisked behind me, filling the summer day with the majestic sounds of honking horns, which someone once described to me as urban bird chirping. The day was a spring-like seventy-two degrees with only a few clouds in the aqua sky, making it hard to imagine that thunderstorms were predicted for later this afternoon.

Across the table sat Lauren Bowden—her glowing blonde hair surrounding her angelic face. She claimed to be eleven years my junior, although my trusty reporter skills told me that her given age wasn't the same one that was on her birth certificate.

Lauren has been what I'd loosely refer to as my girlfriend for the past year. She's also my co-worker at GNZ (Global Newz), an international cable news network, and as long as I'm playing loose with terms, news might be a stretch when describing my industry as of late. It's been taken over by loud, noise-driven sensationalism that my boss, Cliff Sutcliffe, glowingly refers to as newsertainment. The running joke is that GNZ used to spell news with a Z since they were a unique alternative to traditional news, but now it's because much of their on-air talent can't spell. But that wouldn't be my concern for much longer.

Lauren addressed me in her southern accented voice, "John Peter, Norvell's is world famous for its sushi. It's the only real choice. So for the life of me, I can't figure out why you've been staring so intently at that menu."

I had hoped to buy a few more minutes hiding behind the menu. Usually she was too focused on herself to notice my avoidance techniques. Out of options, I was forced to endure a few uncomfortable moments of tedious conversation. But since I didn't get a word in, I'm not sure 'conversation' would be the proper term.

Our waitress arrived just in time to impede the migraine that had begun to percolate behind my right eye. As usual, Lauren waited for me to order for her. But I was drawing a blank.

"What did you say you wanted again?"

"Weren't you listening, John Peter? I said to order two sushis and two glasses of their best cab."

Cab is what I needed, as in the yellow kind with four wheels to flee the scene. I held a long look on Lauren, before switching my glance to our waitress, who wore a no-frills uniform and a pleasant smile. A complete contrast. Her name was Bridget, which I knew because she had been our regular waitress since Lauren decided that Norvell's was going to be *our* restaurant … at least until another eatery became the trendy place to be seen.

"She'll have two orders of sushi—the hosomaki—and two glasses of your best Cabernet. I'll take a cheeseburger and a bottle of your cheapest beer."

Bridget fought back a grin, gathered herself, and asked me which type of cheese I desired on my burger. I made a not very funny joke about holding the cheese on the cheeseburger, which received a giggle. I settled on American cheese. I'd been to so many countries the last twenty years that American seemed exotic.

Lauren flashed me a dirty look for going against her wishes. Or perhaps for evoking the flirtatious giggle from the waitress. The *why* really didn't matter at this point. She then sent an obvious fake smile in Bridget's direction. She'd mastered both looks. *Who says there aren't usable life skills gained from beauty pageants?* Certainly not the former Miss Beaufort County South Carolina who sat across from me.

I ignored Lauren, seeking the refuge of a daydream. But I was jolted back to reality by an angry twang firing at me from pointblank range. "Are you listening to me, John Peter?"

I've always been confused as to why she calls me John Peter, since that's not what JP stands for. "I'm sorry, you were talking about um … well … you know the …"

She flashed me her most displeased look. "I was talking about our trip to visit my parents in Hilton Head this weekend. It's the Fourth of July, if you haven't forgotten."

I racked my brain to think if it were actually possible that I'd agreed to this. I had interviewed rogue dictators and heartless terror-mongers over the years, but I still wasn't sure I was prepared to meet the people who created Lauren Bowden.

"I did?"

She sighed theatrically. "Yes, first we will stop in North Carolina for my big interview with Lamar Thompson, and then to Mommy and Daddy's place. They insisted we stay with them."

It was best not to argue. She would just claim that my forgetfulness was due to jealousy, since she was able to beat me out for the Thompson interview. The truth was, I would have refused it, due to its tabloid nature. In the world according to Lauren, this would be another example of why I'd become a dinosaur in this business, and my career was "in a dreadful decline." Little did she know that this dinosaur was about to become happily extinct.

The interviewee in question, Lamar Thompson, first entered the limelight twenty years ago when he was a high school basketball star out of Columbia, South Carolina. At the time, he was the most celebrated and highly recruited prep basketball player in history. Lamar chose the University of North Carolina, but he never got to play a game.

On an October night of his freshman year at UNC, two weeks prior to the start of basketball season, it all ended for him. In the spirit of being young and stupid, Thompson and a couple of fellow classmates decided to spend their Friday night pulling a prank. They hid in the wooded area alongside a dark, country road in a small town outside of Chapel Hill. When an unsuspecting car drove by, they tossed a lifelike dummy onto its hood, giving the driver the impression of having struck a real person. It was followed by beer-buzzed laughs of insensitive youth and an exhilarating dash for safety.

It eventually led to a high-speed chase with police, which ended with Thompson's car slamming into an oncoming vehicle driven by Marilyn Lacey. The mother of three was killed instantly.

There were two other people in Thompson's car—fellow UNC classmate Brad Lynch, who died from injuries sustained in the crash, and another passenger who survived, but was never identified due to the fact he or she was a juvenile. But when word got out, it really didn't matter who else was involved, because the only name people were talking about was Lamar Thompson … the next great thing.

Lamar's leg was mangled in the accident, ending his promising basketball career. That was the good news for him. The bigger problem was that he was legally drunk, and despite his claims to the contrary, he was identified as the driver. He served five years in the state pen for vehicular manslaughter. The years following were no kinder to him—he was now an unemployed night watchman with a history of substance abuse.

But the reason Lamar Thompson was once again relevant, was his recent assertion that there was a fourth man in the car that night named Craig Kingsbury, and that he was the one who was drunk behind the wheel. The reason this was front-page news, and screwing up my holiday weekend, was that Craig was now Senator Kingsbury, who had just tossed his name into the ring to become the next President of the United States, and many believe the frontrunner.

Lauren grew annoyed with my distracted pause. "John Peter, where *are you* today?"

The question was not where I was, but rather, how the hell did I get here? My old high school journalism teacher, Murray Brown, always preached that journalism went beyond the traditional who, what, where, why, and how. A great journalist tells a story, and to write the ending, one must return to the beginning. And whenever I return to the beginning of my story it always takes me back to Gwen.